HARD TRUTHS

REBECCA ROYCE

Hard Truths (Kiss Her Goodbye #1)

Copyright @ 2018 by Rebecca Royce

Ebook ISBN: 978-1-947672-63-5

Paperback ISBN: 978-1-947672-70-3

Cover art by CoraLee June

Content Editing: Heather Long

Copy Editing: Jennifer at Bookends Editing

Proofreading Editing: Lucy Felthouse

Formatting: Ripley Proserpina

Published by Rebecca Royce

www.rebeccaroyce.com

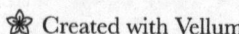 Created with Vellum

Introduction

To my beloved readers,

This is something a little bit different from me. As the cover suggests, it is a Dark Romance. Our heroine is going to go through some rough things in the next three books before she comes out the other end. Please keep in mind that I always write Happy Ever After stories. We sometimes just don't get there until book 3... And sometimes happily ever after isn't all sunshine and roses. Sometimes, it's a dirty, hard path.

Take this ride with me into the darkness and let's see what comes out the other side.

Rebecca Royce

This book is dedicated to the members of Rebecca's Randomness on Facebook. The best reader group ever. Today's Question Is...
You guys make my day.
RR

Foreword

"We are not enemies, but friends. We must not be enemies. Though passion may have strained, it must not break our bonds of affection. The mystic chords of memory will swell when again touched, as surely they will be, by the better angels of our nature."

— Abraham Lincoln

Chapter 1

I washed the bad sex off my body, letting the heat from the shower push away the mediocre fuck of the night before. The payoff had not been worth the effort. Weeks of time spent trying to get Brian Chapel to pay attention to me in philosophy class hadn't resulted in much of anything. 1-2-3 done. Then I'd had to talk to him for the rest of the night about books it was clear to me he hadn't read but wanted me to think he had.

He hadn't even offered a second round to try again. No, I was pretty sure he thought we'd had a good time. I shook my head, letting the shampoo drip down my back. Yeah, Brian Chapel was off the list. I didn't want a boyfriend, just somebody to make me come for the next six months I had left of school. I'd return the favor, happily. Then we could both part ways.

I had things to do, and I didn't need commitment. Just competency.

Touch me on my clit and I was likely to come, stumble around in my pussy like it was a squeeze test and I was going to get annoyed.

Inexperience could be worked with if it was owned.

Enough. It had been a boring encounter, but not the worst. I'd just have to figure out a better system when picking someone out. Maybe someone I didn't have to see in class all the time.

I turned off the shower and grabbed the towel I'd hung on the door. My apartment was small, but it was mine, rented for me by my father after I'd shown him how it was financially cheaper for him to do that than to pay for room and board, and all the fees that made campus housing so expensive.

I didn't have a roommate. This place was all mine. As my dad had let me know that the day I graduated was the day I would be paying entirely for myself, I suspected this was my last time without a roommate, maybe ever. Social workers didn't earn much.

I walked into the living room. I needed water before I could do anything else.

I opened the fridge and pulled out a bottle.

The next thing I remembered was waking up in a bed that wasn't one I knew. I grabbed my head, hoping it would stop spinning if I did. That didn't happen. I groaned, throwing myself off the side of the bed so I could crawl for an unknown bathroom. There had to be some-where I could puke other than on myself or the floor. I made my way to the closest door, and fortunately, I was right. There was a toilet, and it called my name.

For a few minutes all I could think about was emptying whatever was inside of me. I couldn't fathom anything else. Eventually, the spinning stopped, and I lifted my head. Where the hell was I and how much had I had to drink?

I was a two drink girl most of the time. Two glasses of wine, two glasses of beer, or two gin and tonics. I never drank anything else or anything more.

I tried to think. The last thing I remembered was getting water out of my fridge. Then nothing. I'd been in my towel. I looked down. I was dressed. In my black yoga pants and my t-shirt that said *Not Adulting Today* across the front. When had I put this on? Why had I put this on? Was I exercising? It was Sunday. I didn't work out on Sundays. I ate bad food and hated myself for it regularly.

Discomfort filled me and it had nothing to do with my puking, which had to be my least favorite thing in the world. I wasn't a person who lost control willingly. I said when, I said where, I said how—in all things. I got these tendencies from my father. Maybe it had to do with the fact that my mother had taken off on the back of a Harley with an MC President when I was three and never looked back.

Maybe it was just how I was made.

But I didn't wake up in strange beds, alone, feeling like I'd been drugged.

I stood in the bedroom and looked around. The place was ornate but not overdone, which was a hard combination to successfully reach. The floor was white. It was funny I noticed that first, but I didn't know if I'd ever stood on such a pure colored white wooden floor before. The white bedding matched the floor. But the base of the bed was tan, which matched the dresser and the two night tables on either side of the bed.

The head of the bed pressed against the wall where a piece of artwork seemed to have been designed to complement the bed. My gaze was drawn to the small chandelier over the bed. Five old fashioned arms held what looked like candles, but I imagined were actually well crafted holders for small light bulbs.

At the end of the bed was a tan ottoman with orange and white designs. A desk was by the window and it matched the color scheme except for the light green desk chair. Somehow, the different colors didn't seem out of place in the otherwise tan and white bedroom.

Even with all of this, the most striking piece was not the decorations but the structure of the room itself. There was one white column that touched the wall next to the window. I reached out to stroke it. This wasn't a fake decoration. It was marble, and I bet it had structural use keeping the ceiling where it belonged and the house upright.

Okay. I hiccupped, and I tried to hold back my distress. This was clearly not a college apartment or dorm. I was in someone's house, and I couldn't remember getting here. Something was very wrong.

The door on the other side of the room opened. I hadn't seen it when I'd been charging for the bathroom. I retreated a step, narrowly avoiding the corner of the desk.

"You're awake."

The man standing there was a complete stranger, a fact which did nothing to relieve my rapidly spiraling anxiety. He was taller than me, which wasn't easy since I was almost six feet tall without shoes on. His face was oval shaped, and he had short brown hair. His facial hair looked scruffy and dark but clearly maintained. The scruff only covered part of his face, as though he'd drawn a line and shaved above it. The hair was also not enough to be a mustache or beard so he must trim it. His nose was long but not overly large, and his brown eyes flashed something as he looked at me, waiting for a response.

He wore a gray colored shirt unbuttoned on the top two buttons, which he matched with tan pants and black shoes. Formal and yet not nighttime formal. He was fit, that much was clear by how he filled out the shirt. I would put him at around forty years old although when people really took care of themselves, I found it hard to tell. He might be much older. My quick impression was that he was handsome, but for me, so much of that had to do with what happened when a person opened his mouth.

I swallowed. "Who are you?"

He nodded. "Amnesia happens sometimes. Different for everyone. Feeling okay?"

"That's not an answer." Or at least not an answer I liked. Amnesia happened? What the fuck did that mean?

He stepped away from the door. "This is your chance to tell me you feel sick. Otherwise I won't give two shits. You feeling nauseated later? That's your own fucking problem."

Any idea I had that this might be okay, some kind of mix up fled right then. Something very wrong was happening. "I'm feeling fine because I woke up and puked my guts up in the bathroom."

"That was fast. Brush your teeth and let's go."

Brush my teeth and let's go? I felt like some kind of internal parrot, repeating everything this obnoxious douchebag said to me. At least I wasn't saying it aloud. I got points for that. Maybe.

"I'm not going anywhere until you tell me who you are and where I am."

He strode forward, grabbing onto my arm and hauled me to the bathroom. I let out a yell. His grip was unforgiving, and I was sure bruising, while he dragged me the few small feet into the bathroom. "Brush your teeth so you aren't disgusting and then you will walk with me out of this room. Unless you want to be dragged everywhere. I assure you, Everly, you don't want that."

So he knew my name. With my heart in my throat and terror relaxing my anxiety, I grabbed my toothbrush from the holder. I stuttered at that thought even as I did it. That was my toothbrush. My pink handled, soft bristled tooth-brush in the toothpaste holder next to the sink. And my hairbrush was there too. Both of them, actually. I pulled open a drawer. My hair dryer.

No, this was too much. "How is my stuff here?"

"Don't dawdle." He walked away from the bathroom.

With nothing else to do, I brushed my teeth. It at least gave me a moment to catch my breath. I was in a strange bedroom with no idea how I got here. My toiletries were here. There was a good-looking man. He knew my name, and he was an asshole.

If I brushed anymore I was going to make my gums bleed. I turned off the water and set down the toothbrush. Staring at myself in the mirror offered me no help and no answers. There I was, much as I had ever been, save for the wild eyes I'd never seen on myself before. So this was what terror looked like on me.

I wasn't a knockout, but I had a look that some men found attractive. My hair was stick straight black, and I always thought of it as my best feature. Long and thick, I wore it straight down my back and over my shoulders, the same way I had every day of my life. My skin was pale, freckled, mostly over my nose.

My nose was straight and kind of pert at the end. It fit my long face. My eyes were a little bit too far apart, a little too big. I had hazel eyes that looked almost green some-times and a thin mouth. My face was severe. I had the kind of situation where even if I was just being quiet, people thought I was mad.

I wasn't pretty. Not by anyone's standards in magazines or in television. But I was good looking enough that I'd always gotten a man when I wanted one. Despite what some of my girlfriends said, how people appeared had little to do with how frequently they could get laid. There was enough want in the universe that anyone could find a willing partner if they put in the effort.

But right now I was even paler than usual and my eyes were wounded, bloodshot.

What had happened to me? What had that man done? Where was I?

My hands shook, and I gripped onto the granite countertop to steady myself. Okay. I could get through this. I was strong. I'd figure it out.

I walked out of the bathroom with my back straight. The man waited for me by the door. I cleared my throat. "I don't have shoes."

"You don't need them to come downstairs, but you do, in fact, have shoes." He pointed to the closet and the dresser. "Your stuff is in there."

"My stuff?" This time I repeated aloud. "It's all here?"

"Everything that was in your apartment is here now. As far as your landlady is concerned you've paid two months rent and moved out. You're gone." He snapped his fingers. "Let's go. Downstairs now."

My straight back failed me, I couldn't pretend anymore. I sunk to my knees. "You have to tell me what's going on."

He strode toward me. "You want answers, they're downstairs. Move your ass now."

Anger surged through me, but it was better than the terror. I forced myself up. Okay. This was happening. Why? Had I done something?

"At least tell me your name?" I stormed toward him, prepared to kick and scream if he grabbed me again.

"You can call me K."

"Kay? Isn't that a girl's name?"

He rolled his eyes. "As in the letter. You can call me K

the letter. I had heard you were smart. Boy were the reports of your IQ overdone."

I shoved at him. It was probably not the smartest thing I'd ever done, but I couldn't overthink it. I wasn't staying there with him while he insulted and terrified me. Wherever this place was, I was getting out of here. I ran swiftly; I didn't stop to think. The hallway was long, and much as I expected K to follow me and stop me, he didn't. Instead, as I looked over my shoulder to see if he was going to come out the bedroom door, I collided straight into a wall of a person I hadn't seen standing there.

I went down hard onto my rear end. I gasped, staring up at the man gazing at me. He was taller than K had been. If K was maybe six foot two inches then this person was six foot four. They were both plenty bigger than me. Wavy brown hair with a full beard, sharp eyes so dark they were almost black, stared down at me.

"Lost something, K?" He stared at me but didn't address me at all.

"I knew you'd get her, T."

K. T. I knew this time it was the letter. Was this for real? "Who are you people and why do you have me here?"

"Get up, Everly," K said as he walked up to T and me. "Start using some self-preservation. If we decide you're too much trouble, we'll kill you. We won't even think twice about it. So get up, shut up, and move yourself downstairs, now."

T's mouth curved in a half smile. "I'd do what he said. He's hungry. A hangry K is no good for anyone. Trust me on that."

Chapter 2

I didn't try to fight T when he took me downstairs. This letter thing was going to kill me. I had a hard enough time with names let alone trying to remember who was who based on some letter system. Okay. I had to remember this. I'd probably never forget K. He was the first to come into the room. K, the one who told me to go brush my teeth, the one who seemed to be done with me, and I hadn't done anything that I knew about. Okay. Maybe I'd shoved him. But he'd deserved that. He was scary as fuck.

And now there was T to go along with him. T... Why couldn't they use names? T, the man in black. The *huge* man in black. But the problem was that maybe he didn't always wear black. Oh, hell, for now I was going with that. The man in black. K, my bully captor and his buddy T, the man in black.

I'd managed to shove K, but I knew it was because I'd taken him by surprise. I would probably not be so lucky again. My father had taught me to read people's body language, that what they didn't say was sometimes more important than what they did. Right then, I was getting annoyance from K based on the on again off again tic in his jaw. T, by contrast, was calm and easy. He had a lazy gait, but I didn't take that to mean he was actually *laissez-faire*.

We walked together down a long staircase, and I tried to do a better job of taking in my surroundings. Like the room I'd woken up in, the house was a mixture of decorations, which gave the impression of being modern with a classic touch. Had one of these men decorated it?

At the bottom of the staircase, T pointed left, and I walked in front of him, making fast note of the front door. As soon I could, I was making a run for it. I'd go out screaming. Surely some neighbor somewhere would hear me and call the cops. K had grabbed me and hauled me to the bathroom, but other than that it wasn't like I was being dragged around in chains. I'd wait for my chance, and then I'd go out the front door.

Determination made my fear disappear. I was getting out of whatever this mess was any minute, and the police could sort out what had happened here.

Some of my newfound energy fled when I found three more men in the room where they brought me. All of them tall and strong. Why couldn't there be one wimp in the whole bunch? I was a tall, fit woman. I could probably take out a not fit guy who was shorter than me. Use him as leverage. And why hadn't I actually taken those Krav Maga classes when I'd had the chance?

The room was large, several couches, and a large television caught my attention quickly, but it was the men themselves who held it.

K pointed at the tallest of the three. He spoke slowly, like he either thought I was hard of hearing, stupid, or needed time to digest what he said. I didn't guess it was the last one. Internally, I rolled my eyes at the asshole. Outside,

I kept my face passive. The front door beckoned me. I would get out there.

"This is W."

Oh God. We had another letter. I'd hated algebra. It was hard enough to solve for X. Now I had these fucking letters. Okay. I quickly ran through it again. If they were going to use letters as names I had to remember them. K—my dark haired bully captor. T—the man in black. And now W—with the glaring eyes.

He was interesting looking—in the way that I would never forget his face—but not necessarily handsome. Like I wasn't traditionally pretty, he was too severe to be called good looking. His face was oval, and he kept a trimmed beard and mustache. He was dark haired and olive skinned. With thick eyebrows and huge brown eyes, it was his prominent nose that defined his face. This was a hard man. Facial features could be misleading but his gaze was not. He would not be an easy man to speak to. He nodded at me and then looked away as though I were nothing more than a fly in the air he breathed. He wore a light brown suit with an auburn colored shirt he'd slightly unbuttoned. His watch was expensive, but I didn't immediately know the names of his clothing. I'd picked out my father's clothing for years. I knew designer brands for men.

I had a second to try to memorize who he was. It was the glaring eyes I'd remember.

With that done, K pointed to the man who sat on the couch farthest away from me. His legs were stretched out in front of him as though he had not a care in the world. He was the youngest of them so far. Or maybe he just had a baby face. The man had light brown hair and green eyes. He was so good looking he would probably be called pretty. His hair was styled back with gel. He wore a gray long sleeved t-shirt and jeans. He didn't have shoes on, just gray socks. Unlike W, he didn't even nod.

"That's J."

J—who seemed to be right at home here. Casual J.

And finally K—how was I already getting used to this initial thing?—turned to the last man. He stood by the window, watching me with hooded eyes. Usually I found men who had man buns to not be my type but this man would be everyone's. Probably even people who didn't like men sexually. He had blond hair, long enough that it was in the already noticed man bun. His eyes were blue. Like everyone except J, he had facial hair. Had they all just gotten back from a camping trip where they couldn't shave or had I missed the trend where rude kidnappers had to have facial hair? Like the rest of them, he was muscular and good looking.

"D." K finally provided. "Now you've met everyone."

D—the blond dude with the man bun.

I quickly ran through them in my head. I was getting out of there as fast as was humanly possible but I had to be able to tell the police. K—the bully who made me go brush my teeth. T—who wore all black. W—glaring eyes. J—the casual one in his socks. D—man bun.

I didn't say anything. They had done this, they could explain to me why. Or not. I could run for the door. They hadn't blocked it. Had none of them considered that I might make a break for it?

J shook his head. "You didn't show her the house."

He spoke with a lazy casualness. He really seemed… calm.

"I'm not the tour guide. I went to get her and had more than enough hassle for my trouble. You want to show her around, have at it." He crossed the room to the bar in corner and poured himself a whiskey. I could go for one of those, just as soon as I got out of here. I'd drink the bottle. Forget my two drink rule.

J rose slowly. "She's thinking of running. That tells me you haven't shown her the house. I think before we go any further, before we explain to her what has happened to her life, she should see the house. Then she'll understand. It will make things simpler if she understands."

"I don't care what she understands. This is happening." T shrugged crossing to where K had poured the drink, presumably to pour himself one.

W sighed. "It's a good idea." He snapped his fingers and it took me a second to realize he'd done so to get my attention. His eyes continued to glare. Was he fucking serious with the snapping? "Go upstairs. All the way to the top. That'll be two sets of staircases. All of those rooms are empty right now. Go in. Out on the balcony. Then you'll see. Come on down after that. You can go wander around outside if you want to. When you've worn yourself out from the futility of planning escape, we'll tell you what we expect from you and why you're here. But not a minute before. There's no point in speaking to someone who is plotting a ridiculous escape attempt. I don't want to waste the breath."

D strode forward, his man bun catching my attention again. "You could jump from the balcony if you want to. It'll kill you. Even should you manage to survive a fall from that level, there are rocks everywhere. Hitting the ground would kill you. That's always an option. Jump, if you want to."

"Fuck." K shook his head, a laugh in his voice. "Did you seriously just say that?"

These assholes could all choke on their own stomach bile for all I cared. I turned like I was going to do as I was told. No one blinked at that, which told me they were used to being obeyed. That was fine by me. I wasn't taking a tour of the house. I ran to the front door and out, slamming it behind me.

It was sunset, and I'd lose the light soon but that was okay. I didn't intend to be out very long. I was barefoot, but I ran like I had on my running shoes. At that moment, I couldn't have cared less about stubbed toes or torn up skin.

Cold air stuck me, and I shivered as I looked left and right. In the back of my mind that struck me as odd. It wasn't cold in Louisiana in March. Were we having a cold spell I didn't realize? I ran hard out the front door and abruptly stopped. I had nowhere to go if I continued forward, not unless I wanted to run straight into the water.

The house was flat against a rocky beach. My heart beat faster. Where the hell was I? I didn't wait to consider that but ran on. There had to be a road somewhere. It must be on the other side of the house. I darted left and ran hard, following the line of the house to the other side. No, there was no road. On this side there were trees. Lots of them. None of this made sense. How could there be no way to get to this house?

They must traipse through the woods whenever they came and went. It seemed like a huge effort for them to make each time they departed or arrived. I didn't care about the logistics.

I ran.

Until I had to stop because I had run almost the entire length of the island. I didn't have my phone or my watch on me to calculate exact distance, but I was a runner, and it felt like about three miles. I was on an island, containing just the big house. As far as I could tell, there was nothing else.

It had fallen fully dark. I could swim, but I didn't know where the closest land was or if that was even safe to do. I put my hands on my knees and tried to breathe. It wasn't exertion making me out of breath but sheer panic.

Thunder boomed in the sky a second before rain pelted down on my head. It was cold rain, and I shivered. I had to face facts. I was in this strange place, wherever it was, with five guys who went by initials. I had no memory of getting here. The weather was drastically different than it had been at school.

I was royally screwed.

Okay. I stood up straight. I couldn't stay out here and freeze to death. The temperature had dropped degrees just since I'd been outside running. If I hadn't been moving, I'd probably have frozen by now.

My feet tingled, my digits letting me know what my brain had finally realized, this wasn't working.

I limped back to the house, trying the door handle. Fortunately, it was open. All hope wasn't lost. I was a: not dead. If they wanted to kill me they could have done so by now. As long as I wasn't dead there was hope. And b: they had to get supplies sometimes. They had to get on and off the island. I would figure out how to make that work for me. I wasn't a wilting flower. I would get away from wherever here was.

"She's back." T called out, coming out of a room I hadn't been in yet. The smell of food wafted toward me, and my stomach growled. Between the vomiting and the running, I was starved.

He looked me up and down. "You're drenched."

"It's raining." That seemed an obvious answer.

He sighed before he stormed in front of me and opened a closet. "There are clothes in here. Not yours but you may use them for the moment. Change in the bathroom, there. Then come in here and join us for dinner. We weren't going to hold it much longer. None of us settle for cold or burned food. If you caused either of those things to happen, you'd just have to starve for the night."

I'd never gone without food, and I wasn't a fool, that didn't sound very fun. I needed answers, too, so I hustled, doing exactly what he told me to do. I arrived in what proved to be the dining room to find all five of them sitting around a round table.

It was a funny look for a dining room and not one I'd ever seen before. Dining room tables were long, at least where I came from, and had two heads of the table. There was an empty seat next to D, Mr. Kill-Yourself-If-You-Want-To, and I sat down next to him.

A woman came in, wearing a maid's uniform and holding a tray of food. Behind her, an older man followed, holding a second one. I nearly gasped. There were servants here. I made a quick note; maybe they'd help me. Maybe I could make something happen.

The two served bowls of soup before exiting without a word of acknowledgment from any of the men.

Surprisingly, considering his dismissive gaze earlier, it was W who spoke to me. "Did you wear yourself out? Have a good look? See any of the local wildlife?"

"Wildlife?" My voice cracked, my throat feeling a little bit like sandpaper. I hoped I wasn't getting sick.

He drummed his fingers on the table while everyone else started eating their soup. I took a page from the rest of them. It was delicious, creamy. I thought I tasted squash and apples.

"I'm going to level with you," W spoke, and I set down my spoon, waiting. "You are here, Everly, because we need your father to do something for us. As soon as he does it, you can leave."

My mind buzzed. My father? I hardly saw the man. He had done his best to raise me, but as a single parent who owned his own accounting firm, he'd been busy a lot of the year. I stared at W for a long moment. "I'm sorry. You want my father to do something for you so you're holding me prisoner? What is this, the Bronze Age in France? You can't just take a person prisoner to compel their parent to perform some kind of task. And what could you want from him? He's a small town accountant in Louisiana specializing in basically widowers and divorcees."

K shook his head. "I'm afraid not. But we aren't surprised you don't know about what your father actually does. If you knew, it wouldn't be secret."

Seeing as I was in this house, in the middle of somewhere I didn't know, with five men who had kidnapped me, I was willing to suspend my disbelief on this subject. "Is my father in the CIA?"

"The CIA is nothing." D threw his head back.

"Less than nothing." K groaned, taking a spoonful of soup into his mouth. "The CIA is ants marching. The NSA, the FBI. Nothing. Nothing. Nothing. People have no idea who's in charge."

My body had gone cold. Conspiracies had never been my thing. Illuminati was not confirmed, they didn't have aliens in Area 51, Lee Harvey Oswald killed JFK, The Moon Landing wasn't faked, and there was no Reptilian Elite.

I shivered. Maybe my shoeless run had been ill thought out. I really didn't want to get sick right now. "Who's in charge? Little green men?"

W smirked. "We are. Or more specifically, a group called The Alliance. Your father is a member of The Alliance."

Now that was too far. "Is it possible you have the wrong person?" A girl could only hope. "My father is a small town accountant. He isn't running the country."

"World," D corrected. He must have finished his soup and pushed it away.

I put my head in my hands. I couldn't hide it. "I am in the presence of crazy people. Crazy people have somehow kidnapped me. I… Are you all suffering from the same paranoid delusions? I have the deepest respect for people with mental illness but this is too much. Did you all escape from the same institution? Is there someone I can call to help you?"

"Everly," J said my name, and the room was silent until I looked at him. "You should never have known about this. We were raised in it, as your father was, and as any son he had would be. As it is, he only had you, so his family line will die with no son to carry on the line. Unless you have a son, in which case it'll go to him. Your father seems like a small town accountant. He is not."

The two servants who'd come in before re-entered and cleared away the soup bowls. The men were evidently not concerned with speaking in front of them because they continued. This time it was K who spoke.

"Think about it. If you were going to control the workings of the world, who was rich, who was in power, who lived and died, would you let your presence be known? Would you be obvious? Or would you hold non-descript upper middle class jobs that earned you enough to be comfortable, enough you could hide your riches from others."

I hated that what he said made sense. This was supposed to be ludicrous. It wasn't supposed to inch into the back of my mind. No, I refused to go down this path. Conspiracies were insidious for a reason. They sucked people in, made them believe in nonsense.

"And my father is one of those people? You five sitting here with me are the powerful Svengalis moving the workings of the world while you eat apple soup at a circular table?"

T shook his head. "Did you taste the apple more than the acorn-squash?"

I could have growled. "That's not really important right now."

The next round of food was placed in front of me. It was a good thing I ate everything and didn't have food allergies because no one had asked me ahead of time. The plate was filled with quinoa, green lentils, steamed kale, sweet potatoes, microgreens and a spicy peanut sauce. All of that was at the bottom of the plate while tender steak rested on top. It was delicious, but I almost choked on it thinking about the conundrum I found myself in.

They really believed what they were saying. None of my friends would have put together a hoax like this. I didn't think the best prank players in the world could have fathomed this.

I chewed my steak slowly to give myself time to contemplate what they'd told me. Finally, I spoke. "So what world events have you personally controlled in The Alliance? I mean, things aren't so great out there right now. Unemployment. Poverty. World hunger. People killing each other. Children being gunned down in school. Plague. Homelessness. It doesn't seem like you're doing such a good job."

J nodded. "You're thinking altruistically. That's a mistake. The Alliance is not designed to take care of the world. It is to keep and improve upon the status quo. All of those things you said are absolutely true and then some. If you have never been to a third world country then you likely don't have a real sense of truly how bad off the world is. You've studied social work so perhaps you have more of a kind soul than most." He waved his hand in the air. "Or maybe you just didn't know what to major in. I don't know, and I don't care. There are lots of truths in the world, some you haven't imagined."

He had my attention. "Like what?"

K answered for him. "Like the rich keep getting richer. The economy crashed. It weeded out the pseudo-rich. The truly top percentages got even wealthier. People took power, positions they'd been promised. The herd was trimmed. Whatever it looks like, whatever beautiful Pollyanna ridiculousness the ant masses hold onto that things might get better are always bullshit. Because behind it all, behind every decision, every election, every dollar spent is The Alliance. Waiting. Watching. Moving things."

I wasn't hungry anymore, and I'd only eaten a few bites of my food. "I can't accept that. Not at all. If that was true, someone would know. Someone would have exposed this. People would know."

J smiled at me. "Would they? We took you from your apartment in the middle of the day. We took all of your things, transported you unconscious, and not a single person looked at us sideways. People see what they want to see, Everly."

"You shouldn't even know about this." D sighed. "Women aren't included in The Alliance. This is a men's club. Women's lib isn't real, not in the real world, not in the one where it matters. But you're here and so you'll know."

I gained information every second with these Letters. K was a bully who liked to explain things. T cared about food and wore all black. He glared a lot. W smirked and snapped his fingers. J owned this house, which must be why he was so casual here. And D said sick things like jump and kill yourself, or we might kill you.

Several thoughts dawned on me at once. "Say I accept this nonsense as true."

K shook his head. "I knew you were going to have a mouth on you."

I ignored him and continued. "Why tell me any of it? Why let me see your faces? Are you really intending to just kill me?"

"You will never say a word to anyone about this time. Not ever. By the time you leave here, when your father collects you and takes you away, you will understand the importance of keeping your mouth shut for the rest of your life. There will never be a time you couldn't be gotten to, there will never be a place that your grandchildren couldn't be hurt. You will never say a word, Everly."

My hands shook, so I put them in my lap to hide that. "Why not just tell me your names?"

"That's for your sake, little girl." T spoke. "We are the bogeyman. It's always best not to know what to call him."

"Or we might kill you. If you seem like too much trouble. There are other ways to motivate your father. This seemed the most humane." D got to his feet. "I'm going for some air."

With that, he left the room, but I guessed we weren't done. J spoke again. "This is my home you're staying in. One of many I own. It is three miles long. There is nothing on it but this house, as you have seen by now. I'd still encourage you to check out the view from the top floor. It's breathtaking. Lake Champlain is gorgeous in all weather. This island, like many around here, is privately owned. No one comes here without my permission. The water can go from still to treacherous in a heartbeat. Keep that in mind before you try to make the swim. The closest land is several miles from here. You'll be my guest here and treated as such up until the point you disappoint us. Do that and all things will change for you. I really only have one rule."

I didn't like the sound of any of that. "What's the rule?"

"Stay out of the basement. What's down there is none of your business. Wander the grounds. Use the house. Read the books. There's no internet for you to use here, no cellular service should you find yourself suddenly in possession of a phone. Get comfortable, Everly, and stay out of the fucking basement."

Chapter 3

I still didn't believe them. How could I when it was so clearly utter nonsense? I shook my head. "I have no interest in whatever might be going on in your basement. Trust me on that." Unless it was a way off this island, in which case I was going down into that basement the first chance I got. "But you have to be wrong. Maybe this is all real. Maybe you are all big giants of the world and you really control things. My father is not. Maybe it's someone who has the same name."

Jeb Marrs couldn't be that common of a name, but maybe there was one more person. Another accountant who pissed off a bunch of self-aggrandizing assholes. Maybe they just had the wrong name altogether.

K shook his head. "Do you remember what happened to your mother?"

"She took off on the back of a motorcycle with the president of the local MC club and never came back." I could still see her waving to me as she drove away. Once she'd turned around she'd never looked back, as though I was a complete afterthought.

He nodded. "Yes. And then your father had her killed with the help of The Alliance."

"No." I didn't even hesitate in my answer. My father was many things, but a killer was not one of them. No way was my balding, serious, nervous-tic father a murderer. Nothing they could say was going to convince me of that.

K sighed. "Okay. Everly, what happened to your face when you were four years old?"

I sucked in a breath. "How do you know that?"

"Because I do. I know everything. There isn't a single thing about your life that I can't know. You're an ant. Your father is a player, albeit until recently a small one, but you are an ant. I can know anything I want to know about ants." He lifted his eyebrows slowly. "You do remember what happened to your face?"

I looked down at the table. "There was a Chihuahua. We had the sweetest pit bull at home. I thought all dogs were like him. Toto was his name. I wanted to go over the rainbow. I..." I forced myself to breathe. "I ran up to a dog on the street. It wasn't friendly. We couldn't even blame the owner. No one told me it was okay to touch her. I just did. And she went at me, tore into my cheek." I touched where the bite had been. I hadn't thought about it in years. But I could almost feel it now. I'd been terrified before I'd been in pain. And I'd been so afraid of dogs after that we'd had to rehome Toto.

"That's so interesting." W smiled. "You don't even have a scar. Not even the smallest one."

He was right. Not even a mark where the skin had been torn from my face, where that dog attached itself to my skin and didn't let go. It had taken three adults to get it off me. Not even a dot.

I shrugged. If they had a point, I wished they'd get to it. "What's your point? I was young. Kids heal."

"Not like that they don't." Why was W smiling like that? "You had the benefit of a procedure done by a man named Dr. Roy Alaniz."

How did they know that? I didn't even remember that anymore. They must have read some sort of file on me. "Again, your point?"

"Dr. Alaniz has invented a procedure in pediatrics plastic surgery that is about to be unleashed on the world next year. Then all little boys and girls who get torn to shreds can grow up to be hot like you, Everly."

I didn't focus on the hot word. Much as I would usually love the compliment. I had a feeling he was just throwing out some more nastiness, and if I pushed he'd tell me I was ugly. Better left alone. I tried instead to look at what was really important here.

"Was he in trials for it with me?"

W shook his head, slowly. "Not even a blip on anyone's radar."

"Then how did he do it for me so many years ago?"

He took a sip of his water. "The Alliance has been financially compensating him nicely to ask him to wait until next year to announce it."

That didn't even make any sense. "Why would they do that?"

"There were financial considerations. Patents. Timing. People to put in place in pharma companies and on medical boards. Media buyouts. And clinics to create. Intellectual property. Lots of reasons." W shrugged. "That's how it works. Your cheek got fixed. And your father went from minor player to kept man. He was fine until he wasn't. Now he has to undo what he's done and be punished. You, Everly, you're our sacrificial lamb."

I rose to my feet slowly. "I am not going to be dragged to the top of any hill and butchered. I'll…"

J laughed. "You'll what? Go to bed, Everly. If you need something, let us know. Or better yet let Constance in the kitchen know. Either she or Marco. They work for us. They'll get you whatever you need. I don't want you coming to me for tampons or whatever."

I looked away. "Exactly how long am I staying?"

"Until Daddy plays ball."

That was just vague enough to make me want to puke.

"Don't you five have jobs or something? You're going to just stay here with me?"

J pointed at the door. "Bed."

Apparently I was going to have to get used to being ordered around.

———

THEY REALLY HAD BROUGHT ALL my stuff. Even my stuffed dog Scooby, that I'd had since childhood. It was flat, with an indentation where my head used to go when I made it my pillow for the night. I'd kept the childhood lovey with me over the years more as a keepsake but now, twenty-two years old, grownup, and living mostly on my own, I held onto Scooby like he might still chase away my nightmares. Five nightmares. In alphabetical order. D, J, K, T, W. It was perfect they'd given me initials and not names to call them.

D—the one with the man bun who said the most provocative things, like I should die or kill myself.

J—this was his house. He seemed bored.

K—he spoke the most, and he didn't like to be told no; he'd be a bully when he had to be.

T—the man in black who'd helped me get out of my wet clothes and then rolled his eyes at me.

W—the glaring eyes and the smirking mouth.

Having names implied they were members of the human race. These five were not. They were something else. They were… I didn't even know what. I slumped down in the bed. If they'd brought all of my things, they could have packed up my bedding as well. I didn't like these. These sheets were scratchy. I'd always been a total baby when it came to where I slept. I liked soft things around me at night. If that made me a spoiled princess then so be it.

I rubbed my cheek. I didn't have a scar. I'd not thought about the dog bite in years, but now with all their craziness running around in my head, I couldn't stop considering what they'd said. Was it possible? Was my father in something called The Alliance that somehow ran the world? Like freemasons on crack.

I groaned. I had a million questions. Scratch that, a million and one questions. They weren't going to be answered tonight. I was officially kidnapped. In my whole life, I could never have imagined this happening. We weren't rich enough for me to be worth this to anyone. Or at least that's what I thought. Maybe we were. Maybe there was a hidden cache of money under my father's bed where he kept the gun he'd used to shoot my mother in the head.

I turned off the light in the room. I'd contemplated locking the door before I'd discovered there wasn't a lock. I turned the light back on. Maybe I could move some furniture in front of it.

I got out of the bed. I'd somehow push the dresser in front of the door and move it when I wanted to get out. I'd put some muscle into it. I could count it as my workout for the day, my weight resistance to go with the cardio I'd done running like a maniac around this frozen tundra. My feet had still not forgiven me for the mistake.

A gunshot sounded, and I jumped, leaping back onto

the bed. I covered my mouth with my hands like I could stop the sound and then thought better of it. Maybe it was the police. Yes, they'd come to save me from this madness. I rushed to the window, prepared to scream but what I saw stopped me.

Lights from the house illuminated the front yard. D was outside, shotgun in the air, firing at the lake. As I stared, wide mouthed watching, I let myself *hear* the sounds outside. Something was cracking. What was that? He shot again, and I once again jumped. I wasn't entirely used to the sound of shotguns, but I'd certainly heard them before. Our neighbor had once taken out a gator that got in his pool. An argument had ensued after that about whether or not he should have shot that gator or called animal control.

I rubbed the back of my neck. Why hadn't I appreciated normal? I stepped back from the window. I was going to learn something in every moment here and catalog the knowledge I gained into an escape plan. What did I know? There were guns in the house. D might be completely out of his mind. He suggested suicide and murder when it came to me. He shot at the lake.

I had to add this to what I knew about D—said mean things and shot guns into the lake. He might be the craziest out of all of them.

They didn't want me in the basement. That meant I was going to have to get down there when I knew I couldn't be caught. There were two people working here, maybe they could be persuaded to help me. Surely, they could leave if they wanted to. This was J's house. Supplies had to be brought here. Maybe I could get away with whoever provided the food.

Hope wasn't lost. With that thought in mind, I went back to the idea of moving the dresser. I ran to one side and pushed. This wouldn't stop a bullet, or at least not for long. But it would give me a second. To do what I didn't know but I'd figure it out, even if it was jumping out the window.

The dresser wouldn't move. I tried again. That was when I saw it was bolted to the wall. I sighed. They'd clearly taken into account that I might try to move this dresser and had prevented it. I was going to need tools to undo it.

A flash of despondence almost took me to my knees, but I pushed it away. They didn't want to kill me, at least not yet, and even when D had threatened me he hadn't had malice in his blue eyes, which either meant he didn't mean it or he was a sociopath.

I'd planned to sleep in my clothes in case I had to run, even my shoes, which I had finally gotten out of the closet. Now that seemed sort of silly. I had nowhere to run. A better plan was to act like I obeyed. They wanted a sacrificial lamb, well I could seem like I was behaving. When they weren't watching, I'd get the fuck out of this place.

With that thought in mind, I set about to act like I was going to be calm and normal. That started with taking a shower. For being the only structure on an island there was plenty of hot water, an abundance of electricity. They must have an incredible system here. I closed my eyes. Well, of course they did. I internally rolled my eyes. They were rulers of the universe. They would not do without hot water.

A thought snuck into my consciousness. If the water broke, someone would have to fix it. Maybe I could get away that way. There were a million small things that might add up to escape. I just had to keep thinking about it.

I finished bathing and turned off the spray. I was about to step out of the shower when it dawned on me there might be cameras in the room. I sighed. This was going to get old, fast. I grabbed my towel and dried myself inside the shower with the curtain still drawn. It was useful to have my own toiletries. I brushed, flossed, and used my deodorant and moisturizer. My reflection was slightly better than earlier, although I was still wounded looking.

With my towel wrapped around me like a lifeline, I walked out and opened some of the drawers. Things weren't exactly where I'd have put them but good enough. I found my pajamas. The air in the room was cold, or at least cooler than I was used to in Louisiana. I never thought I'd miss Baton Rouge. My plan had always been to get out of there and go to someplace bigger after college. I hadn't thought about where I would go, just that I would get away.

Now I wanted to go back more than anything.

Truth was, I didn't know where Lake Champlain was. I sighed. There was clearly a gap in my education. I was somewhere cold. That much I knew. Somewhere it was still cold in March. In my ugly brown pajamas, I crawled under the covers, drawing the scratchy material around me. I reached over to turn off the light, scowling the whole time.

This sucked.

It sucked. Sucked. Sucked.

I didn't know exactly why—or maybe I fucking did—my paternal grandmother's face moved across my vision. She was a foul woman. I'd detested her. For a while, after my mother left—or maybe died—she'd moved in to help us. That little while had turned into ten years. Eventually, she'd left to live in Florida with her miserable sister and her smelly cat.

I loved cats. Just not that one. And the feeling had been mutual. That cat had hated me, too.

But my grandmother had been full of pearls of wisdom that she shared, constantly. I rolled my eyes at the thought. She would tell me—if she hadn't died five years ago and been slightly eaten by her cat before they'd found her in her bed—that this was my fault because I'd been having so much sex.

I groaned. She could go fuck herself. Wherever she was. If there was anything at all. I didn't need her in this mess. I needed her as far away from my stream of consciousness as possible. I forced my eyes closed. Maybe this would turn out to be a horrible dream.

Maybe it would all be gone in the morning.

▭

I WOKE WITH A GASP. A loud mechanical noise sounded in the room, and I covered my ears as it assaulted my sleep. What the hell was that? I jumped out of bed. The clock said eleven, which meant I'd only been asleep an hour. I rushed to the window in time to see a helicopter landing on the beach not far from where I slept. Lights blared on the beach both from the helicopter and a spotlight that seemed to be coming from the house itself. Three figures walked out toward it. I recognized Constance at once, since she was the only other woman here that I'd seen. The man next to her had to be Marco and in front was... I didn't know the guys all that well yet, but it looked like J to me.

Something about the way he tilted his head to the left gave him away. A man jumped out the helicopter, and J said something to him. I couldn't hear it, but people spoke with their hands. The blades stopped spinning and the noise stopped. More men jumped off the helicopter. They all wore black. I leaned closer to my window to watch. What was going to happen now?

Constance and Marco walked to the helicopter, and along with the men in black, unloaded boxes. The whole thing was over in ten minutes, and then the men got back on the helicopter and left. I sighed. That was probably the day's supplies. Or maybe the week's. If I wanted off, then the next time it arrived, I was going to have to figure out how to get on that thing when it came.

I crawled back into my bed. After a while, sleep took me again. If I dreamed, I didn't remember.

———

I WOKE up with sun blaring into the room. I hadn't shut the shades. That was a mistake. Now I was awake and it was earlier than I wanted it to be. Truth was, much of my gumption had fled in sleep. Without coffee, I was pretty useless most of the time, and this morning it just made me want to stay in bed for the rest of the day and pretend none of this was happening.

But the sun wouldn't leave me alone, and soon I crawled out of my uncomfortable bedding and made my way to the bathroom. I cleaned up and then got dressed in something I wouldn't wear to the gym. Someone had dressed me in my workout clothes the day before, and I couldn't even deal with that. Which one of these guys had dressed me?

No, I wouldn't go there in my mind. It wouldn't do any good. I'd talk about it later. In therapy. Or with a lot of alcohol. For now, I'd put that aside. Yes, I officially had Scarlett Syndrome. That was a real thing. It had been in a textbook I'd had to read during one of my early psych classes. I'd think about it tomorrow...

Except I didn't really function like that. Never had. I was a look things in the eyes kind of a girl. I couldn't deal with this tomorrow. I had to... I didn't even know. What did I have to do?

Finally dressed in my jeans and a long sleeve-shirt, plus the addition of my socks and sneakers, I made my way down the stairs. The house was quiet, which was just what I wanted. I could snoop. Maybe find the basement.

I wanted to at least know how to get down there, so when the time came that I could sneak down, I'd know how. I found my way into the kitchen where Constance was busy working over the stove. I smelled eggs and my stomach grumbled. I hadn't eaten much of my dinner. Still, food was the least of my concerns.

She turned toward me and raised her wooden spoon in my direction. "If you are here for food or coffee you are in the right place. If you are here to ask me to help you can shove it down your throat before you even get started."

Well... that was certainly telling me. She wasn't going to be my ally. At least not right off the bat. I nodded to her, ready to speak, but she continued.

"And, don't ask me to explain things to you. I'm not going to. My job is to feed you and keep your room clean. The whole house. Marco and I run things here. You want answers, well there are five young men out there who can give them to you. Not me. And you don't pester Marco either."

I nodded. Young men? They were older than me, that much I knew. Maybe next to her they were youthful. I didn't want to blow this moment, not when things could change. I was a stranger right now. Whatever had happened to lead her into working for these... monsters...

she could alter her viewpoint. What I needed to do was make her my best friend.

"Yes, ma'am." I thickened my southern accent just a little so that it might sound more charming. "I understand. Is there coffee?"

She raised an eyebrow at me. I could see the wheels turning in her head. She had expected me to argue with her. When I hadn't done that, she wasn't sure what to do with me. Or at least that was what I was guessing, since I couldn't read minds.

Constance pointed to the table behind them. "Coffee brews all day. J…" Her voice trailed off. "J drinks it all day."

She'd almost used his name. I moved past her to pour myself some. As I stood sipping it for a second, I could believe all would be well. Caffeine had that effect on me. Every morning it reset my whole mood.

I leaned on the counter. "Can I help you with anything?"

She waved her hand in the air. "Never."

I blinked. "Never?"

That had to be a new answer for me. No, thank you was something I was more accustomed to. Or sure you can do… Never?

She shot me a side-eyed look. "This is my job. It's not yours. You aren't getting in my way." She scooped some eggs onto a plate and handed them to me. "Now get out of my kitchen. If you want more coffee you can come back in."

Just then Marco came in from the back door. His movement caught my attention, and it was a second before I realized he was signing. I knew ASL. My next door neighbor growing up was deaf. I wouldn't call myself fluent, but I could understand a lot. Right then, he asked

Constance what she wanted him to do with the extra water. She answered him silently with her hands telling him to put them in the basement.

Well now, that was interesting. I looked away like I didn't understand, trying to keep my gaze and expression vague. If he didn't know I could understand, that might be better. I sipped my coffee and left the kitchen, making my way quickly to the window so I could observe where Marco went. He walked a distance next to the house before vanishing out of sight. Now, I knew. The entrance to the basement was on the outside of the house.

I would just make my way out there as soon as everyone was busy. Holding my plate and my coffee, I walked to the dining room table. For a few minutes, all I did was eat. I didn't think about anything else. Sip. Chew. Swallow. Repeat. Repeat. Repeat.

The eggs were delicious. Whatever else Constance would prove to be, she was a wonderful cook. I'd have to tell her. Unless saying so was going to make her tell me off again. I didn't have the slightest idea how to handle this.

A noise caught my attention a second before the front door opened and then closed. K walked in. He was in sweat pants and a long sleeve t-shirt. They were both gray and his sneakers were black. Sweat glistened on his brow. He must have been exercising.

He turned toward me. "Oh good, you're up."

"Why is it good?" Maybe I hadn't had enough coffee yet. They'd kidnapped me. Maybe there was no such thing as enough coffee for managing that.

"Because I need you to speak to your father. Stupid asshole is going to get his daughter killed."

My body went cold with his words. "Do you think you might be willing to treat me with the smallest amount of humanity and not speak about my death as if it's no big deal to you?"

K shook his head. "I'm not sure. You're more human to me than most because you are your father's daughter, and even though he's a scumbag, he is Alliance. That makes you, sort of, part of the group. But you really don't register to me as all that important."

I sighed. Ask a question, get an answer.

Chapter 4

It turned out the no cell phones rule was just for me. There were cell phones. K had one, and as he lifted it up to call my father, there was a moment where I thought about grabbing his and running for it. Then I remembered D was somewhere in the house with a gun. Being that blatantly defiant to the rules would likely land me in a body bag.

K looked at the phone after he dialed. A second later my father's voice sounded. As K held the phone, staring at it, I had to presume he was on video and not just the phone. Not unless K's superiority to the rest of the human race meant he didn't know how to talk on the fucking phone.

"Remember what we talked about, Jeb. We're not using names here. You blow that and this is over."

There was a long pause and then my father spoke, his voice tight. "Let me see her."

"By all means." K passed me the phone, and I took it from him.

My father's face stared at me through the phone. He'd

been my only parent, my only caregiver. When I'd been sick, he'd seen to my needs. Other people had their mothers to talk to. I had my stiff, sometimes unyielding father. But he'd been there. My grandmother had cleaned the house and scolded me. My father raised me. He'd never let me down.

Tears flooded my eyes. We weren't very mushy-gushy with each other. He tended to be stiff upper lipped, and I tried never to be in a situation where I had to feel much of anything to begin with. But this was different.

"Dad."

He nodded at me for a second before he spoke. "You're alive."

"For now. They keep threatening to kill me. But yes, for now, I'm alive." I sniffed, wiping at the tears coming down my face.

"They have you in that hideaway in Vermont." He sighed, looking away for a second. "They won't kill you as long as I do what they want and you don't cause trouble. You're my family and that makes you Alliance. As a rule, we don't kill each other except in extreme circumstances."

And right there was my answer. Any doubt I'd had that this whole experience could be a mix up or that I could be just surrounded by lunatics fled. This. Was. Happening. I steeled my back and stopped my tears. They wouldn't help now. The cavalry wasn't going to ride in to save me and *deus ex machina* didn't seem likely. I had to deal with this and that meant I needed answers. And I needed them fast before K took the phone away from me.

"Start talking, Dad." People weren't perfect. I could be furious with him when I was off this island in Vermont. I'd already learned something I didn't know before. Lake Champlain was in Vermont.

"You were never supposed to know this. Women aren't in this world."

I cleared my throat. "That much I've garnered. More please."

"Careful, Jeb," K warned from next to me. My father couldn't see him but he could hear him.

"What you need to know, Everly, is that I will do whatever I can to make this go away. You will be returned to me and you can get back to your life. In the meantime, you don't need to know the details of what has happened here. It's better if you don't. Minimally, there is a power shuffle in The Alliance and you are in the hands of five men who think they should be in charge. They won't be. Certainly, not after this. But they'll get what they want in the meantime. Don't trust them. This will take some time. Some of the things they want date back from before there were... computers. Please be patient and know I am working hard on getting you back."

There was still something I had to ask. "Did you kill Mom?"

He winced when I asked that. "I see they've been talking."

That wasn't a no. That wasn't a horrified look that told me this couldn't possibly be true. No, that was pretty much a yes. My hand shook.

K grabbed the phone from me. "We're aware that what we're asking is next to impossible to get, but that's what you do, right Jeb? You make the impossible possible. You can talk to her again when you come pick her up and not before. I'd let you kiss her goodbye, but that is obviously impossible. I'm not doing daily proof of life. This was your one time. You'll have to wonder if she pissed us off enough to lose her life. I guess that's the price you pay for doing

39

what you did. Wondering if you're working like a dog to save a person who is already dead."

He shut off the phone. "Any device in here with communication capabilities is coded to only respond to the owner's fingerprints."

"You really seem to have gone out of your way to assume that I'm capable of devious thinking. Of planning. I suppose I should be flattered, considering how little you think of women."

I turned on my heel and headed back to the table and my coffee. I didn't expect him to follow me, so when he did, I had to force myself not to react. I sipped my now lukewarm coffee slowly.

"I don't have a low opinion of women."

I set down my drink. "Yes you do. All five of you made that abundantly clear yesterday. Your whole Alliance that is running things is apparently stuck in the Dark Ages and you five along with it."

His smile was slow. "You're not the least bit afraid of me, are you?"

"I actually am. Terrified. I tried to move my dresser into the way of the door last night to see if I could keep you guys out, and it's nailed to the wall. I'm getting dressed behind shower curtains. And D is firing bullets into the lake while black helicopters arrive in the middle of the night. I'm stuck here. You're not all crazy. I'm scared. Yes, feel better?"

He was silent for a moment. "Your dresser is nailed to the wall?"

That was the part that he focused on? "Yes."

K shook his head. "That's not something we did purposefully. I can promise you that."

Well, that was… interesting. "The dresser didn't nail itself to the wall."

"No, it didn't. Hey, J." He called over his shoulder, and a second later J sauntered out of the living room.

He leaned against the door. "You bellowed?"

K rolled his eyes. "Our guest says her furniture is nailed to the wall. Did you do that?"

"Absolutely not." J shook his head. "Out of curiosity, how did you notice that?"

"I thought it might be wonderful to block you guys out of the room. Bar the door."

J tilted his head to the side. "Smart thinking. We are pretty awful people." His smile was slow. "You never do know what we might do. It might even make sense to give you a lock that only you have the key to."

They were being… really nice about this. Or at least not terrible. My internal alarms were sounding. They were clearly about to say something shitty. Except J walked toward the kitchen door and opened it. "Hey, Constance, send Marco here, please."

Did he say please to her? Big bad run-the-world people apparently spoke politely to the ticked off lady in the kitchen. I really had to get on a handle on these guys, and fast. I also couldn't help but admire his ass as he walked. Internally, I groaned. It was bound to happen. I'd always admired men's physiques. Ever since I woke up sexually, I'd been hard pressed to keep my eyes to myself. I was good at pretending that wasn't the case, and that would be a good thing, since the last thing I needed were these five noticing.

Marco came out of the kitchen and J started to sign to him. I looked at K. If I was going to lie about this then I'd start now. "Do you know what they're saying?"

He shook his head. "I don't speak ASL but J is fluent."

He really was. Most hearing people like me, if they signed, they flummoxed through the experience or mouthed the words while they did it. J didn't speak aloud.

He and Marco communicated in utter silence, the movements of their hands fluid and practiced.

I watched as though I was just interested and tried to keep a blank look on my face. I missed some words, but the gist of it was that Marco had nailed the furniture to the walls because he had been told that Jeb Marrs' daughter was coming, and he'd assumed I was a child. Nailing or bolting furniture to the walls was a childproofing measure.

I almost smiled, but I didn't. At least it made sense now. Marco went on to say he would unbolt the furniture, but J stopped him. Rather than that, he should go ahead and install a lock I could use on the door.

And just like that it was settled.

K crossed his arms over his chest. "Settled?"

"Just a mistake. All fixed. Lock going on the door." J raised his eyebrows, his gaze meeting my own. "You can keep any of us out."

"Thank you."

"What were the other concerns? Oh, you're getting dressed behind your shower curtain and D with the gun."

J shook his head. "There aren't video cameras in your room. Or anywhere in the house. We're not that interested in what you're doing."

With that remark, J left. I guessed he didn't have anything to say about D with the gun.

What did I know now? K didn't like to be argued with, he was the one communicating with my father, and he took offense at being accused of being a misogynist.

J solved problems. He signed with his deaf employee.

K sighed. "D is complicated. We all are, but he's the most overtly off. Stay away from him when he has the gun. He's not coming in your room. That's the last thing on his mind. I'm going to go shower." He nodded at me. "You'll be okay if you don't fuck this up."

What did this mean if K thought I should stay away from D? How fucked up was D?

If I didn't fuck this up. I nodded. He didn't have to know I was getting out of here as soon as I fucking could. Before I turned away, I saw Marco. He stood in the doorway, watching me. With a nod in my direction, he left. That was odd. But then again, this whole experience ranked among the strangest I could imagine. Why should he be any different?

━━

I WASN'T USED to having nothing to do. With no agenda for the first time ever, I took the stairs to the top of the house and did what W had suggested the night before. I could look at where I was from the top. Of course, if I'd done this instead of darting out of the house I could have spared the bottom of my feet the ordeal they'd been through.

If I let myself notice, they really, really hurt. But I was good at pretending I didn't have pain. My father had been busy. Unless a Chihuahua mauled me, I didn't bother him with small stuff. I walked into one of the empty bedrooms. It didn't have furniture. The space was empty except for the black window treatments. They drifted slightly from moving air in the room. The vents were still on, pushing heat into this part of the house despite its lack of occupants.

I could hear my feet on the wood floors, making creaking sounds with each step I took toward the balcony. My room didn't have a balcony or the view this room had. I looked straight down at the lake. This side of the house showed the rest of the island. I opened the door and stepped onto the balcony. A cold wind hit me, and I shivered. March was obviously still a very cold time in Vermont. I could see the other side of the island and the lake there, too. In daylight, it was obvious the water was frozen. In the far distance I could see another island. Even if it were summer, it would be too far to swim.

I wasn't much of a swimmer. I knew how. I could certainly make my way across a pool, but I wasn't going to count on my ability to go miles. But maybe I could get a boat. Maybe there were some, somewhere, I could find them. I knew how to row. I'd done it with a boy I was dating because he liked to go out on a river on the weekend. I'd wanted to fuck him, and he'd wanted to paddle around in a lake. I'd paddled, and when he'd gotten his fill, we'd had at it—sometimes in the boat, which had been a challenge since I'd insisted on wearing a lifejacket the whole time.

Maybe I could row my way out of here. I chewed on my lip. Maybe they were in the basement.

Still, that wasn't going to be a fast exit. I had to wait for the ice to melt and who knew when that would be. Unless I could just walk out onto the ice. That was a thought. I'd read in a book once where people drove onto the ice. Was this thick enough to do that?

I was going to find out. Immediately.

I left the balcony, closing the door and then locking it behind me. A strong wind would blow it open if it wasn't closed, and I'd bet we got lots of strong winds here. I made my way back to my room. I hadn't heard anyone the night before coming or going, but they said all the bedrooms upstairs were empty which meant the Letters had to be sleeping on the same floor as me. Or the first floor. Or the basement. While I was at it, I was going to officially find that door to the basement.

I stopped in my room to grab my coat. The door was

open, and the door handle was different. I bent over to look at it. I could now lock it by pushing in a button on the knob. Next to the bed was a key. There might be another key, but for the moment I was going to believe they had no desire to come in my room at night.

I hoped I could sleep better tonight knowing it was locked.

I grabbed my coat and made my way outside. How did a person know if the ice was thick enough to walk on it? Did I put my foot on it and just see? I buttoned up my coat. How did people get through January or February if it was this cold in March? My coat wasn't going to get the job done. I must have been really worked up yesterday not to notice.

That didn't seem to be the case today. I was fully aware of the temperature outside. Eventually, I reached the water. Or what would be the water if it wasn't so frozen outside.

I stared at it. I was a Louisiana girl. We had some colder days in Baton Rouge but never anything like this. Not even in our coldest parts of winter. I don't think it was this cold when it snowed. I shivered. Okay, maybe I was being dramatic.

I finally got to the edge. I didn't know what I'd expected to see, but I didn't have an aha moment where I suddenly understood if the ice was thick enough or not to walk on. I picked up a rock off the ground, and I threw it at the ice. It didn't crack. Was that a good thing or a bad thing?

"It's freezing out here."

I jumped as W spoke. I hadn't heard him approach. How early did these guys get up? I hadn't slept late and so far at least three of them had been up and out before me.

"It is." I agreed. What else was there to say?

He stepped toward me. "This is not my weather. I was not built for this weather."

"Are you from somewhere warm? Like me?"

He nodded. "I was born in the United States, in Georgia, actually. But I was raised in Saudi Arabia. Well, raised for ten years. Then back to the States. At that point it was southern California. So no, I'm not used to this weather." He looked past me. "I suppose if I was trying to get away from here I might try to walk on the ice."

I sighed. "Don't act like you read my mind. This is obvious."

"It is," he agreed. "I would never claim to read minds. Although I've been trained to understand what people are thinking most of the time. It comes with The Alliance. So if I was going to try to get out of here I would contemplate running on the ice. All I can tell you is what J told me a month ago. The ice may be thin right here on the edge. I wouldn't risk walking on it. If it cracks under you and you end up in the water you're dead. I, for one, am not going in after you."

I shook my head. "My father will do all that work to get back a dead daughter."

"True."

"If he got me back at all. I mean, who would fish out my frozen dead body? That would be such an aggravation." I dramatically rolled my eyes.

W threw his head back and laughed. "Truth. Come back to the house. It's cold."

"I have nothing to do there." I'd spoken the words, and I couldn't take them back. "I can't imagine that I'm going to sit around here for the next few months and do nothing. What am I supposed to do?"

He nodded. "You want something to do? That's not going to be too hard to figure out. We'll tell T. He is very good at finding things for people to do. I'm sure we can work that right out. Keep you as busy as a bee."

I should probably have kept my mouth shut. He nodded in the direction of the house, and I walked toward it. "I just can't... believe this is happening. I'm not sure I'm processing this. I think I might be in some kind of long-term denial."

"I don't know if twenty-four hours counts as long-term." He laughed again. I wouldn't have pinned him as someone who did a lot of that. "I remember when I first found out. Like you, I wasn't supposed to know."

That didn't make sense. "Why is that? You're male. I thought that was the trick here. Be born with a penis and get entrance into a secret society to rule the world."

"It's a little more complicated than that. For example, if you were to have a son, he'd have entrance. It doesn't die with the birth of just girls. The next boy born gets entrance, which can make it complicated in the event that several generations go without a male born."

I didn't want to be fascinated with this, but I was. "How does that work?"

"There are people in The Alliance who are tasked with handling that. I've never personally been to one of those interventions. But it happens."

My mind whirled with questions. "What happens if a person is born female, but is transgendered. How does that work?"

"They get entrance. It's not that complicated. Men get entrance."

I pointed at him. "But you just said you weren't supposed to know. So clearly there is something else going on here."

"I'm the second son. I have an older brother. He was born three years before me. He knew from the time he could understand, usually that's when a person is twelve, that he was Alliance. Dad trained him for the role. I was never supposed to know anything about it. But go and get yourself killed in a skiing accident and guess what? Second son suddenly has to be Alliance ready." He shrugged. "That was a great sixteenth birthday present. Both the death and the membership on the same day."

Wow. That seemed… intense. I didn't want to feel for this man. He was one fifth of the team keeping me prisoner. And yet I did. I wasn't an idiot. It would be useful for me to make him a friend, and I was sure he thought the same. Better to keep me compliant if I believed he gave a shit.

Still, my stomach did turn over, thinking of the pain he had to still deal with.

He put a hand on my arm. "Don't feel too badly for me. I'm rich and powerful. And it was a long time ago. Twenty-two years, actually. Time moved. Fast."

Well, that answered another question. He was thirty-eight years old. I'd have placed him right about there in age. "Big plans for your fortieth in two years?"

"Why yes." He nodded. "I plan to be celebrating my one year anniversary of taking control of the world."

And there it was. The Alliance was a new concept to me. But it was real. I could never forget for a second, even if they all turned out to be laughers with sad stories, they had an objective, and it was to rule the world.

I answered his statement from earlier, even if it didn't require a response. "I can't get my head around it to be honest. I'm not sure I can really deal with the idea that the five of you walk around ruling things."

"The ruling council does, actually. We're members. We play important roles but for now we are not in charge." He smiled. "Very soon we will be."

We'd arrived back at the house. W leaned forward, and he opened the door. He brushed by me, smelling like Giorgio Armani cologne. I knew the scent well. It was one of my favorites on a guy. If I came across it in a bar, I took a second look to see who was wearing it. It was expensive, so guys who wore it were few and far between. But this man was older, rich, and even if his face wouldn't grace the cover of magazines there was something about him that screamed sex.

In other circumstances, I'd never have shoved him out of my bed.

I walked through the door and nearly collided with T.

"Just the man I wanted to see." W pulled me out of the way before I could hit him. He set me to the side.

T smiled but there was no joy in his eyes. "Do you have a problem?"

He didn't like the idea that there was a problem. That I could tell from the way he used that word.

W shook his head. "Not like that."

"Okay." He shifted his stance slightly. "What's up?"

W put his arm around me, which was really odd. I stiffened. "Girl needs something to do."

T blinked. "Are you kidding?"

"No, she's going to be here for months. And wandering the island all day every day isn't going to work for very long."

T pointed at the library. "Books. We have books upon books. Go read."

"Go read?" I had to answer. "That's what I'm going to do for months? Read?" Actually, that sounded like heaven. Of course, it depended on the book.

"I'll find something."

Why did I talk before I thought? Twice now I'd really stuck my foot in it.

Chapter 5

T, who once again was in an entirely black outfit, told me to sit myself down, and since it didn't seem like I should be arguing right at that moment, I did as instructed. He left the room without a word, leaving me alone in the dining room. Marco walked out of the kitchen and stared at me for a moment before he continued on silently. I almost signed to him. I really didn't like not telling him I understood him. It seemed sort of like lying by omission.

But then I remembered I was in a spider web. I was twisting and turning, trying to get out, not get pulled in deeper.

K was the chattiest so far, although W had been pretty talkative down by the water. He hadn't glared at me, so maybe I had to take glaring eyes away from what I knew about him. K—the man who didn't want to be accused of not liking women. W—the man who had become a member of The Alliance at 16 when his brother died. J—who signed to his deaf employee and had my room fixed. T—who was once again wearing black and who was apparently going to find me something to do. D—with his man bun maybe shooting at ice somewhere.

The Letters held me prisoner because of some kind of internal trouble in The Alliance. An organization I hadn't even known existed until yesterday. Tears swarmed my eyes, and I blinked them away. I wouldn't cry where they could see me. I'd spare myself that kind of humiliation.

T returned, pausing in the doorway. I sat back in my chair. "Do you always wear black?"

He nodded. "Most of the time. I prefer it, always have."

"Are you some kind of vampire?"

He held a manila folder in his hand and scooted down the table next to me. "That would be sort of obvious for a vampire, wouldn't it?"

"Like it would be obvious for members of The Alliance to be famous people like presidents or prime ministers."

His smile was slow. "Exactly. You can't be what you need to be if everyone notices it. Not unless you want to be a celebrity. As for the presidents and the prime ministers? They work for The Alliance, even when they don't know it."

I sighed. "And you just run things? From here? In J's dining room."

"Not from the dining room, no." He set down the folder. "You wanted something to do. Here is something for you to do."

He opened up the folder and I stared inside. There was a stack of papers in it. When I looked closer, a stack of resumes stared back up at me.

"Hiring someone for the kidnapping business?"

A corner of T's mouth lifted in amusement. "I didn't kidnap you. I mean, I suppose I did. I was part of the decision to take you, but the actual kidnapping was D's job.

And I guess to answer your question, no, I am not hiring someone to kidnap people. I am hiring someone, yes. I want you to go through this. There are, I believe, five hundred resumes here. I want you to put them in a yes pile and a no pile. Just divide them. Yes. No."

I stared at him for a second. "I've never hired anyone for anything in my life. I've practically gotten on my knees and begged for summer internships. I've never... been on the other side."

"Now see?" He made a tsking sound in his mouth. "Never beg. Never beg anyone for anything, Everly. For the rest of your life, you will remember that you are Alliance. Oh, maybe just on the outside, but you'll know it. And your attitude will be different because of it." He leaned forward just a bit. "They'll be begging you to work for them."

I waved my hand in the air. This was ridiculous. "Because I had the pleasure of being kidnapped by the five of you?"

"Because you had the luck of having the wool taken off your eyes so that you could know the truth of the world."

I should just shut up but that wasn't my way. "While I get to live here taking threats to my life?"

He ignored me. "Go through these. Yes pile. No pile."

I guessed my total ineptitude at this was not dissuading him. "What is the job for?"

"I'm not telling you."

My head hurt. "You can't seriously expect me to hire someone from a pile of resumes if I don't know what the person is expected to do."

"Sure I can. Work it out. Read their qualifications. Decide who you'd hire to do something for you."

I grabbed his arm when he would have gotten up. He stared at it for a second, before he hardened his gaze, as if daring me to keep holding on. I didn't stop. Respect with these guys would be hard won. If I was truly to be stuck here, I wasn't going to be a wilting flower.

"This is bullshit right? Something you made up to give me something to do? I'm going to spend hours looking at resumes, and at the end you'll throw them in the air and say something like aww, did you think that was real, how ridiculous."

He paused before answering. "Maybe I will. Maybe I won't. But you'll do the task because you want to. You're intrigued. Can you figure out what I need to hire for a job you can't know about? Or you can go in the other room and see if J has anything to read that won't bore you to death. He really, really likes ancient Roman history. I know that you're bright and intellectual. That we saw on your resume. You might like a week or two of pottery. But you're always going to wonder what you would have found in here."

Damn him for being right. "What do you do when you're not holding people hostage to get their fathers to do something for you?"

He grinned. "I'm a teacher, Everly, but that won't tell you anything about this job I'm hiring for. Good try though."

I hadn't been trying to manipulate that information. I wished I had been that smart. I was really not doing well with this sneaky thing.

"You hate me right now. I can see it in your eyes. You have very expressive eyes." I rolled those eyes right in his face, and he grabbed my chin, forcing me to look at him. What did he want to see? I'd give him the complete opposite. T abruptly dropped my face and stormed from the table.

I breathed hard like I'd been through a race. That was very… odd.

A noise caught my attention before D strode into the room. He was in jeans and a long sleeve t-shirt. Strapped to his back was a deer. A dead, still bleeding deer with a head wound. I jumped, pulling my feet up against me on the chair. He didn't look up at me, just continued to carry his dead deer through the room, the blood coating the floor as he walked through the dining room with his kill.

I tried to swallow. Well, I guessed that answered a question I hadn't asked. Did D ever kill anything when he shot his gun or was it just an ice filled lake taking his bullets? Yes, he did. I really did have to be careful. He'd been the one to kidnap me. I didn't want to end up being the next thing strapped to his back, bleeding on the fucking floor.

I shivered and grabbed the resumes. Even if it was bullshit, I'd do it. Anything to not think about this mess I'd landed in for no other reason than the circumstances of my birth.

━━

I STUDIED the resumes for hours before I started trying to sort them into anything. The problem was that there wasn't anything the same about any of them. I had expected some sort of sameness that would indicate what the job was. Like if everyone studied psychology, maybe it had to do with that.

But there was nothing so easy to help me determine what I was supposed to do.

The people had no names. They were numbers on top of a page. Sometimes I could determine if they were male or female. If someone listed they had once been the beauty pageant queen of Tulsa, Oklahoma, that gave me a pretty good indication they'd been a woman at least when they'd won that pageant. But it wasn't like there were a lot of those indicators. No names. Just schools and job history. Nothing to create a trail.

I finally had to give up on that. I started reading the resumes and asking myself if there was something about that person I'd find interesting to have around. If they'd done something that was quirky or interesting, they went into the yes pile. If they seemed very mundane and hadn't really presented an interesting picture, they went into the no. Of course, I could have been missing the best-qualified person in the world since I didn't know what the fuck the job was.

And there was the nagging problem of wondering if anyone would actually want to work for T if they knew who he was to begin with. Maybe everyone should be in the no pile.

It took me another few hours to go through them and then to move through the piles once again just to be sure I was comfortable with my totally ridiculous assessment in the first place. When I was done, I went looking for T. None of them had told me where to find them and not since D and the deer episode—a problem Marco had been scrubbing off the floor ever since—had I seen any of them.

The house was quiet. So they were either all in their rooms or in some secret location—like the basement —together.

When they weren't in the library, something that looked like a study, or the living room, I gave up trying to find them. At some point maybe I'd need to know whose bedroom was whose, but today was not going to be that day.

I found Constance in the kitchen. She was chopping onions. Immediately, my eyes started to water.

"Hi, I'm so sorry to bother you. But I need to find T. Do you know where he is?"

She didn't look up. "I'm not his keeper. They don't tell me where they're going, and I don't ask."

Well, that was no help at all. "I'm not feeling well. He left me with a project. I have to get it to him."

Marco, who must have come in the room without me noticing, knocked on the table to get my attention. I turned toward him. He motioned me forward, and I followed him. Constance sighed before she signed to him, letting him know the smartest thing he could do was not get involved in this mess.

He ignored her, taking my hand and bringing me outside with him. I shivered. If I'd known I was going back out here, I'd have grabbed my coat.

I'd wanted to see the basement, and apparently, Marco was bringing me right to it. He put out his hand, and I took it to mean he wanted me to stop, to wait. I almost told him I could understand him but didn't. I wasn't ready to start giving up what little control I had of things. Self-preservation was the name of the game.

I stopped. He walked forward and knocked on the door. Then he waited. The door swung open and J came out. Well, at least now I knew where they were. He asked Marco what he wanted and the other man communicated my need to see T. Only he didn't say T. When Marco signed his name he spelled out T's name. Usually, when someone had been around for a while they could be gifted a name by the ASL community. It was a special honor. I didn't have one but I'd only ever been on the outskirts of things.

It seemed that T was as well. I pretended not to watch as Marco spelled out T's name. His hand moved quickly through the spelling. *T.R.A.C.E.*

I stored this fast. I would still call him T. He didn't have to know that I knew, but T had suddenly become the man in black who gave me a job and whose first name was Trace. Or maybe it was his last name. This could all be last names. No that didn't feel right. His name was Trace. Trace something.

J told Marco he'd grab Trace. Marco was going to be the key to this. He was a nice man. He'd helped me, he was clearly a caring individual. He might help me get out of here. I would make it up to him for lying. Somehow.

As J disappeared back into the basement, Marco turned to me, a questioning look on his face. Did he know that I understood? I smiled at him, doing my best impression of a vague doll. Trace came upstairs. Now that I knew it, the name really worked for him.

Trace. Trace whatever his last name was with his wavy dark hair, his constant black clothes, and his face. I had to remember. T was Trace. The second I blew this it was all over for me. They'd clamp down on Marco and that would be that for secret information.

"You need something?"

I held up two different folders. The ones filled with the yeses in one hand, and the noes in my other. "I'm done."

"We're going to see each other at dinner shortly. Couldn't wait? I'm right in the middle of something."

My stomach clenched. "I'm not feeling well." I wasn't even lying. I had a headache right between my eyes. "I'm not going to eat. I wanted you to have this. I could have waited until tomorrow I suppose. I don't know the rules for any of this."

He took the yes folder from me, and then the noes. "What did you use to decide?"

"Well, since I was given oh so many rules to use and told such important details," I made sure he heard the sarcasm in my voice, "I just had to go ahead and decide from the small details who might be interesting to have around every day."

He lifted his lids slowly. "Well done. I'll take a look. The small details are always what matter. In life. In all things. Particularly when dealing with The Alliance. Small details. Now, you said you don't feel well. What's wrong?"

"I have a headache." I stepped back. "Might have something to do with being kidnapped and held against my will, kept from my family, all that good stuff."

He nodded. Knowing his name had humanized him. Trace actually seemed like he might be a person who could be reasoned with.

"It's interesting about your family isn't it? I mean your father knows we have you, he knows where we have you. And yet there won't be any police arriving, the FBI won't be raiding the house. He won't even show up here himself. He'll do what we want to spare your life… but I'm wondering just how important you could possibly be to him. Maybe the whole fixing your face incident was as far as he was willing to extend himself."

Anger surged through me, and I poked him right in the shoulder. "You're an asshole."

Forget Trace, he was purely T. And I'd add bully to the category that I had him in now. He and K could share that title together. Mean bullies.

"Am I? Or am I just asking you to confront the truth of this situation? You're smart. I can tell. Ask yourself about your father. He had your mother killed, and he's abandoned you here. I might not be so anxious to return to his loving embrace."

That was it. I was done. I'd promised myself I wouldn't cry, but then again I'd made lots of promises to myself I hadn't managed to keep over the years. I'd promised myself I wouldn't order dessert when I'd had to go up a pant size. I'd broken that. I'd promised myself I'd run an extra mile but I'd gone home after doing my minimal run. I'd promised myself I wouldn't buy another pair of shoes I didn't need, they were sitting in my closet.

Tears flooded my vision. I let them fall. He'd seen them. If I ran away that would add insult to injury. "And now that I've seen, you can congratulate yourself on pointing out just how pathetic I was in my delusions and in how you took the clouds from my eyes to show me just how alone I really am."

"We're all alone. From the moment we're born until we die, we're alone, Everly. Love exists, but most people have a pathetic facsimile they accept out of fear of being what they've always been." He shook his head. "Trust me. Nothing has changed just because you can see it for what it is."

I put my hands on my hips. "So you're what? Seeing yourself as my savior, T?"

I wasn't prepared for him to kiss me. I would have expected him to hit me first. It turned out that a kiss could be just as punishing as a slap when it came down to it. T grabbed me by the back of the neck and took possession of my mouth as though he had every right to do so. I'd been kissed before. Many times. But none of it had been what this was. It was in that second that I realized I'd only ever known the kisses of boys before. Trace was a man.

A pissed off, punishing man.

His lips didn't gently press to mine. No, they hurt me. I squirmed against him as though I would get away, even as my body craved more from him. In seconds, I had stopped fighting. He dragged me closer, not asking me if I wanted more but taking from me as though he had every right to do so.

T never gentled the embrace. It was angry when it started and just as furious when it ended. He stepped back, and I nearly fell over before I righted myself.

He didn't say another word before he left me standing there on the lawn in the now much colder night, slamming the basement door behind him as he disappeared into their world. I blinked. My head had been so clouded. What had happened to Marco? Where had he gone? I didn't even know.

But I was alone in the cold Vermont night on an island where nothing made sense.

I wiped my eyes and then my mouth. He had tasted like mint. I loved it, and I hated myself for loving it. What was the matter with me? This had to be early onset Stockholm Syndrome.

Except for the fact that T was hot. He'd have been hot anywhere I encountered him. Of course, I would never have encountered him because he was close to forty, and I only ever saw mediocre boy-men in bars.

My headache, which had dulled outside, reared back to life in a major way. I ran in the house and got to my room as fast as I could. I closed the door but didn't lock it. Why? I wasn't even kidding myself. If Trace was to suddenly decide he wanted to come into my room, I was going to be more than okay with it.

I laid my head on the pillow. I didn't have any painkillers, which wasn't surprising because I hadn't purchased any for my apartment. D couldn't have deposited it in J's house for me if I didn't have it. Why hadn't I gone to the pharmacy?

I groaned. I used to get headaches a lot but hadn't for years. This had to be stress related. I rolled over. It was going to be a long night.

I must have fallen asleep because a knock on the door

woke me later. It was hard to wrench my eyes open, but I managed. I made my way to the door to find J standing there.

"Hi."

I had to find my voice. "Hi."

"You missed dinner. T says you have a headache." As if mentioning it made it flare back to life, the pounding, which had dulled, rushed back into existence.

"I do." Why was he bothering me about this?

J held out his hand. "I realized you might not have what you need."

I practically ripped the medicine out of his hand. "Thank you."

"You're welcome. Take some and if you find yourself hungry, I've asked Constance to keep food for you tonight in the fridge so you can warm it." He stepped back. "Feel better, Everly. I know you've had a long day. Good work with T's job issue by the way. Hugely well done."

I wanted to ask him more about that, but I also wanted to take my pills. "Thanks. I need some water."

He stepped into the room, looking around. I guessed he intended to stay for a minute. I made my way to the bathroom and poured some water into a cup. I took the pills. I really needed them to work fast. Sometimes, the time between taking meds and the onset of relief were the longest of the whole ordeal.

I walked back into the room. He stared out the window. "Nice view from in here. I have the other view. I never come to this side of the house."

"It's huge." What was I supposed to say to him? Thank you for giving me a nice room to stay in while you hold me hostage?

He nodded. "Initially, the whole thing was built so a great-grandfather could take people bird hunting. As far as the locals are concerned, that is what we still do here. We kill birds."

"D killed a deer today."

J nodded. "Yes, I heard all about it. Quite a mess he made hauling that thing through the house. D can be downright savage, but he means well. Most of the time. I guess we'll be eating venison. Not my favorite game. But it is local. And we imported the damn things to shoot them last year, so I guess it's good he's hunting them before they run out of food and starve."

I sat down on the edge of the bed. "I don't have the slightest idea what to say to you right now."

He turned around. "Are you comfortable in here?"

"No." If I'd been a guest I'd never had said that. My southern manners dictated certain behaviors. I hadn't had a mother around and my father didn't notice small things, but I'd had plenty of women to teach me what was and wasn't to be said. Not once had anyone dictated to me the proper way to speak to the man who held me hostage. He wanted to know if I was comfy? Fine, I'd tell him the truth.

"What's not working?" He looked around.

I shook my head. "The sheets are horrible. The comforter is scratchy. I hate them."

J leaned over and touched the bedding. "You're right. These are awful."

I blinked. I'd kind of thought to piss him off. After the incident with Trace, my every response was raw and miserable. I didn't expect him to agree with me.

He looked up. "I'm going to find out what happened to your bedding. If we don't have it, we'll get you something better. You might be here awhile. I don't want to sleep on that. I don't blame you."

This was too much. "J, I'm your prisoner. You could lock me in a dungeon and leave me there to rot on gruel."

"Everly, let me tell you something. If the rest of The Alliance were to find out what your father did, they would come for you and that is exactly where you would find yourself. I've been in those places. Be glad it's only us blaming him for now."

I had been kidding. "There can't really be dungeons left. I mean, not in the civilized world. Sure in places I would never want to be, but there aren't dungeons here in your basement or wherever you live when you're not here, right?"

I didn't know why I wanted to know, but suddenly knowing felt pivotal.

"There is no such thing as the civilized world. We only pretend there is. That's not the question you wanted to ask me."

I swallowed. "Sure it is."

"No, it's not. You wanted to ask me what your father did. What crime or wrongdoing did the man commit to land you here, stuck with us, trying to figure out your way?"

I supposed I did want to know. It was hard for me to think of my father at all. As T had pointed out, he wasn't the man I'd thought him to be. I didn't know how to deal. "Well, I know he kills people. I know he has basically abandoned me here. So yes, I suppose I ought to know. What did he do?"

"He altered documents that prove membership in The Alliance. All of us can trace our right to be in The Alliance to before Christ was born. He fabricated things, questioning the succession rights of over two dozen members. All people who stand against a certain faction. Now, the majority of our members don't want this kind of problem. They'll stand with truth because they know tomorrow it could be them who finds themselves suddenly in question.

That's what your father did and that's what he'll have to undo. He has to prove that we're true members. He has to show he lied."

He was basically going to audit the membership of a secret organization to prove he'd committed fraud? "Can't you all just present your papers? I mean, if it were that important I'd think you'd keep your lineage or family trees in a vault somewhere."

"We do, but our papers are being called into question. He's going to go get the originals and he's going to do whatever he has to do to show how he lied. That's what your father did. And when he is done we will take control of The Alliance and let you go."

That really did seem like quite an undertaking. "Since before Christ was born, huh?"

I leaned back on the bed. I wasn't going anywhere anytime fast.

Chapter 6

J made no moves to leave my room. Did he want to talk? I was still dealing with my pounding head. "Wouldn't it make sense to have a historian look for the proof you guys need and not, say, a small time accountant?"

"Your father has been dealing with billions of dollars for years. He's not small time. And he made this mess, he can fix it. He's handled ancient documents many times. Jeb decided he wanted to play with the big time Alliance members. He picked a side. The wrong side. And now he's made his bed. Or yours as the case may be. With scratchy sheets."

I couldn't help my smile. That was sort of ridiculously cute. I didn't get the impression from J that he did ridiculously cute very often. He rocked back on his feet like he couldn't believe he'd done it either.

"What do you do when you're not locking women in towers? Sorry, houses."

He blinked. "You make it sound like you're Rapunzel. I promise you a haircut if you want one."

"Thanks." He had successfully avoided my question. "T told me what he did for a living."

"Did he now?" His voice went up with the question. "What did he say?"

I quickly got the impression that maybe T wasn't only a school instructor. "He said he's a teacher."

"That he is." J nodded. "I suppose he didn't go on to say what he taught. I'm a doctor. I can be vague, too."

I rolled over onto my stomach. "And doctors can just take massive amounts of time off and stay in a house with me?"

He shook his head. "I'll be going back and forth. We all will. After this week it's unlikely you'll have all five of us at the same time. Do you get a lot of headaches?"

"Only under stress." I told him the truth.

"Right." He closed the distance between us, then put his hand on my head. It was a bizarre moment. I still had no idea what J wanted. J, the casual homeowner, who was kind to his staff and had me locked on his island, was a doctor. I'd once read the phrase "undressing me with his eyes" but I couldn't say as I'd ever had that happen before. Although his hand stayed right where it was on my head, I felt naked. It was hard to explain otherwise. Somehow, with just his eyes on me, J had stripped me bare.

He let go of me and stepped back. "You would respond, wouldn't you?"

The tone of his voice could best be described as intrigued.

"To what?" My throat had gone dry.

"If I touched you. Right now, you would respond."

I didn't deny it. If I squirmed, I was pretty sure my panties would be wet. "I've always liked sex."

"Always? In your massively long life you've always liked

sex?" His voice was low, still gentle. "You're barely out of diapers."

I shook my head, which moved his hand slightly. He stroked my forehead with his thumb, and I wished it were a different part of my anatomy he touched. "You can tell yourself that if you want to. If it makes it easier not to see me as a grown woman."

J dropped to his knees, staring at me from next to the bed. I missed his hand on my body. He didn't say anything, so I spoke again. "How old are you, J?"

"I'm thirty-five."

I had thought he was younger than the others. Not by much, but I supposed if he thought I was young then every year counted with him. "Is it true men get better in bed as they get older?"

His smile was fast. "You're wicked, Everly. It's too bad that women can't be Alliance. You'd fit right in." He got to his feet. "To answer your question, if a man has to brag about it, he's not any good. You'll have to wonder how I would have answered your query that was meant to provoke me."

"Did it?" I rolled back over. "Provoke you?"

"Here's the thing. I have a certain… taste… when it comes to women."

I continued to try playing it cool. I hadn't intended this, but now I couldn't seem to stop pushing at him. If I ended up with him between my legs I'd hate myself in the morning but love it in the moment. Why did I want to fuck these guys? Why didn't I want to gouge out their eyes? It might be more helpful. This wasn't some novel from the 1980s. My magic pussy wasn't going to suddenly make him decide to let me free as it gave him a new outlook on life.

I was more likely to end up dead in the basement when he got sick of fucking me.

Still, I'd poked this bear. I couldn't let it go. "What would that certain taste be?"

"Ever been tied up, Everly?"

I sat up straight. "No."

It wasn't lost on me that the night before I'd wanted to bar my door and now I was talking about kink with J like this was the most normal thing in the world. What was the matter with me? I was going to see a counselor when this was over. Still, heat moved through me at the thought, and I suddenly wondered why I had never been tied up during sex. Why hadn't I done this?

"Well, maybe someday you will."

I wished there was innuendo in what he said, an indication that he meant that perhaps he'd be the one doing it, except his eyes were distant, and I wasn't sure he was thinking that at all in that moment.

He turned on his heel and left fast, shutting the door behind him without slamming it. I didn't know why I fixated on that detail, except my father always slammed doors whether he meant to or not. I settled back down on the bed. I wasn't going to sleep. Not for a while anyway. Not when there was suddenly an image of J and a rope to occupy my active imagination.

━━

I MUST HAVE EVENTUALLY DOZED off still dressed, because when I woke up, my head didn't pound anymore. The medicine had worked. I sat up in bed. Something was, however, banging away, and it took me half a second to realize it had to be D outside again, shooting his gun off into the lake.

I groaned. No, this wasn't going to continue. I didn't know the man at all. I'd spoken to him the least out of

anyone, and certainly when the others brought him up, it was always with a certain amount of trepidation associated with him specifically. But if I was going to be here for months, it couldn't be every night the deer-dragging, man-bunned Alliance member's shooting ice with his shotgun woke me up. No, this was going to stop now.

I grabbed my coat and my shoes, the only things I'd managed to take off, and ran down the stairs before making my way out the back door. The night was lit up from what had to be every light in the house illuminating at the same time. Maybe The Alliance wasn't concerned with energy conservation. If I hadn't been knocked out because of my headache, I'd have turned off my light.

I wasn't quiet in my approach, but he either didn't hear me or didn't care.

"Hey," I shouted at him. I faced his back as he aimed at the ocean. He fired into the ice. A crack sounded, ice flying into the air with a splatter in the distance. Someone could get seriously injured if he kept up this shit.

D didn't turn around.

"I said hey." I stormed to him, and when he didn't turn, I grabbed his arm to turn him toward me. His head swung around first and a second later he had that gun pointed right at my chest. The big barrel of the sawed off shotgun lodged itself right above my left breast.

Well, at least he knew where he was going to shoot it.

I should be terrified. Any sane person would cower in terror, but for some reason I felt nothing but calm. Maybe that was why I grabbed the shotgun and yanked it out of his hands. It was a stupid move. But that was how I ended up with his gun in my hand.

We had a moment where we stared at each other before I pulled the gun back even farther, pointing it at him. I hadn't come out here for this. I just wanted to tell him to stop shooting the thing in the middle of the night.

Yet, somehow this had happened. I'd handled guns before. I liked new experiences, and I'd had boyfriends who hunted and target shot. I'd gone along. Still, this struggle for the gun that I'd won, temporarily, was not one I wanted to see the end of. D was stronger than me. I'd surprised him. If he wanted it back he was going to take it easily.

"Let's calm down." My voice sounded strained to my own ears.

"You're the one holding the gun." D sounded quieter than the few times I'd heard him speak before. He spoke barely over a whisper. "You know what they say about guns? Don't hold them unless you're prepared to fire them."

I shook my head. "I don't want to shoot you. This is the last thing I ever intended to do tonight. I'm not even sure how this happened."

"Are you prepared to shoot me?"

I didn't want to answer that because I didn't know. I'd never considered shooting anyone. "Were you going to shoot me when you jammed it in my breast?"

I could still feel the hot muzzle where it had pressed against me. Right now the feeling was real but it might quickly become a phantom feeling I'd have for a long time. Assuming I got out of this alive.

He nodded once. "Yes. Not a great idea to startle a crazy person with a gun."

"Not a great idea for a so-called crazy person to have a gun." Why was I doing this? Why had neither of us moved? My feet needed to work. I had to walk away. Take the gun and walk away from D. Surely, one of the others would... do something about this.

D grabbed the end of the gun or maybe it was more accurate to say that he pressed the end of the gun against his head. I sucked in a breath. What. In. The. Ever. Loving. Fuck.

"Would you shoot me, Everly? Would you put that bullet between my eyes?"

His blue eyes. Blonde man bun and blue eyes. He might be beautiful if he wasn't so fucking cracked.

"What are you doing?" I tried to pull back but he held on tight. His head right against the end of the gun. There might be another name for the hole where the bullet came out. I didn't really care to remember it. Sweat dripped down my back. If I could go back in time and tell myself to stay in my bed, I would.

"I think you would. I actually see it in your eyes." He smirked at me. "You would pull the trigger and blow my brains to kingdom come. Get yourself covered in the mess of it and then go have a cigarette."

I tried to breathe through this. "I don't smoke."

"Only when you drink."

How did he know that? I swallowed. This was not the time or circumstance for that question. "I don't know. I don't know if I could shoot you. How's that for an answer? Let's not find out."

"You would." He narrowed his eyes. "Do it."

"What?" I choked out my answer. "That's not fucking funny."

He didn't answer right away. "I'm not laughing. Or joking. Fucking do it. Put the bullet right in my head."

I shook my head. "Enough of this." I yanked the gun back, hard. "This isn't suicide by Everly. You want to blow your head off, you feel free to go right ahead, but I'm not doing it for you." I finally took the step back that I should have immediately taken. Then another. For good measure, one more. "Why do you want me to blow off your head, D?"

A muscle ticced in his jaw. "It's Derrick. If *K* wants to go around thinking that not knowing names puts some distance between us, he can go ahead and do so. My name is Derrick. You can know it."

I stored that info. Derrick was the man bun and death wish. I'd put that in the back of my head with Trace. Of course, I could actually say Derrick and not Trace, since Derrick told me his name, and Trace didn't know I knew his.

"Answer the question." He wasn't going to redirect this by telling me something as trivial as his first name. Not after that stunt.

"This life? It's fucked up. Every once in a while I think it might be okay to get the hell out of it."

He'd hardly be the first person to think so. I wasn't licensed to be a therapist. I didn't even have a degree. I hoped someday to change that. The plan had been social work then a master's in psychology. That didn't mean I had a clue what to do right now.

"You should talk to someone about that. There is help and services. People who care." There really were. "I'll even help you make the call."

He shook his head. "I'm actually not suicidal. Not until after I get my revenge. You weren't going to shoot me. You thought about it. You might have done so if you'd ever really believed I was going to hurt you, and you have the capability to do it." He pointed at my eyes like he could see something there.

"I think you might be seeing me wrong."

"No, you see you wrong. Of course I could have been off, and then I'd be dead. Can't have that happen until I've done what I set out to do."

I was so tired of trying to piece together puzzles, and I'd only been at this for a little over twenty-four hours. Maybe I'd finally reach a place where I didn't care. I wasn't there yet. "Which would be what?"

"Killing the five assholes running The Alliance. Painfully. Slowly. And making sure they remember her name when I do. Each one of them is going to say it before they die."

I could see my breath when I exhaled. I hadn't noticed it earlier. Maybe that had to do with the events of this evening, but I noticed it now. We stood there breathing. The night so cold we could see our breath in front of us. I wondered if he noticed, but I wasn't going to ask.

"You loved someone and they killed her? The Alliance?"

He looked out at the lake for a second. "My wife. J's sister. This was her favorite spot."

Well, I'd gotten more information than I'd expected to. Derrick had been married to J's sister. She was dead. That at least explained what the two of them were doing here. Sort of. Most people didn't meet at a dead relative's favorite spot then map out a revenge plot. "Were you in The Alliance before? Or did you learn about it when she died?"

"Before. Her father would never have allowed her to marry anyone who wasn't Alliance. It worked out nicely. She shouldn't have known about it, but the whole twin thing. J didn't keep anything from Alyssa. Anyway, after they remember her, they can all die. Badly."

I shivered, and I didn't think it was from the cold. "Why did they kill her?"

"Because I said no." He stepped back. "Enough of this. You're freezing."

I held up the gun. "I'm keeping this. I'm not listening

to you crack the ice with bullets every night. Find some other way to miss her or honor her or whatever this means to you. My room is right there and this is miserable enough."

Derrick put his hands on his hips. "You aren't how I thought you were going to be. I watched you for a week before I decided how to bring you here. I'd never kidnapped a woman before so it was a challenge."

"Oh, I see. So we can add stalking to your list of crimes. Kidnapped. Drugged. Stalked. You're really adding them up." I shouldn't ask. I should tell him to fuck off. Only, I'd opened up this box, and I was fully invested in the madness now. "What did you think I would be like?"

He shook his head. "You're lost. Most of the time. You walk through life, but you have no idea where you're going. Now? You're lit up."

"This from the guy who just held a gun to his own head after he jammed it on me." I should never have asked. "If I'm lit up it's from adrenaline. As I said, I'm keeping the gun, Derrick."

He shrugged. "I have several."

"So the orchestra of gunfire isn't going to stop?"

His smirk came slowly. "I guess you'll have to see. Put the gun under your bed. You'll shoot it someday if you have to. Of course, you might murder us all in our beds. But then how would you get off the island? I don't think you can take on the helicopter pilots. They're all military. Or swim for it. Not for months and months. You'd starve."

Wonderful. Fuck him. I wasn't lost. I'd always known just where I was going.

Hadn't I?

And what did it really say about my level of ridiculousness that it never occurred to me to shoot any of them, even as I held the gun in my hand? I had to work this shit out and quickly.

This whole thing had gotten dark. Or darker. Fast.

SURPRISINGLY, after my altercation with Derrick I'd slept fine. Thinking about J and his ropes could keep me up a bit, but dwelling on dead wives, gun violence, murder, revenge, and wondering whether or not I could end a life, didn't cause me to skip a beat. Maybe I really was as lost as Derrick said I was.

I woke when the sun came up, feeling refreshed. If I was going to stay here indefinitely then I was going to have to make this work for me. That started with taking care of myself. I ran every day. I wasn't going to stop now.

My feet were still pretty angry at me from my run shoeless run two days earlier. But they were healing. I put on my running clothes, making note that someone had washed them. That had to be Constance. I'd thank her for the effort. Of course that also meant that she'd gone through my stuff. If I did manage to ever hide something in here, I'd have to remember that. I had a gun under my bed. It wasn't like I'd stolen that.

I sighed. I'd have to work this stuff out, and I should have noticed that the bed had been made the day before. I needed to pay attention to details. Like I'd done for Trace with his ridiculous job.

I walked down the stairs and made my way outside without seeing anyone. Even knowing it wasn't the best thing in the world to do, I always ran on an empty stomach. The second I had food in me, I didn't want to do it anymore.

Despite the cold, I ran as hard as I could. The air was

different than at home, and it burned my lungs, made it harder to do. Still, I persevered, and when I finally returned to the house, I was proud of myself for making the effort.

The empty house was full when I entered. All of the guys were up, sitting around the table, and Constance hustled about, pouring coffee.

Derrick jumped up when I entered. "Was just getting worried about you out there. It's going to snow."

Was it? "Isn't it March?"

J nodded, but his gaze was on Derrick, his brow sloped like he had an unasked question. "It snows here in March. Sometimes April."

I wasn't cold at the moment. "I'd have turned around at the first sign of snow. I'm not a cold weather person."

Constance poured coffee and placed it down on the table. As no one claimed the mug, I assumed it was for me. I took it as Derrick touched the chair next to where he'd been sitting. "This one's yours."

"Thanks." I sat down in it just as Marco came through the door, putting a plate full of eggs in front of me. I thanked him, too.

Derrick took his seat as T looked up from a book he was reading. "Do you want another job today, Everly?"

I was just about to answer him when Derrick answered instead. "She's with me today."

I was? "What does that mean?"

"It means you're with me." He was apparently not going to elaborate on that. "I've told her my name. Given her a shotgun. And I'm going to take her into the basement."

My mouth fell open. He was?

K leaned forward, his eyes narrowing as he spoke. "You did what?"

"Which part is confusing? I didn't tell her your name. You can keep with the letters if you want. But she's going to call me Derrick from now."

K pointed at him. "We agreed."

"I changed my mind. I never played well with others. You know that. We have the same objective. That doesn't make us a team. Eat your eggs, Everly. They'll get cold and you just ran miles. You need the protein. Also, probably some carbs. Here," he rose and headed toward the kitchen, "I'm going to make you some toast."

J sighed loudly, rubbing his eyes. "What did you do to him, Everly?"

"What did I do to him?" Was he serious with that? "What could I have possibly done?"

I wasn't going to tell them what had happened the night before. It felt… private. And maybe that was ridiculous. I shouldn't have been having private moments with one fifth of my captors, particularly the douchebag who had been responsible for getting me here to begin with. But really, what did I care?

"I'm Warden." W spoke for the first time that morning. "I don't like hearing my name as W. Feel free to use it, too. I'd like to hear my name spoken on your lips. Maybe called out in my bed."

I spit out my coffee. Where had that come from? T and J had both made moves on me, but not W.

Derrick came back in just then, placing the toast in front of me. "You'll need your sustenance. I'm going to show you how to ruin the world."

Chapter 7

I hustled to keep up with Derrick as he practically ran to the basement. The change in him from the night before was huge. Had he slept very well? Had he not slept at all? His eyes were clear and the anger that had seemed to radiate from him by the water was gone.

"Am I walking too fast, Everly? You're tall. You can keep up."

"Hey, Man Bun," I called at him. "You're even taller than me, and I ran three miles this morning after days off and being drugged. You could try a little bit of manners and slow down."

His grin shocked me even as his hand came up to touch the back of his hair. "Like that, do you?"

"I didn't say that." I hadn't disagreed either. I was just not going to comment either way.

K charged by us, blocking the door as Derrick would have opened it. "Don't."

"I know this wasn't your plan, K," Derrick rolled his eyes. "But I think she needs to see life for what it is. I think it would be beneficial for the rest of her life for her to go down there."

Particularly if there was an escape route, like someone had dug a tunnel under all the islands that led back to mainland Vermont. That would be very helpful. Not that I was counting on it. But it was possible. The Alliance was real therefore all reasonable expectations of what could and couldn't be were out the window for me.

There could be tunnels just waiting for me to traverse. And fairies. And little green men ready to take me on space adventures.

"My thinking in keeping the letters, in keeping her out of the basement, in bringing her in only the bare minimum when it came to what is happening here, was that so she could have a life. So she could go back to being an ant again and live a good, little ant life. You take her down there and there is no going back. She'll have no control, no ability to do anything about any of what she sees. It'll eat at her the way it does people, and that will be that."

Derrick shook his head. "Are you thinking Everly is going to be able to return home after this and get back to her degree, to her parties, to sleeping with random men who don't get her off, and that all will just be well for her?"

"Hold on," I had to insert myself into that statement. "Were you watching things I did in the bedroom? How gross are you?"

He smirked at me and shook his head. "I was not. But anyone watching you walk home after that night with the boy could have known you were disappointed. You had "I was not fucked properly" all over your face."

I took a deep breath. "I suppose I could try to deny it, but it was really bad."

"Ninety-nine percent of the guys you're going to fuck

at that age are bad. They have to get a little bit older to get control over themselves to make it good for you. Unless they're one of the few that really got laid in high school and don't just pretend they did."

It took me a second to realize that statement had come from K and not Derrick. I think D might have been shocked, too. We both stared at him, neither of us speaking. K rolled his eyes. "It's just how it is."

"Was that how it was for you?" Derrick grinned. "Because I remember getting the job done pretty well."

K shook his head. "Please. You were paying for pussy back then. They'd have told you anything."

"I never paid for it."

K stepped away from the door. "Buying a girl an expensive tennis bracelet after you fuck her is basically the same thing."

I didn't need to hear them reminisce. I really didn't. But it did tell me they'd known each other a long time. It wasn't just J that Derrick knew well. K could comment on Derrick's sex life. I took my chance and stepped around K, grabbing the door and rushing down the stairs.

"Hey," K called after me. "Everly, I know you have no reason to believe me, but you really don't want to do that."

Oh, but I did. I was here, and I wasn't going to live here without knowing what was in the basement. My eyes had to adjust from the sunlight to the lower wattage, and I instinctively reached out to grip the banister on the stairs. I tended to be clumsy when I was off kilter and changes in light did that to me.

I ignored K and continued down the stairs. They were made out of wood and they were noisy, creaky, when I stepped on them. Like something out of a ridiculous horror movie. But that was where the oldness ended. The basement was the most modern spot in the house. Down here, there were computers and screens everywhere I looked.

I made it to the bottom as K and Derrick followed me down. "Guess there's no Wi-Fi problem down here."

"We have contacts. It's as good as anyone can have anywhere in the world," Derrick supplied. Ju—sorry, J, he knows the right people."

He'd almost given me another name but I couldn't focus on that right then.

"You know, K, if you really wanted me to be able to live my life undisturbed, the thing to do would have been to have left me alone to begin with."

Derrick laughed. I was really amusing him today. "But honey, we needed a sacrificial lamb."

I shook my head. "I'm not meek or easy to bleed."

"You are." K said walking past me. "The problem is you just don't know it, which makes you even more vulnerable."

I walked toward the computers. They were all on. Numbers flew by, and I tried to make quick sense of them. It seemed like each monitor had something different on it. I had taken statistics classes in abundance, but I had no idea what I was looking at.

The screens weren't better. They seemed to be focused on people. Sitting, walking, running, and driving cars. They were no one I recognized.

"This is where you ruin people's lives and run the world?"

A shout sounded from somewhere down the hall. Neither K nor Derrick responded to it. I turned toward the sound, eventually finding myself in another room filled with screens. In this one, there were people tied up, injured, beaten, and one man I thought might actually be dead from the angle of his head. I covered my mouth with my hand to stop from screaming.

"Help me," the scream came again from a man on a screen to my left. He had a bag over his head.

"At any given time," Derrick said as he entered the room slowly. "The Alliance has hundreds of people captive. Tortured. Killed. Sometimes it's the ants, as K likes to refer to them. Sometimes it's their own members. We're watching a few of them right now."

I rubbed the back of my neck. "Because you are… gathering intel or you're getting off on it… or what?"

"We're not getting off on it." K leaned against the door. "I don't have a thing for torture. None of us do. I suppose there is a time and a place. But Derrick over there lost his wife because he refused to participate in the darker side of things." He stared at Derrick. "See? I can share private information, too."

He shrugged. "I already told her that last night."

"Fuck. How much did the two of you talk?"

I ignored them. Let them banter. There were people in pain, in terror, and they were on a view screen. We stared at them like a spectacle. I could hardly breathe, but I sought calm. I'd wanted down in the basement, and I was here. Now, I had to understand just how far down the sick, distorted rabbit hole I had fallen with these guys.

"Why are you watching them?" They hadn't answered that, and so help me, they were going to.

"Right now we're out of favor. The five of us were never… popular, per se. But we were on the councils. Not the ruling council, mind you. But advisory positions. Our voices were heard. They've managed to sideline us without killing us. That's interesting. Also, more important is why." K pointed at the screen. "Why do they have these people? They don't know we're watching them or they'd cut it off."

I rubbed my eyes. "Why don't you help them?"

"Why would we do that?" Derrick didn't sound sarcastic. "Maybe they're very bad people. Maybe they're terrorists. Child rapists. Part of what The Alliance does is keep order. Occasionally, things go awry in the world. Chaos is not good unless it's chaos we create. That's the party line anyway. Lately, things have gotten very bad, control of events moving too far from what we'd want. Just another indication it's time to change the status quo. Why should we help those strangers?"

Okay, I'd had enough. I walked past them. I was powerless right now to help anyone but it wouldn't always be that way. So help me, I'd find a way. When I got out of here, I'd spend my life trying to free people from The Alliance. I'd devote myself to it. I'd wanted to help people. Well, this was how I'd do it.

"I told you that you couldn't unsee it."

I took a long breath. "Yes, K, you did."

"Fuck it. Just call me Kade."

"I'm going back to my room. If this is what you wanted, Derrick, you've succeeded. You have officially shown me how the world gets destroyed. Just a bunch of people watching torture and terror and doing nothing about it."

He furrowed his brow. "That wasn't what I meant."

I didn't stop to answer him. My room seemed like the best possible place to be right then. In fact, I might stay in it permanently until my father got me out of here. My father, a member of this nightmare—who knew where I was and wasn't storming the place to get me back—could finish what he was doing, and I'd go home.

Then I'd figure things out. In my room, with the sounds of those people screaming, pleading, still ringing in my ears I looked under my bed. The shotgun was gone. I shouldn't have been surprised. Derrick was the only person who could have thought it wasn't a bad idea. I might snap and kill them all.

I'd been skirting a line this whole time, and I might have just crossed it. The five of them were spending their days in the basement, watching people suffer. And I hadn't even asked about those numbers on the computers. What were they? I didn't look at the rest of the basement. There was probably more. Maybe they had their own captive prisoner down there. No, I was the prisoner, and I was free to wander an island I couldn't get off of until I either went mad or my despicable father rescued me.

Talk about awful choices.

I climbed into the bed. I didn't have to be strong all the time. I was still sweaty from my run, but I didn't even care. This was too much. It just was.

━━

I WOKE up and went back to sleep all day. No one bothered me and that was fine. I'd be good with this lasting for months. I'd eat if I had to and otherwise I would sleep. Time would pass. I wouldn't make any more trips down to that basement.

Why had Derrick brought me down there? To punish me? I had all kinds of names now. Derrick. Kade. Warden. They'd told them to me. I knew Trace. And it was only J left, who was Ju something or other. Knowing them hadn't humanized them to me. Now they were just evil people watching evil people do terrible things.

The world was in chaos? What did that mean?

And if they'd been ousted by The Alliance did that mean they were or weren't involved? Too many questions, and I didn't think I should ask for answers.

I hadn't liked the way the basement resolved itself.

Outside, the helicopter landed. Did it come every other day? I didn't get up to look at it. Derrick hadn't shot up the lake tonight or at least I hadn't heard it. I'd been pretty heavily asleep. Maybe he had. Or maybe he'd just found a different location.

I rolled over. I'd go back to sleep.

A knock sounded on the door. I thought about not answering it. The clock said it was almost midnight. Who wanted me now? In the end, curiosity won. I swung open the door. On the other side, T waited.

"I heard you had a rough day. You've been in here over twelve hours."

Did he have a point? "Yes, and?"

"Pack your bag. You have ten minutes. Enough for three days away. Some of your nicer clothes. Things you'd wear to a job interview or a funeral and something for a dinner. Don't do anything passive aggressive like just pack your sweatpants. You won't like how that ends for you. As though you were taking a weekend away. You won't need a coat, but you'll want it until we get out of here. Hurry up. I don't like to be kept waiting."

I shook my head. "What in the hell are you talking about?"

"We're going somewhere for three days. Ten minutes. You can shower when we get there. Hurry up."

He closed the door, and I methodically started to do what he said. Where was he taking me? I'd seen the basement. That wasn't something he'd wanted. Was he going to kill me? No, he could have done that now. He didn't have to tell me to pack. Did they need me out of the house for some reason? I sighed. I wasn't going to find out if I didn't pack my bag.

I opened the closet. They'd really brought all my

clothes. Derrick did like details. That much was obvious, considering that the closet was almost exactly as I'd set mine up at home. Had he taken photos and then recreated it, or did he just have a photographic memory? Was that a real thing?

I packed a bag. I had two suits I interviewed in so I grabbed those. Dinner? I didn't know what kind of restaurant, but black pants tended to work for everything. If I didn't need a coat wherever this was, I'd use a black top and a sweater just in case the restaurant was cold. I also shoved in jeans, pajamas, a t-shirt, a bathing suit for good measure, and my toiletries. The fact that they'd brought my suitcase at all meant that someone must have thought I was going to need it.

I made his ten minute deadline. He took my hand, even though I hadn't offered it, and handed my bag to a person I didn't know.

"Where are we going?"

He put his finger to his mouth. "I don't think anyone will hear you over the helicopter, but just in case, I'm not dealing with the others right now. They won't like me taking you, and I just don't give a shit. They took you to the basement. All rules are over."

A thought dawned on me. "Are you letting me go?"

He shook his head. "No. You're still ours until your father comes through. I'm just taking you on a field trip."

We climbed onto the helicopter and T actually bent over to buckle me in. "It's going to get loud when we take off." He picked up some headphones. "You'll put these on to protect your ears. But first you're going to take this pill."

I stared at his hand as it opened, revealing a small white pill in it. "What is that?"

"It's going to knock you out. We have places to go before we get where we're going and I don't trust you enough to let you see those places. Not yet anyway. You're proving surprising. You can take the pill, or I can shove it down your throat."

I laughed and that must have surprised him. "What if I couldn't swallow pills? Oh sure, that's the shoving it down my throat thing. Sure, I'll take your pill because of the sweet, charming way you asked me to, and because I don't give two shits about the places you don't want me to see. You're evil. Evil people and evil places. You can all sink into the ocean."

His smile was slow. If he cared what I said, he didn't say a word. I opened my mouth and he placed the pill on my tongue before he brought a bottle of water to my lips. My hands worked just fine but maybe he thought I'd spit it out or refuse. I settled against the seat while he placed the headphones over my ears.

Fine, I'd sleep through whatever this was. I'd never particularly wanted to be on a helicopter to begin with. I hated flying on a good day and that was on an airplane.

T lifted one of half of the headphone just slightly off my ear. "My name is Trace, Everly. Probably best if you don't call me T when you wake up."

"I knew that." Let him think on that for a while. "But I'm not telling you how. And, you should know, T, that I fully intend to try to get away from you the whole time we're out there."

He nodded. "You'll fail if you try. You're also not going to want to, but you'll have to trust me on that. What we're doing? It's going to be like a train wreck. You won't be able to look away." He pulled out his phone and texted something. The pill must work quickly because already my mind felt fuzzy. "I'm letting the others know where you're going and when you'll be back. Feeling it?"

I nodded, closing my mind. "Whatever. I don't need a play by play. It's not like I have any say in any of this."

"You came. You didn't shout when I told you not to. You climbed on the helicopter. You didn't spit the pill into my face. You're no wilting flower, Everly. I think the truth is that you want to come. We've piqued something in you. Maybe it's not something you like. Fight against it if you want to. I don't blame you. You're in this now. You were right away, but since you went into the basement, now you're officially ours and for the next three days you're mine."

He hadn't mentioned the kiss we'd shared. He was right. As disgusted as I was, there was part of me that was completely transfixed with all of it. My head felt sideways. It was hard to think. "Did you cause September 11th?"

"No. I didn't. And it wasn't Alliance. That was… chaos."

I supposed that was something. "Have you ever made an airplane crash?"

"Not personally." That didn't make me feel better. Did that mean someone else had? He put the earbud back over my ear. I guessed that was my cue to stop talking. It was okay.

I closed my eyes. "You guys are drugging me so much I might become addicted."

If he said anything, I couldn't hear it.

━━━

"EVERLY, OPEN YOUR EYES."

A warm breeze hit my face, along with a voice telling me to open my eyes. I scrunched up my nose. No, I wasn't ready. "Don't want to."

"I know. But you need to. Time for some water and to

wake up." It was T's insistent voice making me give up my nap. I wrenched open my eyes. I'd fallen asleep on a helicopter and now I was… I looked around, trying to make my brain work. The sun was bright, the colors vivid. The sky above my head was blue and cloudless. "Where is here?"

"That's a funny way to put it." He pressed a bottle of water to my mouth, giving me a sense of déjà vu. He'd just done that. Or maybe not. Maybe a lot of time had passed. I drank down the water, and he pulled back the bottle, finally handing it to me. "Where is here?"

He leaned back in his seat. We were in an open air taxi, driving fast on bumpy roads. A beat from the radio caught my attention as did the man who drove the car. I couldn't see or hear anything but his dreadlocks and his voice singing with the radio.

"This is St. Croix. We made a few stops before getting here. Don't worry, you didn't snore."

I hadn't been concerned. If I snored that was his problem for knocking me out. "And no one blinked at you hauling an unconscious me around?"

"If only that was the strangest thing I'd ever done." He shook his head. "No one saw us who would have blinked at it. Feeling okay?"

I looked around. Everything was kind of pink. "Why are we in St. Croix?"

"I need to check on a client, and you can help me more on the project you've been working on."

I rubbed my eyes. The truth was I could go back to sleep again. "Still tired."

"You'll throw off the drugs soon enough. We should be able to fly straight back, so I'm not going to drug you again."

"Aw, but T, maybe I need my fix. What will I do if one of you is not knocking me out like Sally Sleeps A Lot?"

He stared at me with his head tilted to the side. "Is that some kind of toy? Sally Sleeps A Lot?"

"It might be. I just made it up."

Trace's smile was fast and big. "You're acting more like yourself. You'll be fine."

I leaned forward. "What if I wasn't? Would you bury my body here on the island? Leave me here to decay on the side of the road? Ship me in a coffin to someplace they'd never identify my remains?"

T tugged on the end of my hair. It was such a simple gesture. "You make me wish I could have met you under different circumstances. I would have liked to hear that mouth of yours say things to me across a table with you having no idea how fucked up I am."

I pushed away that image. I knew he could kiss. I wanted more of that. I wasn't in J's Vermont house, but I was still a prisoner. How far did I want to push this? The answer was pretty damned far. "How fucked up are you?"

The taxi driver took a hard left, and we were suddenly on an even bumpier street. Trace smiled at me. "Just as fucked up as I have to be. How fucked up are you?"

I leaned over and kissed him. Maybe it was the drugs addling my brain. Maybe I was too tired to care. Maybe I just really liked sex and needed to admit that I was probably an addict. Whatever. I didn't care. I pulled back to stare at his dark eyes. Trace, the man who always wore black, with his all-seeing glare and his nasty words, stared back at me like he was desperate for air and I was oxygen.

"Just about that fucked up. I might have sex with you, Trace." I said his name, liking how it was to say it to him. "But that doesn't mean I won't run away in the middle of the night."

He shook his head. "You won't. But if you do, know there is nowhere you can go that I won't find you. You're mine."

"For the next three days? Or is it two now?"

He held up three fingers. "They start now."

"Great. Did you bring me to the Caribbean so you could fuck me without the others being around?"

T shook his head slowly. "No, but it's a side benefit for sure."

Chapter 8

The taxi eventually stopped at a small hotel. Trace got out and offered me his hand. I took it and let him help me down to the ground from the open aired vehicle. The sun did feel nice. I lifted my head to be warmed by the sun. I supposed I should consider myself lucky. I wasn't on the ground somewhere with a bag over my head being watched on a video screen in their basement.

We walked together into the lobby, and T checked us in. I could start screaming at any time. I was sure at least some stranger in the lobby would help me. There had to be one person who worked here or was on vacation who would take pity on me.

And then what…

I'd get away. To go home to my father? To be captured again? To be mistreated the next time? Oh, I could rationalize why I stayed quiet until I was blue in the face. The truth was I remained quiet because I just did. I wanted to see what was going to happen next, why we were here, and what we were doing. I wanted to have sex with Trace.

Of course, I could probably find a really good vibrator

and get that job done, too. Sex was pretty disappointing most of the time. T would be fine followed by a hot shower to wash away my disappointment.

"Everly." He held out his hand, and I took it.

If he was surprised I didn't make a scene in the lobby, he didn't say anything. The bellboy had my bag, and T handed him some money before we got in the elevator. "I thought you were a teacher. And that The Alliance didn't draw attention to themselves."

"I am, and is there something I've done that makes you think I've drawn attention to myself?"

I shrugged. "The knocked out girl in the taxi."

"You had a pill and a drink on the airplane. A lot of people show up in the Caribbean half out of their minds."

I supposed he had a point. "What are we here for you to teach?"

"Well, specifically we're here for you to shower and change your clothes. Then we'll get to what we're doing here."

He opened the door to the room, and we walked in. Like the island itself, everything was bathed in pink. The windows were open and a breeze off the ocean flowed into the room. He pointed at the bathroom. I didn't have time to admire my surroundings, apparently.

"When you come out, your clothes will be here. Change into whatever you brought that looks like an interview outfit. Don't be long about it."

I shook my head. "Always rushing me around. Am I getting interviewed? What's the position? Am I going to be locked up so you can watch me tortured?"

He did not smile at my jab. "I hope not. People don't come out of there alive. I'd hate to see your light go out like that."

On that disturbing note, I left him there and went into

the bathroom to do as he said. I scrubbed the grime off my body. Why was I so okay with all of this? Maybe I wasn't. Maybe I was two seconds away from having a huge mental breakdown. I got under the hot water. My body was edgy. Maybe the drugs.

I washed myself quickly. If I'd been alone, I might have given myself a fast orgasm. But for some reason I didn't. I didn't like the idea of Trace accidently hearing me, which was stupid because I really did want him to give me an orgasm, which meant that he was going to hear me come. Okay, the truth was that I wanted him to do it. Not my own fingers.

Could he? It was few and far between men who could get the job done. Maybe I just had my standards too high. Maybe most women just didn't...

I finished up as quickly as I could, knowing that for the rest of the day I would smell like this different shampoo and the hotel soap. They were both slightly coconut-y. I turned off the water and dried off.

There was a blow dryer in a bag on the counter. The robe was soft. I tried to focus on those small things. The humidity in the air made my hair take longer to dry, but I stayed with it until I had it completely straight. Wrapped in the soft white robe, I went back into the hotel room.

T was out on the balcony. He leaned over, looking at the ocean. His arms were spread out in front of him while he looked down below. I could see that he'd rolled his black sleeves up until they were at his elbows.

Fuck. He was really hot. Why couldn't he be an ugly captor? The hard line of his back begged me to walk forward and wrap my robe-clothed body up against him. Of course, I didn't. We were walking a line together and that would have been far on the other side of it. That was girlfriend, relationship action. It spoke of intimacy, of me noticing that he was tense and wanting to do something about it.

I wasn't there, and I never would be.

The suitcase I'd brought was open and unpacked. Had T put away my clothes? I went to the closet. Sure enough, everything was hung. Maybe he'd paid the valet to do it. In any case, I grabbed one of my two interview suits and got myself ready to go. It was a black suit, and I paired it with a pink collared shirt I was glad I had. It sort of matched the décor of everything.

As it was too hot for them, I didn't put on stockings. My shoes were going to pinch if they swelled from the humidity. I hoped we were going to air conditioning.

I walked toward the balcony. T hadn't moved. He still stared down at the ocean. He must have heard me, but he didn't turn.

"I'm ready."

Trace turned slowly. "Nicely done."

He walked toward me. For a second, I thought he might touch me or pull me to him. I swallowed, anticipation filling me. What was T going to do? Instead, he moved around me back into the bedroom where he grabbed his own jacket. "We're both going to sweat if we go open air again so I'm going to ask them for a closed door ride."

I sighed. "Trace, can you tell me where we're going?"

"I was just going to." He unrolled his sleeves, which was disappointing. I liked him like that... Trace was handsome but remote. That made him seem human.

I waited, and finally he spoke again. "The man we're going to be going to see is what I would call an asset. He's not Alliance, he doesn't know anything about it. His name is James Robert Michaels. Heard of him?"

I shook my head. "Should I have?"

"Not necessarily, but it wouldn't have surprised me if

95

you had. He's a financier who made all of his money in hedge funds. For the last few years, he's been trying to figure out what to do with his time and his money. He's only thirty-five. The idea of retirement seemed wonderful to him. He was tired. Now, he's bored."

I had followed that. "Okay."

"For some time, we have been moving him toward making the decision we want him to make."

I'd understood that, too. "So you're manipulating him."

"Yes. He's finally at the point where he is about to make the jump. I should be the one to push him over. He and I have been doing this dance for a while. You're going to help me get him where I need him to go."

"How am I going to do that?" I knew next to nothing about any of this. How did they want me to tell someone how to spend their money?

"He likes beautiful women. You're going to sit there as my assistant. Not say much. It'll be nice and distracting."

I wasn't sure I was okay with this. "What are you forcing him to do? Destroy the lives of everyone in a third world country?"

T scowled at me. "Rocket fuel."

"Rocket fuel?" That was apparently the last thing he was going to say on that subject before he stormed out of the room. I sighed before I followed after him, and when we got into the elevator, I grabbed his arm. "Tell me why you're doing any of this? I mean, I thought you weren't technically Alliance anymore."

He shook his head. "We're going to be leading this mess soon. I'm not giving up all the work I did making this happen for the last ten years. They don't care about James Robert Michaels. It was always my project. They never saw the potential in this."

The elevator opened, and he shook his head, indicating he wanted me to be quiet, so I shut my mouth. I supposed we couldn't go around just discussing The Alliance everywhere we went. Trace took my hand in his. He'd done that a few times now like it was the most natural thing in the world. I was getting used to it, which was a problem because I was absolutely sure it was a calculated gesture and not just an easy thing between two people who were attracted to each other.

There would be nothing easy between us. Not ever. This whole mess was complicated, and I had to keep my head on straight, or I might very well lose it.

━━━

JAMES ROBERT MICHAELS lived in a large house overlooking the ocean. My initial thought was that it was twenty degrees colder inside the house than it was outside. I shivered and was suddenly glad for the jacket I'd left on with my interview suit.

We were shown into the living room that had two hundred seventy degree views of the ocean. Whoever had built this spot meant it to impress, and it did that, for certain. I was a prisoner of some men who had been kicked out of The Alliance, and right now I was being held captive in a beautiful home on St. Croix. Not to mention J's house had been gorgeous in Vermont. I was the most spoiled kidnap victim ever.

"Dr. Trace Hill, I finally got you back to my house. What has it been, two years?"

Trace hugged him back like they were old friends. "Well it isn't like I haven't been seeing you. I just haven't been *here*."

I'd obviously not known T long, but this was an incredible shift in personality. Gone was the glaring man in black. He still wore black, but he was really… charming. I actually winced. I didn't like him like this. Give me the real pissed off deal any day of the week.

This Trace was kind of smarmy. I tried to focus on what I'd learned instead of focusing on him. He was Dr. Trace Hill. I could Google him. He'd told me he was a teacher. The doctor meant he was probably a professor of something. I didn't get to continue to figure this out because my attention was suddenly needed.

"This is Everly. She's a college senior, and she's working with me right now. She doesn't have a degree in chemistry or aerospace design, but she takes great notes."

Awareness swarmed over me the second James Robert's attention rested completely on me. It was like slugs crawling all over my skin.

"Why hello there," he said, extending his hand. "Welcome. I'm glad to have you here. Good for Trace to have some… company. And such pretty company it is. Sorry, guess I shouldn't say that in this modern age. I've had a couple drinks already today." He spun on his heel. "You're both in black. This is St. Croix. Who wears black in St. Croix?"

"Well." I smiled. "One has to always be ready to go to a funeral."

Trace snorted and then covered his mouth. He shot me a look that was somehow both amused and warning at the same time.

James Robert shrugged. "I say live as though every day was my last. But now I can't stop thinking about something you said to me."

T lifted his eyebrows and loosened his tie. "Something I said? What could I have said?"

I was suddenly grateful T had never manipulated me.

Or at least I didn't think he had. Why would he have bothered? I was stuck doing what he wanted. I knew what Jim-Bob, which was how I was going to think of this asshat from now on, was about to say before he did.

"Rocket fuel."

I clenched my teeth. This man was retired at thirty-five years young. He was smart, even if he was an asshole, and he was clearly loaded. And T had convinced him somehow to invest in rocket fuel. Did he want to build a bomb launched from space?

I ended up taking a seat. For all that I was supposed to be taking notes, I didn't have a notepad or tablet. Jim-Bobby—maybe I liked that one better—hadn't noticed. I didn't know what justification T even had for being here. Were we on a social call? Why would he have brought his assistant? Why was Trace Hill, the college professor from who knew where, here in St. Croix?

I could sink this whole thing. I could ask. I bet that would throw the plan into pieces. Was I here helping Trace do something that would hurt people?

Jim-Bob—I was sticking with that—brought Trace a drink and turned back to me. "Want one?"

"I'll have what he's having." At least I knew that way the bottle wasn't poisoned. Although, I doubted that T had brought me all the way here to poison me. I went cold. Was this some kind of... nightmare situation? Were they going to drug me—I knew T did that—and then let Jim-Bob have his way with me?

I jumped to my feet, startling both of them. Trace tilted his head to the side. "All okay?"

"I need some air. Thank you anyway, but I'm not going to have a drink. Headache, I guess." I didn't wait for anyone to answer me but ran out the front door. If I kept running, there would be someone to help me. Unlike J's island. This was a big place in the Caribbean. Fuck The Alliance. I'd count on the sensibility of real people. They'd…

"What freaked you out?" Trace walked toward me. I could hear his footsteps, but I didn't turn to look at him, my eyes down the bumpy road where I should already be running. Why didn't I run? What was the matter with me?

I might as well tell him the truth. "I decided the alcohol was poisoned. Or drugged. And you were going to let Jim-Bob rape me."

He touched my back with his hand. I could feel it, even through the suit material. "I have done many, many bad things in my life. I have never turned a woman over to a man for abuse. I can promise you that."

I turned toward him. "You're a wonderful liar. Manipulator."

"I am." He didn't disagree and that was remarkable. "But you have already seen who I am without those lies. I have no need to give you to him. I'd never have done it. Not even to get him to invest in the rocket fuel. And we're already where I wanted to be."

"Why does The Alliance want him to invest in rocket fuel? Are you going to use it to hurt someone?"

He pushed my hair off my shoulders. "Going to get to Mars in the next twenty years. We want a specific company to do it. Jim-Bob, great name by the way, will connect well in an accidental meeting with the founder of that startup very soon. Others working on it will fall apart. That's okay. Don't feel badly for them. They're very rich and they've done less than reputable things. You found the person who's going to introduce JB to that person. That's what you went through the resumes for. He's going to be hired in the bottom rung of that startup tomorrow. And in five years… he'll introduce our host to his boss. Not one of them will ever know we did this. Long game. By then, I'll be one of the five running The Alliance. I'll know I sent the right people to do the right jobs."

I swallowed. "He's an ass. He's the right people?"

He nodded, slowly. "He's not going to Mars. He's funding the fuel." T tugged me to him, and I gasped. "He's watching through the window, and he thinks we had a lover's spat right before we got here. I didn't mean for you to be the co-ed I was fucking, but I had to improvise. It seemed easier on you than asking you to pretend you were afraid of the ocean."

"Those were the two choices you came up with? Couldn't tell him you'd kidnapped and drugged me?"

Trace's mouth came down on mine, and I wouldn't pretend I didn't want it. Fuck, I really did. His mouth was hard, firm, and all consuming. I closed my eyes and gave into the need to touch his face with my fingernails. His body hardened against mine. He wasn't unmoved by this.

He pulled back. "Fuck. Now I'm going to have a hard on for the rest of this afternoon."

"Good."

He pressed his nose down on my hair.

"How much of this is real? How much are you doing for his benefit?"

"Does it matter?" He stroked a hand down the side of my face. "Feels good, right? Anything we do here, Everly, it's meaningless. You get that, right? We're only in each other's life for a very brief period of time. After that you'll never see or hear from me again. Ever. Don't go and get romantic."

I stepped back. "Trust me, T. I know how to fuck and go. A brief minute of petting that leads to a mediocre orgasm when I could do better myself? Yeah, I don't hold any ridiculous feelings after that."

He lifted his eyebrows slowly. "Wow."

"What are we doing here anyway?" He'd killed the mood and not because I thought I was suddenly going to fall in love with him but because his arrogance could take up all the room on the island. "Why does he think we're here and you need an assistant?"

T ran a hand through his dark hair. "I'm presenting a paper at the hotel. There's a conference going on."

"That's what he thinks?"

He shook his head. "That's what I'm doing. There is actually a conference going on."

Oh. Well, I hadn't seen that coming.

———

A CONFERENCE FILLED with very smart people who all worked somehow in the space industry—that was a thing —proved to be a pretty rowdy party. Trace was a professor and highly thought of at that. With all of that in my head, I finally went back to the hotel room. There was a phone. I could call my father. I could reach out to anyone for help. I didn't.

I needed to accept I was pretty much consenting to this. My journey might not have been my idea, but I was a willing participant now. I wanted to see what was going to happen. And that made me sick in the head. A psychologist would have a field day with me.

I hadn't thought about the fact that there was only one bed in the room but there was just one. I rubbed the back of my neck. The kiss with T had been toe curling awesome. If he had suggested I strip bare on the driveway I'd probably have done it to have him inside of me right then. Now, tiredness rode me hard.

I changed into my pajamas. I hadn't brought sexy ones

and I pretty much thought that moment had passed anyway. There was a couch. I'd go to sleep on it. I grabbed a blanket from the closet and settled in. It wasn't an uncomfortable couch. I had slept in worse places through college. Truth was, I'd been really… uncaring where I plopped down for the night. I was lucky nothing bad had ever happened to me. Well, up until I got kidnapped but that was in my own apartment.

I closed my eyes, reveling in the warm air moving gently from the ceiling fan. Dreams drifted over me.

I woke with a start. T stood over the couch. "What are you doing over here?"

I rubbed my eyes. "Where should I have slept?" Did he want me out of the room altogether? He'd put my clothes in the closet.

"Frustrating woman." He scooped me up like I weighed nothing, which I knew wasn't true, and carried me over to the bed. "In the bed. Why would I put you on the couch?"

My brain hadn't turned back on yet. "So you could sleep in the bed?"

"Do you have any idea how much time I have spent today thinking about getting you off? I haven't given this much brain space to another person's orgasm, ever. That doesn't mean I haven't given them. No, it's just an assumption that I will. But, no, I keep thinking about yours. What it will be like. How you will come. When you will. What you'll sound like."

Oh, I was fully cognizant now. He had my total attention. "Sounds like a lot of buildup. I kind of thought the moment had passed."

"Everly, the boys you've been fucking are such rank amateurs. You stepped into this with a grown man. You want to come? I'm going to make you. But you aren't going to fall in love with me or I'm not touching you once."

I pushed at his chest. "Don't flatter yourself. I'd sooner fall in love with Jim-Bob."

"He'd never get to fucking touch you."

Trace was on me, fast. His mouth came down on mine and this time I held on to his shoulders and met him kiss for kiss. I expected the frantic pulling of clothes that always took place now, but that wasn't what happened. If anything, T slowed down.

He pulled back just a touch to lick at my mouth. His wicked tongue that could cut into me so easily with his words caressed my lips inch by inch. Anticipation had me catching my breath. Well, this was new. I couldn't say as I'd ever had that before and oh…

T was masterful at this, unrushed, his mouth clearly skilled at taking and giving what he wanted. He ran his hand through my hair, once then twice before he skirted back just enough to stare down at me.

"You're so fucking beautiful. I fucking hate it."

I didn't have time to digest that before his mouth came to meet my own again.

Chapter 9

There were a million things I should say to T, but I wasn't going to say any of them. No, because all I wanted to do right then was kiss him. He wasn't easy on me. His mouth was almost painful in how much he demanded. Total submission to his will or nothing at all. That seemed to be what he wanted, what he was telling me without saying a word.

Our kissing was a battle. One of us will win.

His tongue pushed into my mouth, caressing mine. It was the first gentle thing he'd done since we went down this road. I was more than fine with the moment of sweet, but I had no expectation of it lasting.

He pushed me back farther until my back pressed up against the headboard, at no point taking his mouth from mine. Having gotten me there, he moved his hand down further until he grasped at my waist. He squeezed me once. I wasn't sure why, but it felt like possession.

I pulled back to look at him, my mouth swollen in the best possible way. "Hey, you know what, Trace? You should go ahead and make sure you don't fall in love with me, either. Could go both ways, you know."

"Honey, I'm not capable of that kind of feeling. Everyone I meet is a chess piece. Even you. And right now you're right where I want you."

I didn't know how I felt about that. It was super egotistical. He thought he'd done this? Well, I had news for him. I wanted him to and I was always in control of my sex life. Fine, whatever he wanted. His body was making me promises I intended for him to keep.

He smiled at me, but there was no mirth in it. "Don't act like you're tough, Everly. I know you're not. You're soft inside and when this is over if you are careful, you can still be that way."

"Shut up, T." When he talked like that he was the letter he'd been called, not Trace the smart college professor who everyone loved. It didn't matter. I wanted to fuck both of them.

I bit his lower lip and he moaned for a second before fusing our lips together. He moved his hands everywhere he could reach. We were still both dressed, me in my pajamas. Yet, it still felt as though he scorched me with his touch where he managed to hold for a second.

I loved—no, wrong word when it came to T—liked the noises that he made when I rubbed against him. Low sounds in the back of his throat. His noises turned me on. There was no other way to think about it. I liked hearing him get hot for me. Maybe I got off on power. Right then, I didn't give a shit.

He pulled back enough to tug at my nightie. "You are way too hot for such an ugly nightgown."

I smirked at him. "This from the man I've never seen in anything but black."

"I'm profoundly colorblind. Wearing all black all the time means I never have to worry about matching."

I blinked. "Really?"

"Why would I make that up? I can see your hair just fine. The dark, almost black strands really stand out to me. I can see you, just fine. And I know that your nightgown is made for a grandmother. Don't wear it again."

He wasn't going to get to give me clothing orders. Only right then I was doing the thing where I was hung up on the fact that he could see me. I'd find my head later and stop being ridiculous. This was just sex. I never got caught up in pretty words. Right now, they were working for me. I didn't have to overthink it.

I tugged at his black shirt, tossing it aside. He was as buff as I'd thought he was going to be. T—Trace—the colorblind, man in black, with the glaring eyes, the PhD, and the manipulative personality who thought he moved the world like a chessboard. He was going to come between my legs and make me come, too. I could already tell.

I stripped him of the rest of his clothes until we were both naked. He was right. I'd only had sex with men much younger than him before. T was built like a man who was in control of his muscles. He was strong, defined, and he didn't look like he still had to grow any muscle to get bigger. This was a man in control of his body.

He had a dusting of dark hair over his chest. I ran my hand through it and down to touch his abs. His muscles clenched under my exploration. His cock was long, hard, and heavily veined. I stroked him once and he closed his eyes.

His cock grew in my hand but it didn't seem to hurry him. He wasn't pushing me down demanding completion like he couldn't hold off. Trace opened his eyes and looked at me, there was heat in his glaring gaze.

He scooted down the bed, moving away from me without a word. He pressed his mouth down on my stomach, planting a kiss there before he kissed all the way down. Anticipation made my mouth go dry. Was he seriously starting with this? Oral wasn't something the guys I knew offered to do very often. Usually, it took a blowjob first and I'd hardly gotten to touch T for very long.

T lifted his eyes and winked at me. I couldn't help my grin. He planted a kiss on my right thigh, and I shuddered. His breath was hot and I could feel it against my skin. He moved over just a little, planting another kiss on the other side. I closed my eyes. Good God, why was this so... intense?

Why didn't he just get to it already? Shouldn't he be half done?

But no, he'd hardly started. T kissed me everywhere, but my pussy, no bit of skin in the area went uncaressed. He moaned, low in his throat. Yes, I really dug that sound. And he liked this? I squirmed and he put a hand on my knee, just a gentle touch to stop me from moving. Okay, I'd try. It was just hard to... wait.

He ran that hand from my knee, down to where he kissed me and I shuddered. Slowly, ever so achingly so, Trace laid a kiss on my pussy. I could barely feel it. He'd been harder on my skin before. He laid a quick second one there, a harder kiss. This one I felt. Wow. I opened my eyes as he moved slightly on the bed, as though he had to adjust himself to get comfortable. His gaze was heated and he kissed me there again.

"You taste so fucking good."

I sucked in my breath as my nipples hardened. I didn't even know what to say but he didn't seem to need a response. No, T was right back where he had been before.

He licked my clit. With his tongue laid flat over it, he licked it ever so slowly. His movements weren't rushed or hurried, no he took his time and before I knew it my eyes were closed again and I knew nothing but the rhythm of his tongue on my clit. He slowly moved down, applying pressure to it as he went. Every pass increased just a little bit until I panted for it.

I cried out as he hit one spot I'd never known I liked before. He did it again. And then again. I gripped onto the bed. I arched onto the bed, my hips coming closer to his mouth. He didn't stop. Yes, it was like he could read my body. I wanted that and he kept doing it. Over and over until I exploded. Colors passed over my vision as tremors shook my body.

I tried to catch my breath. The intensity of the moment shocked me and I didn't want to…

T wasn't done. I'd assumed he'd move on. But just as I was catching and my body still contracted, he placed a finger inside of me. My body reacted and he took his cue, pushing his finger in to ride the wave of pleasure with me. For some reason, the gentle touch right there inside of me pushed me over again. My hips jerked off the bed and I came harder this time.

His mouth met my own and he kissed me through release. Over and over. I still couldn't think, couldn't breathe. That was the single best orgasm of my life and he hadn't even been inside of me. T jumped off me for a second, grabbing his pants and pulling out his wallet from his back pocket. A second later he had a condom in his hand. I nodded at him. That was the best I was going to do right then for affirmation.

My body felt cold without him near me as though it

was a sudden jolt to my senses. I shivered. Fortunately, he returned fast. I guessed I was needy for a change.

I wasn't usually *that* girl.

I was the woman who wanted to put the condom on him. I sat up to grab the package from his hand, and he raised an eyebrow at me. "Let me."

"Sure." He nodded once and sat back on the bed.

"You're so big." I stroked a hand down him, tip to balls, and he jerked in my fingers. Yes, he was ready for this. And I loved that he'd gotten this hot making me come. His breathing was shallow as he lifted a hand to caress my cheek with his thumb.

I tried to ignore how my hands were shaking and roll the condom onto him. I'd finally gotten him sheathed when he pushed me down under him. I hit the mattress with my back, releasing an oomph. I didn't mind it a little rough, and I didn't think he was even conscious that he'd almost shoved me down.

I was pretty sure he was just that excited.

I wrapped my legs around him as he teased the opening of my pussy with the tip of his cock. I should have known he wouldn't go right inside of me. T liked to play my body like an instrument, and he did seem to be a master at it. I wasn't complaining. After moments of antici-pation, he finally did.

Filled up with his big, hard cock I moaned. I couldn't have stopped myself if I'd wanted to. I was so full right in that second. My body clenched around him even as he pulled out. Where was he going? I wanted him right where he'd been. This time he pushed back inside of me shal-lowly, hitting my clit and pulling back out. I closed my eyes.

I couldn't think, couldn't focus. There were too many feelings going through me, too many sensations. He thrust inside of me over and over but then just as suddenly would stop, lingering for a moment deep inside. I squeezed around him, and he cried out, the smirk I'd come to think of as his crossing his mouth.

I dug my fingers into the skin on his back to hold onto him. He cried out again, his glaring eyes meeting mine. We were lost together. That was what it felt like, and I couldn't say why. He leaned down, grasping onto my nipple and sucking hard as he thrust into me. My breasts burned, and I shouted his name. The bed banged so loudly into the wall everyone on three floors would know what we were doing.

I was going to come, and it was going to be hard. My hands and feet tingled, and it felt like my whole body was going to explode into nothingness. I'd never been able to come this hard with someone else. Alone, yes. This was a first and I...

It happened. I shattered. I clung to him while he finished, not even sure how much time that took. With a whisper in my ear, he called out my name. I held on like he was the only way I could live through this pleasure that somehow came with so much pain.

This might very well kill me. And T would be my executioner.

We panted next to each other, side-by-side, not saying a word. What was there to say, really? That had been... yeah. Incredible. But nothing had changed.

I'd never thought it would. Still, it was impossible not to feel something about what we'd just done together. I couldn't deal with any of it so I rolled over away from him. I'd get myself under control and handle this all later.

I must have slept because the next thing I knew I was dreaming. Or at least I thought it was. I wore a long black gown. It was silk and it clung to my every curve. I'd never owned a dress like it. I couldn't see myself but every time wind hit me, the bottom of the skirt pulled up like it wanted to fly off my body.

I stood on the sand in my bare feet. It was a stark contrast to the fancy dress I had on.

A noise caught my attention, and I turned around to see who came near me. It was Trace. He wore his signature all black. In the way of dreams, despite the darkness of the night, I could see him just fine, and I was sure he could see me.

"Come to finish the job?"

T lifted his gun. "I told you. I'd never hesitate."

He fired, and I jolted up in bed, my heart racing in my chest. Next to me, T slept with his eyes closed. He breathed deeply. Light from the bathroom reached the room. He must have gotten up and done that because it was off before. Maybe he didn't like to sleep in pitch darkness.

Still, it illuminated the room so I could see a little bit and that helped me to settle. Of course, I'd had a nightmare. I'd had mind blowing, stress relieving sex with one of my kidnappers, the absolute reason for my stress to begin with. I pulled my knees to my chest.

The movement must have stirred Trace. His eyes fluttered open, and for a second, he stared at me, but I didn't want him to see the vulnerability pouring out of me just then, so I pressed my head further into my knees.

He touched the side of my leg. "You okay?"

"Just had a bad dream. Shook me. It's nothing. Sorry to wake you. Go back to sleep."

T pulled himself up to sit next to me in the bed. "Light bothering you?"

I shook my head. "No."

"I like to be able to see right away when I open my eyes." He ran a hand through my hair. It was a comforting gesture from a man I was so conflicted about. I could, on one hand, have the best sex of my life and on the other dream he shot me in the head.

I turned to look at him. Any chance I'd had of not looking vulnerable was gone. He'd seen I was shaken. There was nothing to do about it now. "Would you shoot me in the head?"

He didn't answer right away. "In what context is this alleged shooting taking place?"

Well, that wasn't a no. "In my dream, you shot me in the head on a beach."

His hand stilled before he raised it to my forehead. Like a child playing pretend—even though this was very real—he made the shape of a gun with his thumb, index, and middle fingers. Just like that he kept it there pointed against my skin. "I would shoot you, Everly. If I had to. If you gave me reason to. If doing so was essential in some way. I told you not to fall in love with me."

I swatted his hand away. "Oh trust me, no chance of that." I should probably have been running away, but I wasn't doing any of the things a smart, sensible person would have done by now.

He sighed. "I'd rather not shoot you in the head. I like you. I'd like you to continue to live in the world. So don't give me any reason to and we'll be fine."

T rose from the bed and walked to the minibar. "I think we could both use a drink. A stiff one."

In the light I could see what I'd not paid attention to earlier. Trace had scars all over his back. Deep, ugly scars. They crisscrossed everywhere. I knew next to nothing about this kind of thing but it looked like someone had taken a whip to him.

"Who did that to you?" I asked before I thought to stop myself.

He looked over his shoulder. "Training."

"Training? What does that mean?" I was sick of not understanding the world. I knew things. I was on my way to being highly educated. I intended to get a master's degree. I wasn't some idiot who didn't know basic knowledge. Yet, every time one of these Alliance men spoke to me it was like they spoke about a different planet I'd just landed on.

He shook his head. "Let's not do this." He pulled two bottles of small portions of alcohol out of the mini fridge and brought one over. T extended it to me, and I took it. Yes, a drink sounded wonderful. Necessary, even.

T spoke again. "Let's not share sad stories or upsetting stories. Let's be two people who had incredible sex. Really, surprisingly good sex. Let's leave that alone. You don't tell me your darkest secrets, and I won't share with you things that you're better off not knowing. Especially as we're not going to know each other in six months anyway."

I unscrewed the top of the... What was it? I took a sip —ugh—vodka and nodded. "No sad stories."

He hopped into the bed. I bet he gave himself something better than vodka. I bet he had whisky in that small bottle. "Okay."

As he'd been the one to get the booze from the fridge, I supposed he could decide what he drank. I took another long swig of the vodka. It would get the job done.

"You know dreams are supposed to be representations of things. I am not necessarily me in the dream. I may be representing something for you."

I shook my head. "No sad stories. No sharing."

"Fair enough." He smirked. "You are really amazing in bed."

Well, that I could talk about. I side-eyed him. "I actually didn't feel like I did very much for you. Next time, if we have a next time, I'll be more reciprocal."

"Everly," he laughed, throwing his head back. "Are you kidding? That was amazing. That's all there is to it. I could eat your pussy all day long."

My cheeks heated up. "Um...okay."

"Did I embarrass you?"

Now, this I could do. We had lines we couldn't cross with one another, but this I could do. We stayed like that, talking about sex and then meaningless nothingness until we both crawled back under the covers. He liked a little light in the room so he could see immediately when he woke up. Tonight, I felt the same way. It was great to have a little bit of light in the room.

━━━

I WOKE up to the sun streaming through the window. Next to me, T slept quietly. He never moved, hardly made a sound of breathing. But he'd wrapped his arms around me in the middle of the night, and I'd cuddled against his chest. I didn't move for a little bit. This was going to be awkward if he woke up, but right now I'd take the moments before that happened.

I didn't want to analyze why I liked this so much. He hadn't said he wouldn't shoot me in the head. Why was I looking to him for comfort?

That thought galvanized me and I left the bed, making my way to the bathroom. I quickly took care of my morning business and came back out to a still sleeping Trace. He had to be really out of it. I hadn't been particularly quiet in the bathroom.

It was a beautiful Caribbean morning. I'd only seen the Caribbean Sea once before. My father had taken us on a vacation to St. Thomas when I was six. I hardly remembered it. I opened up the balcony and walked outside, letting the morning sun hit me.

It was already warm, but the breeze off the ocean was heaven. I closed my eyes and leaned against the bannister. The crazy of last night seemed to burn off me, even as muscles I hadn't known could hurt ached just a little bit from the sex.

I was never going to regret that. The way it had made me ridiculous afterward, however, that I was going to wish hadn't happened.

"Everly?" T's shout in the room caught my attention, and I whirled around. He was looking around the room, not out on the balcony, and he didn't see me. Trace ran to the bathroom and then back again before I caught his attention.

He stopped abruptly, staring at me before running a hand through his dark hair. I'd scared him. He'd woken up and didn't know where I was. T walked out toward me, a quickness to his gait.

I stared at him, neither of us speaking. "Did you think I'd wised up and run for my life?"

"Maybe." He strode to me as I turned my back on him to stare at the ocean again. I couldn't look at him rumpled and warm looking. It would be too easy to see if last night was a fluke or we could have that chemistry again. It would be too easy to let him bring me to that level of needy once more. And I didn't even know if he was doing it on purpose. If that had been his plan all along.

He'd been running a long con on people for years. I might just be the next diversion in some plan I didn't understand.

Still, T stood behind me a second before he wrapped his arms around me, tugging me back against him. I closed my eyes. If this was him faking it, I was just going to live with the consequences for a few minutes. I did want to be held. I'd never wanted it before.

"I didn't think you'd run away. I just didn't like not knowing where you were. I *should* have thought about you running away. I forgot for a half a second that you weren't here with me because you wanted to be."

I took a long breath. "The problem, T, is that right this second I do want to be here with you. I don't like what that says about me."

He leaned his chin on top of my head. "It doesn't have to say anything at all. It just means that right now you're trying to make the best of things. You're smart. You know running away won't solve anything."

I hoped that was it. "You didn't tell me to bring a bathing suit. I did. But you didn't tell me to. You were going to let me come to the Caribbean with no suit."

He rocked me just slightly. "I can't wear swimwear. I never think of it. Feel free. If you want Jim-Bob looking at you that way."

Yeah, maybe I'd stick to fully dressed. I didn't pretend to not understand him. He couldn't wear a bathing suit because his back was scarred so badly he'd never get away without questions.

Training…

Whatever that meant.

Chapter 10

I spent the morning freezing in JB's Caribbean house, listening to him talk about rocket fuel. He really thought he'd come up with this idea just from a few passing comments T had made to him on occasion. From now on, I was going to pay more attention to what people said to me in passing. Or not. I wasn't really important enough to warrant this kind of manipulation.

I pretended to take notes. Trace had said I was good at that. I shook my head at the memory. *Misogynist asshole.* Of course, with that same nasty mouth, he'd licked me to completion in bed. I shook my head. What was the matter with me? Before this crazy interlude I would have said I was all about female empowerment. Now I was getting sex confused with emotion and trying to make my kidnapper seem okay in my head.

I bit my lip. He really was more than okay. *Fuck.*

Around lunchtime, T rose to his feet. "Well, I've got to get back to the hotel and get ready for my speech tonight."

He had to what? Trace had told me we were spending the day here. Was he done? Had Jim-Bobbery said something that told T we had to leave lest he screw up this path he was on? I got up, a smile on my face. If anyone had noticed that I hadn't uttered a word all day, they didn't indicate it. Maybe that was typical in their world.

JB called a taxi, and soon we were shuffled into it and on our way back to the hotel. After a few minutes, when he'd said nothing, I had to ask him why we'd left. "Something happen?"

He shook his head. "I'd had enough."

I guessed that was going to be it. "When we get back to the hotel, go put on your suit. I'm taking you to the beach."

"I thought you didn't wear bathing suits." I could only imagine the questions he would get about his back from strangers. Whatever this training was, it seemed counterintuitive. If the idea was for them to all have positions of power without being obvious so they could work together to get what they wanted for the overall group, then marking someone like T up would only make him the target of speculation.

Or maybe it had to do with that. Maybe they wanted him to always remember who was in charge.

I could dwell on this all day, and he'd been clear he wasn't going to talk about it.

"I'm going to keep a shirt on. And shorts. We're in the Caribbean. You should get some beach time."

I blinked. "Did you leave your… ah… meeting so you could take me to the beach?"

"Don't overthink it, Everly. Do you not want to go to the beach?" He shifted in his seat.

"I do." Who knew when or if I'd ever be back to a place like this. "Thank you."

He nodded. "You're welcome."

This was a strange turn of events from a man who had

just the night before told me he would shoot me in the head if he had to.

———

WE DIDN'T TALK MOST of the day. Sitting on lounge chairs side by side, we stared at the ocean. At some point he dozed, obviously content with the fact that I wasn't running away. I hadn't actually gotten into the ocean although it had been tempting me. The only thing keeping me out was that Trace wasn't going to swim. It was weird I didn't want to leave him alone, but I was so past the point of odd at that moment I should probably just get over myself and go for it.

I scooted off the chair and walked into the warm waters. It almost felt like a warm bath. I walked out until I was waist deep. I'd not brought a bikini but was instead in my oldest bathing suit, a plain black one piece that was more functional than sexy.

I lifted my head to the sky. This was an okay moment. Life was screwed up. But this was okay. Movement on the beach caught my attention. T must have roused from his nap. His head snapped in my direction, catching sight of me in the water. He lifted his hand to wave, and I waved back.

In other circumstances, this could be a normal moment. He might have been my boyfriend. He was sixteen years older than me, but relationships with that age difference happened often, and he was hot as hell. My older, more accomplished boyfriend who was here to give a speech to his colleagues at a conference. He'd brought me along and we were spending a little time together between obligations.

I liked that version a lot better than the reality.

I dove down into the water before coming up for air and then doing it again. As an only child with no mother and a busy father, I'd been good at amusing myself. Swimming had always been a favorite pastime.

When I'd finally tired myself out enough, I made my way out of the water and back to our chairs. He tilted his head to look at me as I approached.

"You look like sex personified in that suit."

My cheeks heated up. "It's an old, nothing bathing suit."

"Not on you it's not." He linked my wet hand into his. "Maybe tonight after my speech we could come back out here, and without people looking, I could take you back out into that water."

I lifted my brows. "To drown me?"

His smirk was ridiculously cute. "To kiss you in that water."

I caught my breath. "Okay."

I hated that I was going to anticipate that all day. He grabbed a towel and wrapped it around me. "What are you doing to me, Everly?"

I didn't know how to answer that because I didn't have a clue what he was doing to me either. Or what all of this would mean the second he drugged me and put me back on an airplane to Vermont and the reality of my life.

⸻

I DIDN'T UNDERSTAND MOST of what T talked about in his speech, but I listened. I clapped when everyone else did and sat through dinner as his assistant while every one of his colleagues laughed and congratulated him. They all had to think we were sleeping together especially since even I could tell he was constantly undressing me with his eyes.

If anyone thought that was weird, no one said anything about it.

After dinner, in utter silence, I changed back into my black suit and put on a cover up to go with it. In his requisite black outfit—this time shorts that showed off his long, muscular legs—we walked together back toward the ocean, a towel slung over both of our shoulders.

We didn't go back where we'd been but walked awhile until it was quieter. I'd had sex with the man the night before. He had his mouth on my most private of parts. And yet this was making me more nervous than losing my virginity.

He ran a hand through my hair. "Everly." Whatever he would have said next, he stopped as he jerked left, like he was listening for something. "Fuck. Get down."

T threw me down on the ground. I hit it with an oomph. What was happening? I asked him just as a whizz sounded over my head before exploding into one of the palm trees nearby. Was that a bullet? I'd been around guns a lot, even taken Derrick's away from him. But this was different. Someone was shooting at us.

"What's going on?"

"Stay down. It's dark. I don't know if they have night scopes or not. I can't tell yet what they're firing. We might have to run for it."

People rushed at us. Three of them. I thought. I lifted my head to watch. This was like… a bad movie. Except it was really happening. All dressed in black, they had guns strapped to them. I had a moment to register this before T rushed one of them, knocking him to the ground. He had the man's gun in his own hand a second later. That was all

I could register before two men ripped me off the beach. My arm burned where he squeezed it.

"Take her. She'll be useful to get him to do what we want. The mighty Trace finally falls for a girl. He'll never be able to handle us torturing her."

Torture me? Oh no. No. No. No. I struggled for my life. I was taller than one of the men holding me, and I took advantage of it, kicking him hard in the shin as I wrenched my own body weight away from the other man. I got away from the shorter assailant before the larger one punched me in the face. I went down, blood streaming from my nose, my ears ringing. Dizziness assaulted me.

A shout sounded and a large bang struck the man who had hit me before a bullet fired into the shorter man still to my left. The bangs continued. Again and again. Until they stopped.

I tried to raise my head.

"What the fuck, man?" Derrick was suddenly in my vision.

"I've never been so fucking happy to see you." Trace answered him.

I was having trouble following the other things they said. Derrick picked me up, staring into my face. Was I imagining things or did he have a baseball bat?

"Everly," Trace held my face in his hands. "Fuck. They hurt you."

"You took *my* girl and you got her hurt." Derrick shouted at Trace, his words ping ponging around in my brain.

Trace shook his head. "Can we focus on something else here? Everly is hurt. And she's not *your* girl."

Dizziness swept me under, and I thought I might puke. What was happening? I was so confused. That was it.

Nothing made sense except the pounding in my head. The world went black.

―――――

I WOKE up with my head in Derrick's lap. We were in the hotel room, all the lights on, and across the room T stared out the window.

"She's up." Derrick said and T whirled around.

Everything hurt. How was that possible from one punch to the face? I lifted my hand to touch my aching cheek, but D grabbed my hand instead. "Don't touch it. That's only going to make it hurt worse. Pretty sure you're concussed. We're icing your face, and when we get back, which will happen as soon as the plane is gassed, Judson can look at you further. I've been concussed. A lot. This isn't going to be fun, but you're going to live."

"What happened?" I didn't try to move. I believed him. That was going to hurt more.

"You were attacked." Derrick said simply. "Mostly because you were in the wrong place at the wrong time near Trace."

Trace came into my vision, holding a bag of ice. He settled it down on my head. "I've apparently had a kidnap ransom put on me. I had no idea. It just happened. Or, obviously, we'd not have been here vulnerable to attack."

"That's why I came. Or one of the reasons I came. I was also here to retrieve my girl."

Trace shook his head. "I'm not doing this merry-go-round with you again. We settled this ten minutes ago. Trust me, she's not your girl."

"Fucking her doesn't make her yours. Trust me, she's mine. I knew it that night by the lake. She's *mine*."

I groaned. This was too much. I couldn't focus on the

important things with the blasting—scratch that, pounding —in my head. I had to tell them something. "They wanted to torture me to make you compliant, that's what they said."

"Fuck." Trace ran a hand through his hair. "Coming after me like this? In relative public? They're desperate. What do they want?"

"Well," Derrick shifted slightly, and it jostled me. I groaned, and he placed a gentle hand on my shoulder. "Sorry, Everly. Trace, you could let yourself get taken in and find out. Of course you'll never be able to tell us because you'll be, you know, dead."

A thought dawned on me. "Did you have a baseball bat?"

"He always has a baseball bat."

I closed my eyes because the light hurt. "Why? Did you travel with it? Why do you always have it?"

"You really don't recognize him. We wondered. Sorry, Derrick. You're not famous to Everly."

He jerked again, and I cried out. I opened my eyes to plead with him to either stop moving or put me down, but he'd placed a kind hand on my head this time, and I decided to just keep quiet about it. "Should you be famous to me?"

"He used to play professional baseball." Trace supplied. "In the major leagues. For the Yankees. He had a following of female fans. We wondered if you knew him right away."

I stared at Derrick for a second. He didn't seem the least bit familiar. "We don't have a professional baseball team in Louisiana, and I'll be honest, I don't follow it much on the college level. Football is kind of religion in my house. My father. My grandfather. Oh shit, he must be Alliance, too."

"Your father didn't become full Alliance until your grandfather died. Before that we're all just semi-Alliance. But yes, your grandfather was, too." Trace looked tired. He rubbed his eyes. "How does your head feel?"

"Like I'm going to die and you'll have to dispose of my dead body somewhere on this island."

T glared at me. "I'm not disposing of your body. I'd totally cremate you."

Derrick shook his head. "You are such a sick fuck. Ignore him. You're going to be fine. Concussions suck. Yes, I played ball. I knew you didn't know who I was and that was fine by me."

"Did you play with that man bun?"

Trace snorted and then outright laughed, throwing his head back when he did. He winked at me before he stood up and looked at his phone. "The plane is ready. Can you walk? Carrying you onto the island like you were drunk was one thing. Carrying you out might draw more attention. These fuckers. I can't believe they did this." A muscle ticced in his jaw.

"I can walk." Maybe. I hoped.

"You can lean on me." Derrick helped me up. "And you can pass out if you need to once we get you on the plane."

I swallowed. "You're not going to drug me again?"

"Did you drug her to bring her down here?" Derrick shot a look at Trace.

The other man shrugged. "I had to make two stops at secure locations. I didn't want her to see them. I was actually trying to spare her any problems later. So yeah, I let her sleep, and she woke up in the Caribbean. No harm. No foul."

"Don't make sports references. I know you. Watching golf does not give you permission to do that."

Trace shook his head. "That's basketball. You don't own all sports."

"I do. I own them all."

This was going to be a long day. Or was it night? I put one foot in front of the other and leaned on Derrick.

I managed to keep it together until we got to the plane. I even made it through take off. It wasn't until we had been in the air an hour that I started to weep. I hadn't seen it coming. Derrick snored next to me, his eyes closed, his breathing even but loud. He didn't stir with my crying, but Trace woke up. He placed a gentle hand on the uninjured side of my face.

"I am really sorry this happened to you."

I sniffed. Words were escaping me. Was it possible I had brain damage or was this some kind of shock? "Why were they shooting at you if they wanted to kidnap you?" I finally found my voice. "Why didn't Derrick text you or something about what was happening?"

He kissed my cheek. "They didn't hit me. That was a warning meant to take me down so they could get me more easily. If they'd wanted me dead I'd have been dead. I was more worried about them hitting you. And as for Derrick, I think what he wanted was to see you."

Derrick's eyes flew open. "I wanted to get you back. He doesn't just get to take you because he wants you. In the middle of the night while we're all asleep. He doesn't just get to do that. I came to get you and bring you back. And to tell Trace they were after him."

"Just me or everyone?" Trace sat back down in his seat. My head really pounded now. The harder it did, the more that I wept.

"Everyone." Derrick answered him. "Can we really not give her anything for the pain?"

T shook his head. "No. Judson says not until he's at

least seen her. He may want to take her to the hospital and getting caught is not a good idea, obviously. So we'll have to figure out which one."

Derrick sighed. "I'm sorry you're hurting, Everly."

"You beat the crap out of that man with your bat, Derrick, and T, you shot someone."

He held up two fingers. "That many people, actually."

"Then I guess you weren't kidding when you said you could shoot me in the head. You really could." I didn't know what was happening inside of his mind, but he didn't seem particularly bothered by the experience.

"What the hell went on between the two of you?"

I would have answered except the tears overwhelmed me again. Everything hurt. Why was this happening? I was supposed to be studying, waiting to hear from my graduate schools, and planning my life. I wasn't supposed to be on an airplane in this crazy situation, beat up and concussed.

The weeping wracked my body, which only made my head hurt more. T squirmed in his seat. "I never know what to do with tears. I really don't."

Derrick drew me against him, holding onto me. "You can cry on me." I closed my eyes, doing just that. He leaned down, pressing a gentle kiss on the top of my head. "I'm crazy. Out of my mind lunatic. But I'll always be there. You don't know that you want that yet, but you will. Give me all your tears. I've got you."

I didn't sleep. My head hurt too much, but time did move at a funny pace. I was aware of things, and then I wasn't. By the time we'd landed in Vermont and boarded the helicopter, I'd thrown up twice. I couldn't believe there was anything more in my stomach.

Derrick had a hand on my back the whole time, and Mr. I Hate Tears Trace hadn't abandoned me either, even if I was fairly certain I'd put him into his own version of hell. Crying, puking women were not on his list of things he knew how to handle. Well, he could kiss my ass. This was his fault. Sort of.

Judson met us by the door of the helicopter. "Still feel awful? Yes, I can see that you do."

"Does she need a hospital?" Trace jumped down next to me.

"It might have been better to have done that before you put me on that death machine." I didn't like helicopters. I'd decided about halfway through the flight. Or maybe I just hated everything right now.

J picked me up. I hadn't anticipated it, and I must have made some sort of sound to indicate that because he adjusted me quickly so my head didn't jostle too much. "I'm sorry this happened to you. It was my never my intention that you'd be hurt at all. I'm afraid we've dragged you into a hole with us that we have to dig out of now."

"You could let me go. That would work." That seemed to make sense to me, even in my concussed state.

K stood by the door to the house. He must have heard me because he groaned. "We still need your father to do what we always needed him to do. That's the only way this stops."

"Considering she just got shot at and smacked around, I don't think she gives a shit about our problems right now." Derrick moved past us into the house.

"Gentlemen, this is all too much." Warden walked quietly into the room. "Everybody shut the fuck up and let Judson check her out."

I closed my eyes. Time slipped away again.

I must not have gone to a hospital, and I didn't know if that was because they didn't want to take me or if I was okay to not be in one. Judson hovered around me, and at some point I realized that time was moving at its usual pace again. I sat up in my bed.

Judson stared at me. Casual J who had a face that could probably be called pretty and turned out to be a doctor of some kind. This was his house. He signed to his staff. And right then he tilted his head while he spoke to me.

"How are you feeling?"

"My head is pounding a little less. Did you give me anything?"

He shook his head. "I didn't. I'm not trying to torture you. It's not a good idea to give pain meds in the first stage of a concussion. At some point I will give you something. For now, rest is what you can do."

A sound caught my attention, and I turned to see Derrick at my desk, his head down on his arms as he slept in the chair.

"You've made a big fan in Derrick. In Trace too. I think he left to take a shower. They don't leave you for very long." Judson sat down on the side of my bed.

"I know your first name." That might be an asinine thing to say. "All of them now."

He nodded. "Well, then, Everly, it's nice to meet you. Come on downstairs. We've got to make some plans."

Derrick lifted his head. "Because you know how much I love planning meetings."

"I don't know why we bother." Judson rose. "You and Trace have proven you'll just do what you want anyway. I thought Kade was going to have a coronary."

It was both good and bad that I now knew their names. It was easier to think of them as their letters. The Letters watched people getting tortured in the basement. The Letters took me prisoner. The Letters got shot at. If they were really these people—just people—then I had to deal with the fact that they were more than just monsters. They were people, complex, good looking, funny, people—who did monstrous things.

And I was so tied up with them now I wasn't sure I would ever get out. Or if I'd want to.

Chapter 11

The last time I'd been in the living room with all five Letters, I'd been terrified. Now, I was in too much pain to care one way or the other. I slumped down on the couch, not surprised when Derrick sat next to me. He had said he was always going to be around. I'd deal with that at another time. He was hot, even with the man bun, and he'd let me cry all over his shirt.

He'd lost his wife, Alyssa, when she'd been killed by The Alliance. He shot bullets into the ice and killed a man with a baseball bat. Kade actually sat on my other side.

"I know your first name," I told him.

He tilted his head. "I'm the one who told it to you. How hard did you hit your head?"

"I didn't hit it. I got punched. Hard." If I closed my eyes, I could still see it. The fist heading straight for me. I should have at least tried to duck. It had been really fast...

Judson sat down on another couch and soon they all trickled in. Trace didn't sit, standing by the window. Warden was next to J and winked at me after a second.

"I'm going to cut to the chase," Judson said. "We've all

had kidnap orders put on us. I think our cell phones have been compromised. We knew that could happen. That's why we didn't text you, Trace. I think we all hoped that you'd be safe until Derrick got there."

Well, that hadn't worked out the way they wanted. Of course, maybe it did. Trace was fine. Sure, he'd killed two men. But he was perfectly healthy. It was my head pounding, my brain bruised.

J kept speaking. "It isn't safe to stay here. They know we're here, and the bounty collectors will eventually figure out how to get here. I don't one hundred percent trust the helicopter crew to not sell us out for the right amount. I want to get out of here tonight. We're going to have to separate."

I blinked. "So you're going to let me go?"

"No, we just need to move you around until your father comes through." Judson sighed. Why had I started to think he was nice? He wasn't any different than the rest of them. He fully intended to keep me tied to them until he got what he wanted. "We need to split up. You'll have to go with one of us."

K held up his hand. "I think that's the answer. The ruling council clearly knows we aren't going away quietly and that we're going to bring them down. Or that we want to. But I am concerned about her staying with any of us too long. I mean, look at what she's done to Derrick and Trace."

What had I done to them? "What does that mean?" I tried to sit up too fast. Derrick placed a hand on my thigh, stopping me from moving.

"It means what it means. They're both tied up in knots. I don't know what went on with you and Trace on St. Croix, but I can guess, and Derrick is hooked. This is temporary, gentlemen. She is leaving. Never seeing us again."

T shrugged. "She and I didn't make each other any promises and whatever you think you know, Kade, you don't. It's not your business. Everly is free to do as she likes. Period."

That shouldn't have burned, but it did. Not that I expected a commitment from him. I absolutely did not, but the way he made it sound was like it was nothing. Oh man. I'd done it. I'd gone and equated sex and feelings. I kept my face passive even as part of me went cold inside.

"She was never going to be yours anyway." Derrick put his feet on the coffee table. "So yeah, by all means, be stupid about this now. You're good at it, professor."

Warden interrupted. "I'll take her. We'll shift her around until her father comes through. A few months more. Less maybe if he hustles. Could be significantly less. We'll all have to disappear. We have those outs. She'll come with us. Then it'll be over and Everly can go back to her life, knowing that I'm fantastic and that the rest of you are douchebags."

I laughed, but it hurt. Derrick shook his head. "I'm not leaving her."

"You don't have ownership on her, dip shit." Trace's voice was so sharp it could have cut glass.

K sighed. "I rest my case."

"You need a break, Derrick." Judson sat back. "I'm afraid this is some kind of transference from obsessing over Alyssa to now obsessing over Everly."

I expected Derrick to tense with that statement, but he didn't. Not even a little bit. "Wait and see, brother, you're going to be panting at Everly's feet."

He shook his head. "I don't do that."

"We'll see."

I'd had enough. "So we're all just going to leave here and pass me around while my father gets the information you need? Has anyone spoken to him? Is it possible he did this to you? Put the kidnap hit on you."

"I spoke with him yesterday. It isn't him. He doesn't want you dead. Whatever else he is, he understands that putting us in any danger, also puts you in the crosshairs. And the last thing he wants is the ruling body of this fucked up existence turning their attention to you. Your father is on the wrong side of this war, but he recognizes that it is, in fact, a battle. If we're not careful, you're going to be collateral damage."

So not my father then. "I hate to point out the obvious but if you guys need to go into hiding, you could just let me go. I won't even tell anyone. Who would believe me? I have a head injury. Boom, I'm crazy. Easy fix, done."

"Sorry, honey." Derrick laughed. "You're not done with us. Back to the matter at hand," he squeezed my thigh again, this time harder, "I'm not leaving her."

Judson shook his head. "You have something to do. You can't go into hiding. By contrast, you have be so in public they can't take a shot at you. No one is going to grab you from an award show. Go be seen. Everywhere. With every hot starlet out there. Go do the baseball thing. You're still recognizable. That'll be a great distraction to give the rest of us time to get these bastards off our asses. You can't have her with you while you do that. And keep your fucking eye on the goal here. Taking over The Alliance so Alyssa can never happen again."

That was when I remembered Alyssa was Judson's twin sister. Oh, he had a strong objective here too. Maybe I could forgive him for being so centrally focused. What was it like to share a womb with someone and then lose them?

"I will never forget Alyssa. You know that." His voice was low.

J nodded. "I do. Go take care of business, Derrick. You can have your turn with Everly at the end if you're still interested. You'll probably have moved on which will be better for both of you. Trace will cool off, too." When had J gotten to be in charge? It seemed like they rotated through unspoken leadership. Or maybe there wasn't any, really. Trace had absconded with me in the middle of the night. None of them liked it but there wasn't anything any of them seemed to be able to do about it anyway.

"How do you all know each other?" I looked between them. "I mean, I get it. You're all Alliance. Are there like get-togethers? Birthday parties? Bar crawls? Did you go camping? Tubing? Shrimping? I'm trying to understand your dynamics here. Derrick was married to your twin sister until she died. I'm sorry about that, by the way, but how do you know the rest of them?" I addressed Judson, but I was really speaking to all of them.

Judson pointed at Warden. "Our fathers knew each other. We didn't know about The Alliance until we were older. Warden wasn't supposed to be part of it. But we used to see each other regularly because our dads were friends. Warden's father used to give money to the hospital where my father was chief of staff. So he and I have been friends for a long time."

W shook his head. "J was annoying. He was two almost three years younger than me but he used to tag along with my brother and me. Eventually, I discovered he wasn't annoying. He was brilliant. Then I kind of hated him a little bit."

Judson laughed. "Warden has an IQ off the charts. I wouldn't believe him on this. Or much of anything. He lies."

"You're going to make it so she never believes me, and out of all of us, I'm the most likely to tell the truth." He shook his head. "The rest of us met later. At Alliance training."

Training? I thought of Trace's back and the scars all over it. He'd said that happened during training. I filed this away for another time when my head didn't hurt.

"I met Alyssa through Judson. He wasn't at the first years of training with us. He came in the last year we were there. Then he did two years without us. His father hosted a get-together," Derrick supplied, "here, actually. I went. She was there, shouldn't have been considering it was an Alliance party but their father was lenient."

Judson nodded. "Got her killed, thanks to it."

"No, that was my fault." Derrick tensed for the first time in the conversation. "I got her killed."

J shook his head. "No. I did the second I got her involved in something she should have been left out of. Like we've done ourselves with Everly." He pointed at me. "As her concussion proves. Let's hope that's the end of it."

Kade sat forward. "We all became allies of sorts. We saw things the same way. That eventually led to friendships, but like all Alliance members we understand that friendship only goes so far. We're loyal to each other. That's more important than friendship. Like I really don't give a shit if I hurt their feelings. They know I'd kill to keep us all safe. That's more important than if they like me."

Warden laughed. "I like you, Kade. Especially when you've been properly fed."

"Very funny."

Judson groaned. "We have to get out of here tonight. So we need to decide things immediately. Everly isn't going with Trace or Derrick right off the bat." I noticed neither of them objected, and I tried not to feel like their discarded favorite toy. I didn't fool myself into thinking I was going to get a say in where I went. I didn't really care. I just didn't want to be hit in the head again. Or worse.

"She'll go with me. Unless you think you need to watch her, Jud." Warden spoke as Constance came in the room, bringing bottles of water for everyone. She handed one to me, placing a hand on my shoulder and squeezing when she did. Constance hadn't particularly cared for me up until now, but maybe having my head concussed earned me some sympathy.

Warden took a long sip on his water while they seemed to be waiting for Constance to leave. They needn't have bothered. I was one hundred percent certain that woman knew everything going on in this house and then some.

Judson finally answered. "She's okay. I mean, I can give you some suggestions, Warden. But I don't want to know where you are. None of us can share that. Meet back here, but only to trade her off. Two weeks at a time. Then back. I'll go second. Kade after me. Then Derrick."

Trace ran a hand over his face. "I got a day and a half maybe. She was asleep for most of it."

"If her father hasn't finished, you'll go after Derrick. You certainly had enough time to get her damaged." Judson shot Trace a hard look. "And it'll be good for you to get some separation. I'd have expected the run off in the middle of the night routine from Derrick but not from you."

T stalked over to him. "I don't have to justify to you not wanting my years of working James Robert Michaels to go to hell. The details of why I took her with me are not your business. That's between Everly and me. You're certainly preoccupied. What? Disappointed you didn't think of it?"

Judson didn't respond to him. Instead, when he spoke,

it was back to the plan. "If we keep the pass offs here as brief as possible we'll be okay. Stay off the grid, except for Derrick. Do the opposite. It'll make them nuts."

Trace stormed out of the room. These guys might all have been brilliant. They might all have been troubled. They might all have been absolutely right in their feelings about The Alliance. They might have been a million things. But they were a mess.

Someone was going to have to help them pull their lives together if they really wanted to be the leaders of this mess of an organization. I just had no idea who that person could possibly be.

━━

WE ALL TOOK the helicopter together that night. It seemed I was going to be on this thing a lot if I was being dropped off every two weeks. Did J think he could pay the helicopter pilots enough to keep them loyal for those bi-weekly drop offs? I should have asked that, but I'd just had enough.

Derrick was silent, but he wore a pleasant look on his face. Trace wouldn't make eye contact with anyone. He eventually closed his eyes and was either pretending to sleep or doing the real thing. Kade was thinking about something that bothered him. Judson stared at the floor. Warden nudged me before he took my hand.

I hardly knew him. I was going to spend two weeks with him. I should have been nervous, but I wasn't. Maybe it was the concussion or I'd just given up on thinking about any of this. Warden seemed like he cared. His hand was a comfort.

I couldn't hear anything but my pounding head thanks to the headphones I wore. I never thought I'd have wished for Trace's sleep drugs, but right then I'd have taken them happily.

Since that wasn't going to happen, I settled in to go wherever I was being taken and tried not to puke in the process.

That would have to be enough.

———

WE SEPARATED at the helicopter landing pad. Without a word to each other, they exited. Trace went first without a backward glance. He must not have really been asleep because he was the first off the helicopter and he stormed off into the dark.

Kade went next. He nodded at everyone, including me, before he zipped up his coat and walked in the other direction of where Trace had gone. Judson exited, followed then by Derrick who smiled at me before he left. I had to admit, I was going to miss his slightly off kilter way and the man bun that wouldn't work for everyone but was growing on me with him.

Warden and I were last. He hadn't let go of my hand. We walked quietly into the night. I wasn't sure how long I could make it walking, but I wouldn't complain, not unless I was about to fall over. The cold air hit me square in the face, and I shivered. Warden took off his coat and wrapped it around me.

"You'll be cold." I tried to take it off, and he stopped me.

"We only have a little bit to go to the car. I keep one here. I have plans on where to take you and, yes, we will go off grid, but first we're going to a neurologist. He's an old friend. Alliance. On our side. Not hated by powers that be, yet. He'll look at you. I want him to do that before we go. Judson's a great doctor, but he's not himself right now."

I cleared my throat, my breath obvious in the night. "Will it be warm? Where we're going?"

He nodded, pointing to the dark car parked a little bit ahead of us. "And we'll be inside a lot."

"I'm sorry. I don't seem much like myself. I'm... off."

Warden opened my door, and I got into it. Men did that where I was from, and I appreciated that he did. This wasn't a date, but I appreciated the courtesy nonetheless.

He got in the driver's side. "I don't expect anything from you, Everly. If you want to be silent for two weeks, you can go ahead and do so. You got punched in the face so hard it concussed you. This is trauma. K uses the ant phrasing all the time, and I'm over hearing it. But the point remains that non-Alliance people should not be hurt like this. We're not even supposed to do this to each other. We take a vow."

That was interesting. My mother cheated on my father, and he'd killed her. They'd had vows, too. People didn't keep their vows. Warden started the car, and it hummed as it came to life. It was some kind of SUV. I hadn't looked and probably couldn't have told the difference in the dark anyway. I leaned against the side and closed my eyes.

Sleep welcomed me despite my pounding head.

―――――

THE APPOINTMENT with the neurologist went fine. I was going to be okay. That was the bottom line. It was going to take some time. I was given the same dos and don'ts Judson had given me. I really wasn't sure where we were. Somewhere in Massachusetts? Elsewhere? Not knowing our current location wasn't because of my concussion, but because I'd slept the whole way and not paid attention. They liked that my cognitive ability seemed intact, despite the fact that I'd forgotten that Kade had told me his name. I knew my own, who the president was, what day of the week it was, all sorts of things that told them I was okay.

Warden eventually took us to eat on a river somewhere. The sun was warmer here, not Louisiana warm, but less frigid than where we'd been.

I leaned back letting it hit me in the face. "I was in the Caribbean two days ago. So weird to think about. Where am I now?"

He smiled at me. When I'd first met Warden, I'd been struck with the idea that he wasn't handsome. There was something too rough looking about him. The truth was, he was sexy as sin. It came from the careful way he watched me, the intensity of his gaze, the way he seemed to pay attention to everything. There was heat to all of it.

And when he grinned, it lit up his whole face. Oh, he was handsome all right. And he knew it. I took a sip of my water and tried to ignore it.

"You're in Massachusetts." So at least I'd been right about that. "We'll be leaving from a private airport soon."

That much I knew. At least I understood where I was now. I looked out the window that overlooked the river. It was a pretty day outside. "More air travel. I've never flown so much in my life."

"You're jet setting. And think of it this way, you can't do screens right now. You can't read. Nothing to do, but rest. And where I'm taking you, you can rest. As long as you make no moves to get away. That'll just piss me off."

I held up my hands. "I had ample opportunity to run away from Trace and I didn't. I'm not going to do that with you unless you start being some kind of abusive asshole. I'm not going to sit around while you beat me or something."

He set down his iced tea as the waiter came by and delivered our food. I was just doing soup, a chowder that smelled delicious. Warden had more to eat, ordering a burger and a salad. When the waitress walked away, he turned back to me.

"I've never in my life hurt a woman. I won't hurt you, Everly. If you try to run away or cause me any trouble in that direction I'll have to take away some of the freedom I'd like to offer you for the next two weeks."

I set down my spoon after taking a small bite of my chowder. "I get it. I'm brain damaged but not dumb. I've seen what the people after you do. I'd rather not see it again. I'm not going to cause any trouble."

"Good girl." He rubbed my foot with his under the table. I could have kicked him away. I didn't. "Then we should have a wonderful two weeks, even if we're technically in hiding."

I didn't ask him where we were going. If he'd wanted me to know, he would have told me. Instead, I ate in silence with Warden, watching the river and appreciating that my head was hurting less. I supposed at this point, whatever was going to happen was going to happen.

Maybe I was fatalistic at heart.

Chapter 12

We flew on a private jet to Georgia and then changed to a car for hours. When I asked Warden where we were headed, he just said Florida and left it at that. As the state could mean any number of things, I sat back to wait.

W didn't like to talk when there wasn't much to say, and I didn't find staying in silence to be a problem with him. I drifted off to sleep, which happened a lot more than usual with my healing brain. I'd be awake and then hours later I'd wake up not having known I'd fallen asleep. For all his bluster in the restaurant, Warden was actually being gentle with me.

His version of Florida wasn't anywhere I'd seen before. There weren't any oceans that I could see, we weren't on an island, and there were no theme parks in any direction. Instead, we drove down a long, bumpy road—that seemed to be a theme for me lately—and ended up in what essentially looked like a log cabin.

I was wide awake when we pulled up. The cabin was huge with solar panels and a satellite dish on the ground next door. Warden sighed. "I'll be honest. It's not my favorite place in the world. I never set out to live off the grid. However, my father foresaw there might be the need for this someday. He bought the land, and when I inherited, I finished the project. We are, as they say, off the grid here. No one and I mean no one, knows it's here."

I got out of the car. "It's actually beautiful."

"It's functional. I'm not going to kid you, Everly. I'm a spoiled son of a bitch. I like room service. I like spas and casinos. I like fine liquor to go with my fine dining. But this will do for the next two weeks and then for me to come back to. Assuming I can trust you not to even tell the others where I am?"

I held up my hands like I was under arrest. "Look, I get it. I'm always at risk with you guys. Trace made that clear, too." He might shoot me in the head. "I don't need to be constantly threatened to remember all that. I get the idea. I don't want to end up locked in Judson's basement while you watch me being tortured."

He smirked at me. "Judson would never stoop to having someone tortured in his house."

"The point here is that I get it. I won't ever tattle where you are. Truth is, I'm not even sure where this is. I slept so much you could have turned the car around and taken me to Maryland for all I know. You're safe with me, Warden. Even if I'm never really safe with you."

His smirk fell, and he nodded once to me. I didn't know why what I'd said made him upset—I'd really only spoken the truth—but he hadn't liked it. I needed to know Warden a little better before I was so open with him. I chewed on my lips. I'd gotten careless being around Trace and Derrick. They didn't seem to mind if I was slightly flippant with them.

Warden came up behind me. He put a hand on my back. "Let's start over. We've both made our points. From now on, consider yourself safe with me, Everly. Okay? Nothing is going to happen to you while you're with me."

Had I hurt his feelings? I nodded. "Sounds good."

"Great. Now let's go inside my weird looking house. I have homes in five cities. In any one of them I'd show you such a good time you'd forget that anyone else ever existed. Here? You're going to see me out of element."

I walked toward the house, noting the flat roof thanks to the solar panels. The house was on stilts, putting it off the ground in the event of flooding. Or that's what I assumed. Wood paneling covered the outside with a wrap-around porch around the exterior. One room had a balcony on it, too. "When I pictured off the grid, I have to admit, I kind of thought of someone living in a trailer somewhere. This doesn't look like roughing it to me."

"I was born with a silver spoon in my mouth, and if my brother hadn't died, I'd have lived my whole life without knowing that anything was ever hard."

I followed him inside. As we walked in, lights flashed on and an air conditioner started to blow. "Who looks after this place when you're not here?"

"A woman and her daughter. They've never seen me, and they think they're talking to a man named Steven. I called her from a burner phone when we landed in Georgia, and she made sure this was ready. Food in the fridge. Then she left. She doesn't want to know me, I don't want to know her. Bit of a survivalist." He pointed upstairs. "Two bedrooms upstairs, one down."

I wandered around, looking. There was nothing in the house that I could see that identified anyone as living here. It really was a space empty of any personal effects. There were two black couches and a coffee table but not much else. There wasn't a screen to be seen anywhere, which was good since I'd been banned from them until my head healed.

"There is one thing I like a lot." Warden motioned with his head, and I followed him out the back door to see what he was talking about. A giant pond caught my attention. It was beautiful, with floating moss and great big trees with gray branches hanging over it.

"That is beautiful." A thought dawned on me. "You know I'm from Louisiana, right?"

He nodded slowly. "Sure."

"So I have to say this because I don't know how it is in Saudi Arabia or Southern California where you're from, but I suspect it isn't someplace like here, right?"

He leaned against the wall. "Have I mentioned how sexy your southern accent is?"

I rolled my eyes. "Hush. I asked you a question."

"It is not someplace like here. I was born in Atlanta. Moved to Saudi Arabia pretty fast and stayed a decade. Then back here but to San Diego. No, not like here. I consider San Diego home. Why?"

I pointed at the pond. "You don't want to swim in that pond. I mean, I wouldn't. There are probably alligators in it."

"Alligators." Olive skinned Warden paled a second when I said that. "Right. Alligators. I had dreams of fishing in that pond."

I opened the door to step out onto the porch, loving the humid air that hit me. This was like home. Or close. Baton Rouge wasn't New Orleans. We didn't have quite the humidity rate. In any case, it made my bones feel better. I wasn't cut out for the north, although I think if I'd gotten to stay there I could have come to love the beauty of my surroundings.

I tended to be adaptable, as I was proving every day.

"I think we can fish. I'm good at it. But we'll scope things out first and try not to be dumb about it. They can look like floating logs. We'll have to get bait. I bet there's a place that sells it somewhere around here. A long drive maybe, but wherever we're going to go to get groceries."

Warden pulled on the end of my hair. "You're better at this than me. I think it's a good thing you came with me. I might have been eaten by a crocodile."

I rolled my eyes. "Alligator."

"Whatever."

He was ridiculously adorable about this. "They're not at all the same thing."

"To me, they are close enough. How are you feeling? Are you hungry?"

I was, actually. "Awake for the moment and, yes, hungry. I can make us food. Maybe. Depending on what you have. I will admit that I am better at making reservations than dinner but I'll manage."

"You cook tonight, I'll fumble through tomorrow."

Sounded like a plan. Strangest kidnapping ever, but I wasn't going to complain. I'd had a few minutes of a taste of what it would be like if other members of The Alliance had taken me. My father had really not considered the fact that he had a family when he did this.

Or maybe he didn't care. He'd killed my mother.

I discovered quickly that there was warm water if I let the faucet run. And that there was gas to cook with. Pasta seemed fast, and he had it in abundance. I started making spaghetti. It was a good thing it wasn't very complicated because by the time it was finished, I was too tired to do more than serve it.

"Everly." Warden sat next to me after I placed down the pasta with the sauce that I'd opened from a can sitting next to it rather than on it. "Did you wear yourself out?"

I shook my aching head. "This is just ridiculous."

"No, it's not. This is standard. You heard the doctor. Let's save this. Eat later."

I didn't like that idea. "I'm hungry. Even if I face-plant I'm eating it."

"Fair enough." He poured me some water, and we ate in silence, me focusing on staying awake the whole time. I didn't miss that he hustled my plate away quickly and suggested we go watch the sunset together in the living room.

It was pretty coming in over the pond.

Warden shook his head. "I'm never going to look at that pond the same way. From now on, it's an alligator breeding ground."

"Oh come on now, isn't it more beautiful for its dangerous nature?"

Warden nudged me toward him, and I eventually ended up with my head on his shoulder. I probably didn't know him long enough to do so, but he didn't object. "I am going to end up drooling on your shoulder."

"You won't." He didn't seem concerned. "You slept in the car. No drooling happened. Just relax. If you fall asleep, you fall asleep."

As though his giving me permission made it possible, I knocked right out. I dreamed. I was tied up, chains around my hands and feet. I wore gray pajamas, and I shivered because it was freezing outside. I was in Warden's off the grid house but there was no furniture in it. Everything was barren, empty. I'd been alone for days. My stomach clenched with pain, and I'd peed myself. Several times.

The door opened and closed, turning the light back on. Chained to the wall and unable to move, the automatic lighting system had long since turned off, leaving me in the dark. Warden stood there staring at me.

"Well, you're still alive. You must have a lot of body fat to live off of." Warden's eyes were hard. Gone was the charm and only left was the nasty edge. He hauled me up even as my knee threatened to give out. "If you don't drown, the alligators will love eating you. Or maybe you'll do both."

"Please don't do this." I never thought I'd be hoping to be shot in the head.

I jolted awake. The sun was down and the lights were on in the living room. W read a paperback that he dropped as I jerked off of him. "Hey. Are you okay?"

"I…" My heart raced. "I'm sorry. Bad dream."

He put his hand on the side of my face, stroking his finger over the bruise where I'd been hit. "Want to tell me about it?"

"I…" I'd told Trace about how he featured in my dream, and he hadn't denied it was possible. Did I want to know if Warden would feed me to the alligators? "I was tied up in this house. It was empty. I'd been alone for days… and then you fed me to the alligators."

He shifted slightly. "Huh. Now, that would be an interesting way to get rid of a body."

Like Trace, Warden was not helpful with this issue. It did help to know where I stood, even if it made me want to puke.

"I can and have killed someone, Everly. I'm not going to expand on that. But it's not my job to do so usually. Those screens you must have seen in the basement when you went down there in Judson's house? That's my job. I'm the money guy. I make people wealthy or I take it all away. I do that both for The Alliance and for myself. I wouldn't so much kill you as I'd make it so you lived on the street."

I put my head in my hands. "Please don't put me on the street."

"I can't see the need to do that to you. I might do it to your dad. Are you prepared to have him living with you?"

I groaned. "Fuck, Warden." He snorted, and I lifted my hands away to see him looking at me with a raised eyebrow. "I don't even know if I can look at my dad. He killed my mother. How do I live with that? I mean... I hardly remember her. He raised me. But the point is that happened because he had her killed."

"She was unfaithful, yes?"

I kicked him gently with my foot. "That's a little bit extreme. One does not get murdered for sleeping with a biker and fooling around on one's accountant husband."

"One does if one's accountant husband is Alliance."

He was really not letting go on this. "And all those poor women marrying Alliance men and having no idea they've stepped into some alternative dimension of misogyny and delirium. Beware single women. Alliance men don't play by the same rules."

Warden laughed, throwing his head back. "See? You're not afraid of me at all. I mean not in the least bit. So no more nightmares. I wouldn't go anywhere near the alligators to throw you to them."

"Oh, thanks." I sighed. "I feel so much better."

"I have something that might make you feel better. I Googled it at the doctor's office and while the medical community doesn't endorse this at all... and I'm not a doctor... I thought that a little marijuana might make you feel better." He lifted that eyebrow again. I reached out to touch it, stroking my hand over it. He tilted his head. "Unless you don't smoke pot."

I leaned toward him. "Do you?"

"Rather regularly, actually. I prefer it to alcohol. No pain for having done it the next day."

I grinned. "I could be game."

Warden pulled a bag out of his jacket. "Well, then. Let's give it a go."

Who knew that when Warden went on the run he brought with him a bag of happiness?

———

I'D NEVER SLEPT BETTER. Or maybe I had. All I knew was the next morning I woke up on the couch I'd conked out on with no headache at all. I was still injured—hugely, so—and the doctor had warned me that I would feel better way before I was. I wasn't going to go run a marathon. But it was nice not to have a headache.

Warden slept on the other side of the couch. Our legs had gotten tangled up in each other as we'd slept on opposite ends of a too small couch. But it had worked. I guessed neither of us had thought about using the other couch or any of the bedrooms when we'd dozed off in a haze of relaxation.

He'd snored a little bit. It wasn't a loud, obnoxious sound, more like he breathed deep and was really lost in sleep. He was unabashedly breathing. I shook my head. Sun shined through the window. I rubbed my nose, sitting up.

Warden stretched his hands over his head before he opened his eyes. He blinked awake. "Hey."

"Hey, yourself." I patted his legs. "Good morning."

I got off the couch and made my way quickly to the bathroom. Like the kitchen, the hot water took a long time to come, but it did and there was running water for a shower. I took a fast one and dried off. When I came out, wrapped in a towel, I realized I still had my suitcase from the Caribbean. That meant I had my outfit from dinner, my bathing suit, and my work clothes. I didn't want to put back on the outfit I'd been beaten up in on the beach.

I'd been in it too long.

"Not that I don't appreciate the view." Warden had taken off his shirt. He was built like he'd been carved out of stone. I'd never seen anyone as strong. "But is something wrong? I mean, you can parade around in your towel all you want. It just seems odd for you."

He wasn't wrong. "I need clothes. I could put back on my bathing suit cover-up."

Warden rubbed his chin. "No, that won't do. We didn't think of that and you were too concussed to be thinking of anything at all. You need clothes. We'll have to get some. There's a general store not too far. It's a drive, but it's the closest. We can go ahead and go now. I'll supplement some of the food here. I think we might actually need more than we have. Besides, it's not like we have a lot else to do today."

In the meantime, I'd put back on what I'd worn earlier. "What? You aren't going to take away someone's life savings today?"

"The day is still young, gorgeous. The day is still young." He winked at me, turning around to head into the bathroom I'd just exited. I sucked in a breath I was glad he didn't hear. He had almost exactly the same scars Trace had. It was like they wore matching pain on their backs.

Training…

The question was when they'd gone into that training. As young men? Had that made them the kind of people who shot others in the head and destroyed their finances? Or had it simply enhanced their already inherent talents?

Were they the alligators in the pond or had someone thrown them to them?

I shook my head. This was getting way too deep.

I put my clothes on, deciding I'd take the bedroom downstairs unless he wanted it, and I arranged what I did have in the closet. The bedroom was a nice size with a queen bed and a small closet. So far, I'd only seen one bathroom in the house and W had waited for me to use it, so I was going to guess it really was just the one.

I wasn't going to complain. This could have been a lot worse. I walked back out to find Warden coming down the stairs. He carried a sweatshirt in his hand. "Take it. When we get to the store, I want you to put this on and keep your head down. I'm not really worried about it, but anywhere we go that could have a camera could be traced. I don't want to get our faces on camera."

I took the sweatshirt. It was dark blue and hooded. The scent of peppermint hit my nose. I brought it closer. It was one of my favorite smells.

"Do you really think they're searching for me? I mean, as far as they knew I was some chick that Trace was fucking. Why would they be looking for me at all?"

He touched my face where I'd been hit. "Your head is better today isn't it?"

"That didn't answer my question. Yes, my head is better." My stomach rumbled. I was seriously hungry. "Do you think they're looking for me?"

He shook his head. "I have no idea. I would imagine that once you got away they came looking for you. We can only assume it was just the three of them there. But maybe there were two people watching for you guys. Maybe they're now looking."

I supposed that made sense. "I'll keep the hood on."

"Good. Oh, and I don't ever want to hear about you fucking Trace. Or Derrick. Or the bogeyman. Okay? When you're with me, you're mine. I don't share. I don't care what you do when you're not with me. I also don't do relationships but with me, you aren't fucking anyone else. Got it?"

I opened and closed my mouth. "I don't remember fucking you at all, Warden."

"When you say my name it makes me hard."

Well… that was something. I couldn't help it, I let my gaze drift lower. He wasn't kidding. There was a bulge in his pants. I swallowed. "I can see that."

"We haven't fucked yet, Everly. I'm not a monster. Or at least not that much of one. You're concussed. Few more days of you healing and then I'm going to make it so you can't think of anyone else but me. Understand? While we're together, you won't remember anyone else's name."

I pulled on his shirt. "I find the arrogance hot, Warden, but you're setting yourself up to have to live up to a lot of hype here. Most of the time, I find myself disappointed."

He kissed my cheek, holding his lips there for a long second. It felt like he branded me. I closed my eyes for a second until he pulled back.

"You won't be disappointed. And you can imagine that for the next three days." He held up that many fingers. "Glad your head is better. It must be the pot."

I rolled my eyes at him. "Or maybe it was just time and being careful."

"Well you don't know it wasn't the pot." He shrugged at me. "Come on, gorgeous. You need clothes. Let's get them."

I followed him. "You don't know it was the pot. Can't prove it either way."

He put his arms around me. "See? You're not afraid of me at all. I can't think of another person on the planet who'd be holding up as well as you."

THE GROCERY STORE-SLASH-CONVENIENCE-STORE-SLASH-DINER-SLASH-LIQUOR-STORE was huge and the only thing around for miles except for a fireworks store a little bit down the way. The sign outside said it also sold bait. We'd be stopping there on the way back. I did want to see if we could catch some fish.

No one inside the store made any eye contact with each other. We were clearly not the only people there who didn't want to be noticed. A small television screen hung above the cash register, catching my attention. I quickly dropped my eyes. I wasn't supposed to be looking at screens. Still, I'd seen Derrick's face, and it had caught my attention. I couldn't look, so I listened.

The host of the entertainment show called him the Blond Bomber. I smiled. He was that, very blond with his man bun sitting right on top of his head. He'd been seen all over New York with a different model every day. The tabloids called him *back*.

Little did they know what had taken him away in the first place.

Warden didn't look up at the screen. He seemed interested in the collection of old paperbacks in the corner of the room. I needed clothes, and I set out to get them. So Derrick was doing just what he'd been told to.

How far was he taking it? Why did I think that was my business?

Chapter 13

In terms of clothes, I managed to get some shorts, some jeans, and some t-shirts. They were mostly plain and cotton. I grabbed some candy bars, some vegetables, some canned goods, and some hamburgers with all of the fixings for them. I wasn't going to try to cook anything fancy, mostly because I was bad at it, but also because we were pretty limited with what we could actually do from the food store here.

Worst came to worst, I'd eat chocolate all week. Maybe after everything that had happened lately, I deserved to. It would go really well with Warden's ganja kick. I bent over to look at some socks. I did like to wear them to bed. The hood on my head fell down as I stood back up. My heart sank into my stomach, and I yanked it back up as fast as I could, dread settling on me like a cold burst of water.

Were the men with the guns just going to burst through the door?

Warden's hand came down on my shoulder. "You okay?"

"My hood fell," I whispered to him. "I didn't mean it. I'm sorry."

"Hush." He tipped my chin so I looked at him. "Don't apologize for that. Accidents happen. No cameras in this store. Anyone see you?"

I shook my head. "I don't think so, but I wasn't paying attention exactly. I concentrated on pulling the hood back up."

"Good. Then don't worry. Get what you need?"

I nodded at my basket. "Yes. I just don't have any money to pay for it."

"Well, then it's excellent that I'm paying. Come on."

The woman behind the counter chewed gum, loudly. It was more like she snapped it. I hated the sound. Why couldn't she just not do that? Was chewing somehow difficult for her?

"Get everything?" She asked me, not W, even though he'd handed her the cash.

I nodded. "Yes. Thanks."

Blonde haired gum chewer leaned forward. "Your boyfriend is hot."

I almost corrected her. It was on the tip of my tongue to tell her that Warden was absolutely not my boyfriend. But then she clicked her gum again, and I didn't want to tell her the truth. It was as though her annoying gum habits made me want to lie to her. "Thanks. Yes, he is."

I leaned up and kissed Warden right there, leaning against the counter, as though I had every right to do so. "Come on, honey bear, let's go."

"Ah, sure." He took my hand while I led him out to the car. We got out there, and he backed me into it. "If you didn't want to be remembered, that was not the thing to do."

"She was going to remember you anyway. Because you're so hot." I mimicked snapping my gum. "Besides, I'm not good at this. I'm the kidnapped victim. If you wanted someone who would be good at going on the run I'm afraid I'm not your girl."

He shook his head. "I was wondering when your brat flag would show up. Get in the car. Let's go buy bait."

"Sure thing, honey bear." I liked that nickname. I was going to stick with it for a while. Even if it irritated him and maybe more so if it did.

My brat flag? I got in the car and buckled my seatbelt. Well, he could just kiss my ass.

———

WE BOUGHT the bait along with rods and anything else we might need to fish. It was on the way to his home I discovered he'd never done it before. Warden liked the idea of fishing, but he'd never actually been. He might not like this. But that was okay. It would pass some time.

I'd really never stopped to notice how completely dependent on electronics I was. Plus, the fact that I couldn't read was really proving to be a problem. What were we going to do for two weeks? Or what was I going to do? Warden could do as he liked.

"Hey, W." I deliberately used the letter. He'd called me a brat. He was going to get brat for a little while.

He rolled his eyes. "That was Kade's idea. He'd gone and done it before I had a chance to weigh in. You'd never have been calling me W. My lord and master, maybe." He winked at me. "Sorry, you were saying?"

"I was never going to call you my lord and master. Just so you know, honey bear."

Warden side-eyed me. "I don't think I like that better."

I shrugged. "Tough."

"You're going to punish me for the brat comment. I see. I see. Okay. We'll go with honey bear. You had a question, Brat?"

I snorted. It felt good to laugh and to not have pain doing it. "What is your last name? I know Trace's. It's Hill. He was Doctor Hill the whole time at the conference. And I just heard Derrick's on television. It's Norris. Do you have a last name or are you just Warden like Madonna?"

He side-eyed me. "It's Warden White."

"For real?" It was totally possible he was messing with me giving me that name.

W drummed his fingers on the steering wheel. "I'm serious. My mother thought it sounded... distinguished. And American. They were very anxious for me to sound American when I was here. They thought I might make a go of it in the movie industry or something. I don't know. Remember, I wasn't supposed to have this life. I was the extra kid. My father is half Saudi, on his mother's side. He, and then eventually we, spent a lot of time living overseas with family when I was growing up. My mother—blonde and blue eyed farm girl that she was—wanted us to sound like her family, to connect us to them. She always hoped that would make them like us better. Our tan skin was a problem for her family. Other families might not have felt that way. Hers did."

That was such a huge shame. It made my heart clench. Hate within family was completely unacceptable. People's families could be such a beautiful mix of stories, customs, and traditions. It was interesting what was important to some people and not others. "All right then. Two Ws. That is pretty cool. It does sound distinguished."

"Liar. It's ridiculous. The kids used to just say it over and over to be shitty when I was in boarding school."

I rolled my eyes. "Kids can be cruel. You can imagine what they said to me because my mother ran off."

Of course, now that I knew my father had actually killed her made it even worse. He knew perfectly well where she had gone. I shuddered. The longer I sat with this the worse it got. I rubbed my eyes.

He touched my shoulder. "Head hurting?"

"No, I'm just thinking about my mom. I've hated her for years, thinking she abandoned me. She did run off, but maybe she wouldn't have left me. Maybe she would have just been done with him. I'm having trouble with this. He killed her. Maybe you don't get it. You live in a different world than me."

Warden squeezed where he'd touched. "I've lived in the darkness a long time. I'm more comfortable in it if you want to know the truth. In that place, the existence where mothers get killed for cheating, where people die for no reason other than they're positioned wrong on the chessboard of life. It surprises me when people don't live that way. How did you go so long without knowing life sucks?"

How indeed? I leaned my head back against the seat. "I keep forgetting you're my captor. I keep thinking you're my friend."

"I think the same thing until I remember I don't have friends."

Now that caught my attention. "Surely your fellow Letters are your friends. You're trying to take over the world together."

"We're not friends. They don't have friends either. We're in this together, but we're not pals. None of us are going to go get a beer together or remember each other's birthdays."

I shook my head. "I get it. I don't have too many friends. Two girlfriends that I really like. I've always thought less was more. Face it, Warden, they're your friends. Kidnap a girl together and it really bonds you for life."

He twisted his lips but ended up in a smile. "All right, Brat. They're my friends. And I forget you're my prisoner, too. Then we have to talk to the cashier and I remember."

I could tell him that I had no plans to get away. But I'd already told him, and I decided I was in no mood to repeat myself. He could believe me or not. I stared out the window. It really was a lovely day.

━━━

WARDEN WAS NOT A NATURAL FISHERMAN. I ended up dragging a couple of chairs down to the pond. I hadn't yet seen an alligator. Maybe we were, for the moment, lucky. I handed him a beer. "Sit. Fishing isn't going to be the easiest thing you've ever done."

He pointed at the chair. "You're concussed. You shouldn't be dragging chairs. Even if you feel better."

I sat in the chair. "I'm sure you're right. I did it anyway."

He took a sip of the beer I'd brought him. "Feel okay?"

"Yes." I grinned at him. "But thanks for worrying about it."

We sat like that, not catching anything in his pond. I didn't even know if there were actually fish. I could have asked him that but it might have spoiled the moment. We'd go with the idea that there were fish and leave it at that. Eventually, he hooked a fish. It was a tiny thing, and I made him throw it back.

Still, it put a big smile on the day.

We cooked dinner together, and then he read to me from one of the books he'd picked up. It was a murder mystery. I kind of thought I knew who'd done it but that wasn't the point. In the end, I crawled into my bed, listening to the sounds the house made.

I'd been stoned the night before and conked out on the couch. Tonight, I could hear the wind blow and see the flashes of lightning in the distance as they lit up the room. I sighed. I never liked sleeping in new places. I wasn't even going to think about how scratchy the sheets were. What was with people not paying attention to how soft their bedding was? I felt like the Princess and the Pea.

The door opened slowly and Warden poked his head in. "Thinking I could come in and protect you from any alligators that might come in the middle of the night."

I rolled closer to the edge, letting him in. He lay down next to me, drawing me close to him. "You know, Warden, you're the worst kidnapper ever."

"I know." He pressed his nose against the back of my neck. "But you are a terrible victim."

"That's right, honey bear, I am."

He laughed. "I'm going to show you sometime how I actually live. Not this place. You'd love it."

I kind of liked this place a whole lot. I didn't have to think too hard about anything that might make my head go sideways. I could just be here with W and not stop to contemplate why that was so okay. Or if it had to do with the fact that the life I'd been living had been an utter lie. What was I going to return to?

Every day the truth of my existence became clearer and clearer to me.

Still, I had to point out to Warden what he said was

probably not going to happen. "We won't know each other long enough for me to see where you live. You'll let me go —unless you feed me to the gators—and I'll never see you again because you'll be busy secretly running the world. I'll be some kind of ant marching, to steal from Kade."

He was silent, and I wondered if he'd fallen asleep. "I suppose you're right, and I don't like it. Guess I'm just going to have to make do with having you here now."

Warden had told me he wouldn't make any moves to have sex with me for three days, and he seemed determined to live up to that. We lay there in the dark, holding each other, but not doing anything else. He fell asleep first, his nose still on the back of my neck. Each breath he took was like a small tickle, but it didn't bother me. I liked having him there. Like the night before, he sort of snored. It wasn't an outright, obnoxious sound, but he was definitely not a quiet sleeper. It made me grin. It was what Warden sounded like when he was asleep.

Eventually, I fell asleep, too.

I didn't have any weird dreams about dying.

In fact, I woke up feeling really well rested. Warden moved next to me, which was what finally roused me from dreamland. I shifted slightly, and he pulled me against his chest. "Morning, Brat."

I grinned. "Morning, Warden White."

———

THE DAYS WERE long and sometimes quiet, although it wasn't for lack of conversation. Warden turned out to know a lot of stuff. Random things were quick for him to recall. He could easily tell me without blinking what year a country gained independence or what the price of milk was in 2001.

He listened to me lament about when I'd had to take economics and how much I'd hated the class. He'd told me that he couldn't have imagined taking the social work classes I'd undertaken and loved. With my hoodie on, we went to dinner an hour away at a restaurant on the side of the road. I'd never have imagined they had such good pie.

What was funny was that Warden hadn't known either. We were both fish out of water in this situation, but he was maybe having more of an issue adjusting than me. I wasn't sure he'd ever spent any time in the country before.

On the third day, the mood shifted. I woke up in my pajamas that I'd managed to wash the day before in the slowest washer-dryer known to man. Still, it had eventually gotten the job done. Warden stretched next to me. He was clearly hard and not trying to hide it. I'd sort of thought he was the day before, but he'd jumped up quickly, and I'd not had a time to confirm my suspicion. Today, I was sure of it.

He nuzzled my shoulder. "You smell incredible."

"I can't possibly smell incredible in the morning." I laughed. Although he did. If it was possible, I might have been getting addicted to the pure male scent that was Warden.

"You do." He planted a small kiss. "I am going to give you so much pleasure tonight, Everly."

I looked over at him before I ran a finger down the slope of his nose. It was just slightly misshapen. And sexy as hell. "Are you busy right now? Big plans?"

He shook his head. "Tonight. Anticipation is good for the soul. Let's enjoy the knowing it's coming."

I groaned. "If you say so."

Rain struck the roof hard. Looked like we were going to be staying inside today. It was going to be a long, long day. But he was right. I was going to be thinking about it all day.

HE SPENT the day touching me. If I was at the sink, he ran his hand up my arm. If I was sitting on the couch reading, he'd brush the back of my neck gently as he passed. It was day five. The magic number the doctor had given me to return to normal activity had been reached.

Warden still claimed it was the pot. I just thought it was that I had a hard head and time to heal. In any case, I felt better. He sat down next to me on the couch, kissing my shoulder. I shuddered. Warden had been right. There really was nothing like the anticipation of knowing he wanted me, and he was going to show me he did all day long.

He cooked dinner. Warden lied when he told me he couldn't cook. He actually could. W made a great steak. He grabbed the plates before I could clear them and kissed my cheek on his way to the sink. "I could have done that."

Warden shook his head. "I got it."

I leaned back in my chair, watching him clean up after he'd cooked. "You know you're going to have sex tonight. I'm a sure thing."

He looked over at me. "That's not why I'm doing the dishes. I'm doing the dishes because it's my turn."

Was it? "I wasn't keeping track."

"I don't do dishes in real life." He shrugged. "This week has felt like a step away."

That was a good way to put it. And we had one week left like this. "I only have the ugly pajamas."

"I'm going to be getting you out of your clothes. I don't care what you have on when I do so. You'd be sexy in a brown paper bag. The point is that it's you."

I leaned my forehead on his arm. Touching Warden

was easy and that was because of him. He'd done this, he'd made it easy between us. "You say the sweetest things."

"I don't. I only speak the truth. I'm an asshole." He nodded toward the porch. "Go stand there and wait for me a minute. I want to look at the stars with you."

I almost made a joke. It was easy for me to be flippant. I went through life keeping things meaningless. Then I remembered that this was Warden, who took away people's money to control them because the circumstances of his birth arranged that for him, and maybe it meant something to him to look at the stars. Maybe it could mean something to me too if I let myself stop being cynical.

I stepped onto the porch. It had stopped raining while we ate. The air had that post rain humidity feel to it, but the temperature had dropped considerably. It might even have been called a chilly night for wherever we were in Florida. I still didn't know, but that was cognitive dissonance. I could have found out any time I wanted. I just didn't want to.

The sky was clear and there were a million stars above my head. I watched them as the slight cloud cover blowing above me seemed to make the stars dance. A few minutes later, Warden joined me. His arms came around me, and I leaned against his chest.

"I look up so rarely."

He kissed the top of my head. "Well, the good news is that you're young and you have plenty of time to look up for the rest of your life."

"You make it seem like you're so old. I promise you, you're still young and hot."

He squeezed me tighter. "I think I was born old."

I didn't have anything to say to that so I didn't. Who was I to tell him if he'd felt that way since birth? A few more minutes passed when he tugged on me. "Come in. If you want to."

I turned in his arms before I kissed his chin. "I want to."

Warden took my hand and drew me inside. I followed him gladly. The lights were off in the house, and as we walked into the bedroom together, low flickering lights caught my attention. He'd lit candles and they glowed like the stars outside had.

I gasped. "Warden, you lit candles."

"I did." He stood in the doorway of the bedroom. "They're technically in case the solar panels don't draw enough power to light up the night. But let's hope that doesn't happen. I'm using them tonight."

I pressed my hands on his hard chest. "You have a romantic soul."

"I never did. But like I said… this week is just a step away."

I liked that answer. Accepting that I loved this didn't mean I had to give up being my cynical about sex self. I could just take it for what it was and know that life would go back to normal soon enough. I reached up to kiss him, and he drew me closer. Warden gently caressed my lips with his own. He didn't stop there, kissing all over my face. I held on and let him, returning the kisses where I could reach.

Warden laid me on the bed. He came over me, but seemed like he was in no hurry. His hand was in my hair, and he kissed and kissed me until dizziness wafted over me. He was hard, there was no disguising it, and yet his hands stayed right where they were as though we were teenagers not taking this any further instead of what we'd planned for tonight.

I wrapped my arms around his neck, and he stopped

kissing me to stare down. "You are the most beautiful woman I've ever seen."

He adored me with his gaze, and shivers of pleasure danced up my spine at his words as heat pooled in my core. "I can't believe that is true, and yet right in this moment I believe you."

"I'll prove it beyond tonight. You're not lacking confidence. Don't sell yourself short. You're gorgeous."

Maybe he saw me that way. I hoped it was the least interesting part of me. "Kiss me, Warden."

He took directions really well. He kissed me, starting with my lips and moving down to kiss my neck. I shuddered. I didn't know that I'd ever been kissed so long in my life.

Warden started to undress me slowly. He tugged my shirt over my head and then followed with his own. Goosebumps broke out on my skin. Not from a chill, from anticipation alone. He thumbed my bra. "I could look at you all day."

The strangest thing was I was pretty sure I could let him without a moment of hesitation. "You've been looking at me day in and day out. If you're not sick of it now…"

Warden gave me a side smile. "Not sick of it."

He was built like he'd been carved out of stone. I ran my hands over him, touching the dark dusting of hair on his bare skin. He let me trace his muscles even as his body jumped under my touch.

"You aren't the only one who could look all day."

Warden tilted his head to the side. "It might kill me, but I'd let you."

He undid my bra and discarded it. He stroked my breasts, starting with the nipples. Gently, he touched them until they pebbled in his fingertips.

His sweetness undid me. "I won't break."

"I might." He kissed my neck again before he replaced his fingertips with his mouth, cupping my other breast while he sucked on the nipple of the other one. I bit my lip as I cried out. My body burned for wanting him, but I wouldn't have hurried this for anything in the world. We'd never have a first time together again, and we both knew this was temporary. I was going to love every second of it.

Chapter 14

We undressed each other the rest of the way in silence. There was something sacred about the way we were quiet, as though someone might overhear us if we made sound. His cock was huge. Stretched out before me, it made my mouth water.

I would have reached for him, but he whispered in my ear. "Lie back."

I did without question. This whole experience had so far been different than I'd thought it was going to be. He rubbed his fingers over my temples. It took me a minute to realize he was giving me a massage. "You have an incredible mind. No more getting it jostled. Hear me?"

I nodded. His hands were doing incredible things. He rolled them down, tracing over my skin, as though he memorized my body as he went. Warden stopped over my thighs, rubbing me there and then on the other side. He massaged me there, loosening my muscles until I panted. Warden rolled me over slightly, rubbing my lower back. It was like he instinctively knew all my spots, just where I wanted to be rubbed.

By the time he finished rubbing me, I was panting. I was putty in his hands.

He opened a drawer next to the bed and pulled out a condom. As I watched, almost transfixed, he rolled it onto himself.

"I haven't done anything for you yet." Sex was a back and forth. It wasn't me demanding attention and giving him none.

"Are you kidding?" He motioned toward his cock. "You get me any harder, and I might explode. I just got to touch you almost all the places I fantasized about. That's doing something for me."

I leaned back on my elbows. "Next time I want to take you in my mouth."

"Sounds like a plan." He whispered against my mouth before he kissed me hard. Warden slipped a finger inside of me. He found my clit and started to rub slowly in circles. I clenched around his hand. Yes, he'd worked out the rhythm I liked fast. "Yes, just like that."

"I've got you. I know how you want it. I can feel you, I can read you, Everly."

He really could. I lost track of time, the surges of pleasure overtaking me so that soon I had to bite my lip to keep from screaming. He kissed the top of my knee, the inside of my thigh. "Don't hold it back. Give me your noises."

I cried out. I didn't know that I could have stopped it if I wanted to. "Warden." I had to say his name again and again. He hissed in a long breath before he bit down on my lip.

"You know how hearing my name on your lips undoes me."

He moved then, and I spread my legs because I knew what was going to happen and I craved it beyond anything else. Warden pressed inside of me, inching deep toward my core with slow movements. I squirmed. I wanted all of him, fast, but he tormented me with his determination to make all of this last. I wasn't going to ever complain.

"Fuck. You're so tight." He flared his nostrils. "I am going to make this good for you, I swear it."

He already had. I squeezed him tight inside of me. "Warden. Please."

He nodded once. W pulled out and pushed back in all the way, a deep press that had me panting for more. I expected him to repeat the movement, but he didn't. The next time he moved it was a shallow drive that rubbed my clit completely in the thrust. I cried out. Over and over he stimulated me, never doing the same thrust twice in a row. I couldn't think, couldn't keep up, couldn't anticipate.

He'd promised to pleasure me and this was what he was doing. Varying the experience made it seem to last forever, and oh I would have been fine with existing like this always. Finally, when I couldn't handle anymore, couldn't think, couldn't breathe, I exploded around him. I dug my fingers into his shoulders, and he whispered my name as he came.

I'd never heard Everly spoken in a way that made it sound like a prayer before.

Minutes later, Warden linked our fingers together. We both lay on our backs, neither of us speaking. I wasn't sure there was anything to say. That had been… yeah… incredible. He tugged on me until I lay against his side.

Yawning, I pressed my head down on him. I could hear his heart beat. He'd wrecked me in the best possible way. He stroked his hand up and down my back.

"Maybe tomorrow we can go by that grocery store again and get something to barbecue for dinner."

I loved that idea. "Chicken. Sausage."

"Sounds good." He kissed my forehead. "Everly, that was…"

I nodded. "I know. It was."

"Good."

We weren't making a whole lot of coherent sense but that was okay. We didn't need to. Not really.

———

I WANDERED through the store looking at the night-gowns. Warden said it didn't matter what I had on, but wearing the same thing night after night and then just washing it every other day was getting on my nerves. I'd like to be able to change nightly. That didn't mean, however, that I wanted to wear something I'd imagine my grandmother in.

There had to be something else. Like a long t-shirt that would do.

"Glad to see you here again." The woman who had been the cashier the other day when we'd come in spoke to me. She leaned against the wall by a water fountain that had an out-of-order sign on it. She was once again snapping her gum.

I looked up at her. I had my hoodie back on. It would do well to find another one of those, too, so I could return this one to W. He whirled around as the woman spoke to me from where he was looking at baseball hats.

I caught his gaze even as I turned to gum girl. "Hello." I smiled at her. "How are you today?"

"I'm good." She shrugged. "Men came in here asking about the two of you."

Well, now she had my full attention. "Did they? For me?"

She pointed at W. "For both of you. They had pictures.

It was funny. It was of the two of you outside in the parking lot. It was one of them satellite photos. I think. Like something you'd see that looked like it was right off the internet."

Warden was suddenly by my side. He put his hand on my back. "What were they asking?"

"If I'd seen you. They asked my boss, too. But he hadn't because he didn't come out that day."

I set down the t-shirt I'd been holding. "What did you tell them?"

"That you'd been here but you'd left." She shrugged. "What else could I tell them? I don't know nothin."

No, she hadn't. But now she'd know we'd come back. Plus, if they'd gotten us on satellite once, they would again right where we'd parked. Warden didn't flinch. He just nodded. "What did the men look like?"

"They wore suits. Not from around here but neither are you two. That much is obvious."

"Right." Warden turned and walked to the sporting goods aisle. What was he doing? My heart beat so fast I thought it might explode. I couldn't be shot at again. Not ever. That was too much. I...

Why was he grabbing a baseball helmet? He pointed at gum girl. "You. Come check us out. Now."

She was clearly on a break, but with W giving her a pointed look and a command to his voice, she jumped up and even pushed the current cashier out of the way to ring us up.

"We're going to take this. Do you have a car?"

Her eyes widened. "Yes. Parked right there." She pointed outside. I didn't follow where, but Warden must have because he nodded. He pulled open his wallet, a white envelope folded in the middle of the bill holder.

"There's twenty-thousand dollars in cash in here." He

slammed it down. "Count it. It's yours for your car right now."

The woman snorted. "Mister my car is not worth twenty thousand."

"Well then you just made the deal of the century. Take it now. Car. And baseball helmet."

He was carrying twenty grand in his wallet? Was he nuts? Of course, this had proven extremely useful, but who carried that kind of money just around with them? The woman looked stunned, her pupils were huge, but she took the cash and handed him her keys.

Warden grabbed my hand and yanked me hard outside. Gone was my sweet lover who wanted nothing more than to give me pleasure, and in his place this focused, hard-gazed man stood. I had to say, given the circumstances, I liked the change.

"Get in."

Gum chewer's car smelled like old air freshener, and I quickly threw it out the window. If we somehow got arrested for this, they could add litterbug to the list of things I was to go to jail for.

Warden put the car in drive almost as soon as I'd shut the door. "Buckle your seatbelt and put on your helmet."

He handed me the new batting helmet he'd just purchased along with the dirty car. "Why am I putting this on? I don't think it'll stop bullets."

"No, obviously not. But it will help if we get rammed off the road. It might stop another concussion. You just had one. Put it on."

I supposed that made sense. I took the helmet out of the packaging and shoved it on. It was a little snug, but I wasn't going to complain. "Why were you carrying that kind of money?"

"For just this kind of scenario."

I pointed behind me. "You're going the wrong way. The house is behind us."

"We're not going back there. Let's assume they've found it on satellite by now. And fuck, I can't imagine the algorithm they're running that they found us so fast. This is out of hand. No more waiting on your dad. I'm going to show those fuckers what happens when they mess with me."

I sucked in a breath. "Where are we going?"

"San Diego. Well, I'm going to San Diego. I'm taking you to New Orleans. That's where I'd lay money Kade went. We have to let go of the two week plan. Guess tonight is where you and I part ways, Brat."

I swallowed through the pain those words caused me. Like with Trace, I'd known this was temporary, but knowing it, and feeling nothing when they moved on like we'd been nothing together were two different things. If that made me pathetic, then so be it.

If anything, spending time with these crazy assholes was opening me up from the outside in. I didn't know if it was a good thing or bad. But it was happening, and I was powerless to stop it. I looked out the window.

"Guess it is." I patted him on the arm. "Been fun knowing you, Warden White."

"What happened to honey bear?"

I scooted down in the seat, finally deciding I wasn't going to get comfortable thanks to a hole with something poking out of it that dug into my lower back. Oh well, beggars couldn't be choosers. Not even for twenty thousand dollars.

"Not in a honey bear mood, I suppose. Do you think they're after us?"

"Yes."

That did not fill me with a great deal of confidence but

I didn't suppose he'd meant it to. This was reality, this was actually happening. A street sign caught my eye, and I read it as went by. It pointed to the Seminole County Correctional Facility five miles away. Well, now at least I knew where I was, sort of. I'd have to look it up when I had use of a computer or tablet again. Vermont. St. Croix. Seminole County, Florida. Now I was practically going to be back home if we were headed to New Orleans.

I was supposed to be studying for finals and drinking cheap alcohol while I obsessed over graduate school.

"What are you going to do?"

"I'm going to pick apart the finances of all six of those bastards, starting with Nathan Barton." A muscle clenched in his jaw. "We thought we could handle this the way it's supposed to be handled in The Alliance. First we had to prove we really were Alliance, that's your dad. Then we'd fucking take them on the way it's done. I should have spoken up when the shooting happened, but I got focused on having alone time with you. So yeah, time to stop thinking with my dick and get back to real life."

Any good feelings I had left plummeted. Thank goodness I'd gotten so good at holding back how I felt. I would not fall apart in the car with him. "So this is my fault, W? I'll point out that I didn't ask to be kidnapped and no one forced you to fuck me."

He winced. I didn't care. It was awkward with my stupid helmet on, but I looked away from him. I was done talking. Fully and completely done.

Three hours later, I'd almost convinced myself we were going to be okay. He'd drop me wherever with Kade and move on. I couldn't wait to get out of the car with him and even if it took six hours from now at least it was fucking coming.

Or maybe not. Maybe I'd finally get my head on straight and get out away from them.

"Your seatbelt is on, right?" It was the first time he'd spoken to me since he'd pronounced that I'd made him lose sense of things.

I looked down. "As it's been this whole time."

"We're being followed. I'm pretty sure we've been made."

I swallowed slowly. "How do you know?"

"I know." That told me nothing, but I wasn't going to push. "I'm getting off here. We're going to find a place to hide you, and I'm going to continue on my own. I realize this is stupid. You could very easily just leave. But I'm going to point out that your face is now on the radar of some people who will take you to hurt us. The best thing you can do is stay with us until your father clears our name. He won't be able to protect you. He's not high enough up in The Alliance. You'll hate The Alliance having you more than you even hate me right now."

I glared at him. "You could be lying. You guys could have been lying about everything." I knew that wasn't true. My father had confirmed most of it. But I was scared. Sick of feeling like I didn't have control of my feelings and pissed as hell.

"I could be, but I'm not." He shook his head. "I'm going to save your life not your feelings right now."

"Why bother? I'm just another ant."

He didn't answer me, but took the next exit at too high a speed. I grabbed onto the side of the car so hard that my knuckles turned white. I gulped. We were going to be okay. I wasn't dying like this. I had too much to do in life. I couldn't come up with anything right then but so help me I would.

W nodded to the left. "There's a shopping mall. It's

busy. See the cars? It's Saturday. It'll be open late. I'm going to drop you there. Get lost in it."

"And then?" I hated the sound of desperation in my voice. "I can't stay there endlessly. It'll be open late, but I can't live there."

Warden nodded slowly. "Someone will come for you. I promise."

"When?" He'd already sped into the parking lot and was making his way to the door with the sign food court over it.

"I don't know. Soon. Trust me."

That was the problem. Last night I'd let him inside of my body, I'd trusted him. I really had. I'd forgotten how dire things were, how I was in the middle of a mess I hadn't had a hand in making but now had to exist within. Was it his cruel words? Maybe. I didn't know, but I wondered as he skid to a stop, the tires screeching, if I was about to walk into a situation where I was either going to get killed or left with nowhere to go and no one to help me.

"Out. Everly, now. Get lost in there. Here." He pulled a wad of cash out of his pocket. I grabbed it. How much did he carry on him at a time? He'd just handed gum chewer twenty grand for her piece of shit car. Now I had... two thousand in my hand? "Don't leave. Someone will come."

I got out of the car. I had a million questions. I was in the middle of a place I'd never been, in a shopping mall where I knew no one, with no identification, no cell phone, and only the word of a man who had seemed to care for me one second and not give two shits with the same breath. I turned and ran. I was all the way past the cell phone kiosk before I let myself breathe.

He'd wanted to protect me. In the midst of hell, he'd thought about my concussion. Fuck. I still wore the helmet.

It was getting a lot of attention. I pulled it off my head and ran a self-conscious hand through my hair.

I gripped the money like it was my lifeline, and if I wasn't careful I was going to get mugged for it. I shoved it in my pocket. Okay. I maybe looked less… crazed. I knew how to be in public. I was dressed okay. There was nothing about me that should scream lunatic.

I needed some water. I set about to get some.

Four hours later, I'd eaten in the food court and pretended to be interested in every store in the mall. I sat down on a bench. This was ridiculous. I needed help. I was going to call my father. Surely, he would come get me or tell me where to go. He and I could work out this shit. Or I could go back to pretending all was okay. Eventually, The Alliance would lose interest in a nobody like me, and I could go back to my life. I'd never tell a soul.

I'd forget about Warden's soft gaze, which seemed more real in him than his cruel tongue. I'd let go of the way Trace had held me, how he had grinned, the way the breeze had moved through us, and the feeling that he had things to say he never got to. I'd somehow never think of Derrick's intensity and wounded soul, even when I saw him on television flashing his smile and his man bun. I'd never question who Judson actually was, what he meant when he talked about having particular tastes in the bedroom, and how he reconciled being a doctor with being Alliance. I would know I never got to unmask Kade, the most reserved of all of them. I'd know nothing about him except that he was handsome as hell and he was determined to take over The Alliance.

I'd forget. I'd make myself without counseling because knowing The Alliance, if they heard I was talking to someone about them, I'd be a dead woman. I rubbed my eyes. I needed a phone. Were there pay phones or did I need to spend some of this two thousand dollars on a burner phone at the kiosk and call my dad?

Someone plopped down next to me. I didn't look up.

"Everly."

I knew that voice. I raised my head. "D?"

"In the flesh." He ran a hand down my back. "You okay?"

"How are you here?" I was bone tired. Everything hurt like I'd been beat up again.

He shifted slightly. Derrick wore sweatpants and a ratty white t-shirt. His man bun was hidden in his skull cap, and he looked like he hadn't shaved in forty eight hours or so. I'd never seen him this much of a mess, not even when he shot the lake in Vermont. This had to be deliberate so he could sit here in a place like this and not be noticed. Well, maybe not the shaving. That would have taken days.

"Warden managed to lose his tail. He stopped at a convenience store, grabbed a phone he could chuck, and called me. Told me to get my ass here and save you." He stopped his hand on the back of my neck, rubbing gently. "Sorry it took a little bit. I was in Miami. I got a plane. Took half an hour to charter. Anyway, I'm here. I told you I would always be there. I meant it."

I swallowed away my tears. "I had just made the decision to call my father. I had just decided to throw down my cards and see what happened. I should have run away, not sat here like a lamb waiting to be sacrificed."

"No." He leaned over to kiss me on my temple. I shivered from the warmth the gesture caused to the ice forming inside of me. "You did the right thing. We're not heroes or good guys. We've done bad things, and you've been hurt in the process. But believe it or not, we're your best option now. We can't go back in time and leave you alone so now you have to let us make it right, however that happens. Besides, I told you I'd always find you. You're mine. Even when you're also theirs. Trace. Now Warden. Makes me wonder some things. But we'll see. Neither you nor them would believe me. You all think I'm crazy anyway. Come on."

He took my hand, and I let him. "You know that's exactly what a person trying to convince me to stay in victimhood would say."

"You're no one's victim. You may be the most powerful person I know right now. And you're certainly not a sacrificial lamb. Abraham isn't showing up any second with a knife. Come on. Let's get out of here. Unless you're hungry. Want to eat?"

I shook my head. "You're wrong, you know. I'm not Trace's, Warden's, or yours. I don't belong to any of you."

He put his arm around my shoulder. "We'll see. I'm Alliance, baby. I see things before they happen. Don't be fooled into thinking I'm not as smart as they are. We all survived training." The word brought to mind the image of both Warden and Trace's backs. I had to assume Derrick had the same marks. "Baseball is a mental game. And I also kick ass at chess. I promise you. I'm not dumb."

I never thought he was. "How did you explain your beat up back in the locker room?"

He winced. "So you've seen the scars on Trace and Warden. Yeah, didn't think of that. Car accident."

That made sense. Simple explanations that left people with nothing to wonder about. "Was it possible to not survive the training?"

"In a word, yes. Let's do this elsewhere. I've had two attempts on my life. It's why I keep moving. Right now, the powers watching us seem to be preoccupied with chasing Warden. But they'll be back on me. You need to get underground."

I guessed that meant I wasn't going to be traveling around with Derrick. "Where will I go?"

"I'm going to take you to Kade. That'll be the safest. Judson's had some attempts, too. It's a good thing. Let them keep coming. All they're doing is showing their hands. They won't succeed. But Kade is hidden and so, baby, will you be. But don't worry. I'll be back."

At this point, I didn't know what to think. Derrick had come, and it seemed I was on my way to New Orleans. Again. Just this time with a different Letter.

Chapter 15

We landed in a private airport by Lake Pontchartrain. The pilot wasn't Alliance. That was the last we'd discussed it before Derrick ushered me onto the plane. He was just an ant like me, going about his life, totally unaware that he might have signed a death warrant by flying us that day. Only everything had gone smoothly, and we'd landed with no trouble at all.

It wasn't my first time in the airport. My best friend from high school had a brother who was a pilot. He'd taken us here a few times and flown us around. It had seemed like such a treat to be in New Orleans for the day and to fly like we had every right to do so. I shook my head. That felt like someone else's life now.

Derrick didn't get off the plane. I turned as I exited down the stairs to look at him. "Something wrong?"

"You're going. Not me. I have to keep doing what I'm doing. It'll help in the long run. Kade is waiting for you." He nodded toward a blue car parked nearby. The windows were tinted, and I couldn't see in them. "Keep your head down. I think it's fine. They're still after Warden. But I'm going to get them turned back to me. Go. Now."

I took a deep breath. What was it going to be like to be alone with Kade? "Are you sure I shouldn't have run, Derrick?"

"I'm sure. Kade doesn't bite. And remember what I told you—you're mine. Maybe you're also theirs, but you're mine."

I rolled my eyes. I was never going to be owned. Maybe someday I'd share my life, but these Alliance men had another think coming if they thought that they'd own me. I opened my heart up a tiny smidgen to both Trace and Warden. Both of them had stomped on it. No thanks, I wasn't looking to do that again.

With my head down, I ran to the car. I got inside quickly.

Kade stared at me from the driver's side. "You okay?"

"I've been better. But I'm okay. Just a little shaken up, I guess." I stopped talking. This was Kade. He'd had little to no sympathy for me thus far. "Thanks for coming."

He nodded. "Derrick asked me to so yeah, I do it. There are some rules you'll need to follow, but we'll deal with that when we get there."

"Rules. Right." I nodded.

"Good."

I hadn't actually agreed to anything, but apparently he thought I had. Maybe everyone agreed with Kade all the time. Maybe that was just a given. Seemed to me there was a lot of agreeing with Kade and then sort of doing as they liked. That had to be aggravating for him, considering that if they'd listened to him from the beginning, my kidnapping and subsequent situation with The Alliance would probably have gone better.

Not that I was complaining since I'd been the beneficiary of the others breaking the rules. But the truth was if they actually did as Kade said, life might run smoother.

"Would it be okay if I asked a question?"

He made a hard right out of the airport just as the plane with Derrick on it sped away. I never thought I'd miss the very intense D, but as he flew off, a pang of regret hit my stomach. He really did seem to care about me, and I wanted to know more about him. What made Derrick, Derrick?

"You can ask." That wasn't a yes but then again I'd known that nothing with Kade was going to be easy.

"I can also not ask. That wasn't my question. Maybe I should rephrase." This was going to be very similar to what it was like in my ninth grade language arts class with Sister Raphaelea. I needed to speak precisely and mean every word that I spoke. "Would you be willing to answer a few questions if I asked them or would you prefer if I didn't?"

A small side smile appeared on Kade's face. "I'd be willing to hear your questions, but I'm not promising to answer if I don't like the question, don't think the question is appropriate for you to know the answer to, or I just want to be a dick."

I laughed. I shouldn't. He was pretty much being a dick by stating it that way, but his honesty was awesome. And after the day I'd had, apparently funny. To me, at least.

"Fair enough. All right, let's start with which one of you is in charge?"

He drummed his fingers on the steering wheel while he merged onto I-10. "No one is in charge. It's a circle. Let me back up, you must know by now that a circle of 5 run The Alliance."

I had gathered that much, yes. I nodded so he'd continue. "The odd number means one side wins in votes, most of the time. Unless they end up with more than one option on things."

"And who makes the others live up to the vote? I'm not trying to poke a sore subject, but I'm calling you Kade not K."

He grimaced. "I determined that and let them know. No vote was taken. I am hopeful that the ways of The Alliance will mean they are compliant to the system. It works when things are not... so fucked up."

Maybe he was right. Still, knowing Trace, Derrick and Warden the way I did now, I had a hard time imagining them just doing as they were told if they disagreed with something. Maybe I was wrong. Maybe they were good Alliance members and they'd be the perfect five in a meeting. Still, it seemed to me every organization I'd ever known or been involved in had a leader.

I bit my tongue. I wasn't going to push him anymore on this.

Besides, we were suddenly turning off the highway and into a graveyard. Burying the dead was different in New Orleans. It had to do with sea level. The city would flood and anyone buried under ground was suddenly not so buried anymore. No one wanted to see their dead relatives floating down a river, hence they had developed mausoleums: cities of the dead.

I knew my Louisiana history. Everyone who grew up anywhere in the state did. The question was why were we here now? I swallowed through a lump in my throat. "Kade, are you going to bury me alive here?"

"What?" He shook his head. "No. Fuck. You'll see. I have... kind of a hideout."

"A hideout. Like a superhero?"

He shrugged. "Not a bad comparison."

I tried not to laugh and mostly managed not to. Maybe

a little snicker escaped. He had superhero fantasies. Alliance or not, he was still male. The twenty-somethings I knew were the same way. Maybe I should figure out how to get him a cape.

"Seriously, though, what are we doing here?"

He pulled his car over to the side. "We walk the rest of the way."

"To where?" I took off my seatbelt and followed him into the graveyard. "Aren't we exposed walking?"

He shrugged. "We might be if we were anywhere else. I pay the guy who upkeeps this place—and that is exaggerating the term, upkeep, my ass—to let me keep the car here. No one is looking over here. I designed the systems they're using to track us, and I put myself in the hole. Well, one of the holes where it is possible to hide. Here, a spot in Philadelphia. A couple of locals in England. And most of the country of New Zealand."

Well, this was interesting. "Are they just places you want to be?"

"It had more to do with angles of the Earth and satellite and not wanting to interfere with the government's equipment that I also designed." He shrugged. "Anyway, I just knew where to put myself when I made my escape pod so to speak."

Now we were using science fiction terms. This was a whole new side to Kade. Apparently when he wasn't yelling at me or ordering me around, he could be funny. Geeky.

He didn't wait for me, and I followed him quickly from the car for a very brisk ten minute walk through the old mausoleums. They weren't well kept up. In fact, most of them didn't have legible writing on them anymore. Marble was broken, cracked. I sighed. These had been lives. Weather and time had taken away even the dignity of their deaths. Or maybe the whole fucking thing was ridiculous anyway. Dead was dead. No, I didn't feel that way. In my heart, I was sentimental.

Kade walked to a particularly old looking mausoleum, and he took out a key to open it. I stopped. "Are we going in there?"

"Yep. Come on. Don't be superstitious. There are no dead bodies in here. It's a good place to hide."

I shuddered. Warden's safe house had running water and a pond. Kade's was a place where they put dead bodies. I almost didn't follow him. I almost turned and ran. Apparently, I could really be creeped out. But I shuddered and didn't hesitate at the door. He closed it behind us, and lights turned on. I blinked rapidly. I didn't know how this worked most of the time, but I couldn't imagine these things were lit up. Or so... big inside.

"Is this the Tardis?" I asked the question without even considering the audience. Usually, I kept my fandoms hidden, but given the conversation we'd just had in the car, I had a pretty good feeling he would understand the reference.

He grinned. "Not a bad comparison."

The inside was huge, because it went down, down, down. Apparently, he wasn't concerned about the river flooding. I touched the wall. It was steel. Yes, nothing was flooding in here. I followed him down the stairs. Eventually, it was like being in a bunker.

The ceiling was low but plenty big over my head so that I wasn't worried I was going to hit it. Kade was taller than me, and it was closer on him. "How did you have this done?"

I called after him. "I used a crew that is loyal to our side. We worked at night. I don't keep it hidden from those

I trust. Obviously, Warden knew where it was. He was going to bring you here."

"Why don't they all come? Why are they out there when everyone could just be hanging out down here in this... Fortress of Solitude you created?"

He winked at me. "That's not underground. I offered. They don't come. Everyone has their own thing to do. Warden is obviously going to go after the funds. Trace is figuring out what they want. At least I assume he is. No one has heard from Trace in a while. I think we would know if they had him. He tends to go quiet when he wants to get things done. Judson can only go so long without doctoring. It drives him. Derrick we need out in front. So that leaves me."

An air conditioner turned on, making a loud blowing sound. It was like a small jet engine had turned on. I jumped. Okay, this was just really... weird. "You just stay here underground?"

"Yes. It's pretty impenetrable. That gate I closed behind you is a vacuum seal. They'd have to really come at it, and by then the alarm would go off. At that point, the secret exits I built myself, that even the crew didn't know about, would be how I got away. I'll walk you through it in a bit."

Well, at least we weren't going to be stuck in here while the place got raided. "At what point did I become so okay with how strange the world actually is?"

"Maybe it's in your genes. Your father does fine with the weird, too." He motioned for me to follow him again, and I did. We ended up in a small bedroom. It wasn't bigger than a bed, a tiny closet, and a bedside table with a lamp. There was a bathroom attached, too. It was small but functional, or at least it looked like it was.

Everything was very institutional in color. Brown. Gray. Tan.

"Is this where I stay?" A thought dawned on me just as I asked. "I don't have any clothes. I mean none. Everything is back in Warden's house or in Judson's."

He ran a hand through his hair. "Fuck. Yes, of course you don't have any. Well, we can't do anything about that right now. I really don't want to go out of here. That'll have us showing up on the satellites. It was one thing to hide in the car while I knew they were watching Warden. You can wear some of my clothes until I can figure something out."

As tall as I was, Kade was taller. I was going to look like a little girl playing dress up in an adult's clothing. It was fine. I didn't need to be dressed up to wander around this place doing whatever Kade did down here in his converted mausoleum.

"Thanks. I appreciate it."

He waved his hand. "None of this has been your fault. And since it was my idea to motivate your father using you, I suppose it's the least I can do."

"What will we do here? I mean do we just sit here and stare at the walls. I'm good with all of that. Just want to know what to expect. I've had a lot happen lately. I… I would love to have a sense of what to do."

He nodded. "Come with me. I'll show you."

I entered a room loaded with video screens. Numbers shot everywhere. I couldn't follow them and didn't try. This was different than the screen in the basement at Judson's. This looked more like the Matrix movie.

"It's just the algorithms running. I'm searching for the Alliance council. They're also in hiding, just sending their dogs after us. We need to locate them so we can send our dogs at them."

This was a lot of dogs, and since the dogs came with guns and cars, they were obviously not dogs. I would have preferred canines. "Let's call them what they are, shall we? Kidnappers. Assassins."

"Fair enough. See, the thing is that they don't know how to use my equipment like I do. I invented it. I make the satellites do things they can't make it do. We'll find them."

I slid into a chair next to him. "So there's more than just the five of you."

I didn't know how he looked at that screen for so long. It made me sort of dizzy. I glanced at him instead. He leaned back in his chair. "I keep thinking I'll hide things from you. But the guys have told you so much stuff, and I think fuck it, I'll tell the pretty girl everything and work out the shit later."

Pretty? Ugh. I was such an idiot because that made butterflies in my stomach. I ignored them. "Tell the pretty girl. Go for it."

"There is a schism happening in The Alliance. People have seen what happened. Every day more and more of them are contacting us with allegiance, so yes we have people. And some of those have skills that are very useful. Like Derrick. He has those skills, too. He just sometimes refuses to use them."

A previous conversation with Derrick flooded my mind. He'd said no to something and they'd killed Alyssa. I wasn't going to ask about that now. I wanted to stay on topic. "So you find them and your people try to kill them. Why all this effort? You have all this shit. Why not let them have their Alliance and you can form your own club of world dominating secret dudes? You could call it the Society. Then you could do your thing, let them do theirs. Everything couldn't be more fucked up, could it?"

He stared at me, and under his gaze, my cheeks heated. I sighed. Okay. That was dumb, and now Kane could think I was even a bigger idiot than he already did. Scratch that idea. I moved on. Sliding into the chair next to him, I used that moment to try to regroup.

"So who are we looking for? Warden said Nathan Barton." I'd kept that name in the front of my mind. He'd been one of the ones to send men with guns to the beach. I'd never forget it as long as I lived. I wanted the other names. I'd remember them forever. Anger seethed at the thought. It was possible to hate someone you never met, it was possible to wish them harm. I wanted the other names.

Kane smiled. "Warden particularly hates Nathan. The current council is older than us, and they trained us. And Nathan was distinctly hard on Warden during training. Yeah, he'd go after him first. The other four? Ben Gray. Josh Kralik. Marcus Petrone. Henry Laparra. The big five. Nathan. Ben. Josh. Marcus. Henry." He spun in his chair. "They can only search for two of us at a time. Me? I can find all five. They have to come out sometime even if all I'm doing is waiting them out."

I cleared my throat. "Do they know the safe spots?"

"Nope." He smiled before he jumped up. "Hungry?"

He was really at ease here. Much more so than he'd been at Judson's. Also, his clothes were totally different. He'd been so put together there and here he was in jeans and a t-shirt with a stain on it. I wondered if this was much more his environment, if somehow it was possible to be more at home in a converted mausoleum watching numbers on a screen than it was to be in a mansion on a frozen lake. I rose slowly.

He was sexier like this and that threw me. Somehow this was doing it for me.

"So this schism... how does it end?"

His face fell. "One way or the other, people are dying."

Of course they were. These Alliance guys treated life and livelihood like it was nothing. I was never going to get used to it. "I'm not actually hungry. I might go lie down. I've had a long day."

"If you need something let me know. You wrecked Warden and Trace, Everly. Are you going to wreck me?"

I turned to stare at him. "They wrecked me. Not the other way around. I don't even know who I am right now. This person? I don't recognize her."

He leaned against the wall. "The Alliance does that. It gives us rebirth, reshapes us, and molds us into someone else. That's why those people cannot run it. They are destroying it."

"But I'm not Alliance. I'm a woman. That automatically makes me an ant in your eyes." I took a step away. "Or are you rethinking your life bathed in misogyny?"

His smile was slow. "You can be the queen of the ants, Everly."

"Not good enough." And I meant it. I wasn't anyone's ant. "I'm not going to be an ant of any kind."

He cleared his throat. "Well, I can't speak to that. You are surprising, that is for sure. Are you certain you're not hungry?"

"I'm really not." What I needed was time to process these things. "Kade, what happened to the former residents of this mausoleum?"

He took a step toward me. "Are you suddenly worried about poltergeists?"

"I'm a pretty reasonable person, but you don't grow up in Louisiana and not have some good old respect for the idea that there might be other beings around than just you. Even if it's not religion. This city is old. You can almost feel all the energy here, the old energy, still floating around."

Kade put his arm around me. "Come. I'll get you some clothes. I've never seen a ghost, never felt a ghost, have no feelings whatsoever about anything woo woo going on here. You'll be fine."

"You tell me that when the demonic clown shows up and drags you into some other dimension."

He sighed. "You watched too much television as a child." He showed me where his room was, and I waited outside while he went in for some clothes for me. Peeking in, I found it was the same size as my own. The only difference was on his wall he had a picture framed. I knew it right away. It was the *The Scream* by Edvard Munch.

I pointed to it from the doorway. "What does that mean to you?"

"Wouldn't you like to know?" He handed me a pile of clothes. "There are toiletries in the bathroom. You're perfectly safe here."

He had totally not answered my questions about the bodies, and I wasn't going to ask again. Instead, I took his clothes that smelled newly laundered and went back to the room assigned to me. How many bedrooms were here? I'd find out in the morning.

I used the small shower that had hot water and managed not to kill myself when the AC turned back on again sounding like a jet plane taking off. That was going to take some getting used to. I climbed into bed wearing a plain gray t-shirt and listened to the other sounds of this strange place. I was with a man who had turned a mausoleum into a surveillance bunker. How did that happen?

I chewed on my lip. Was Warden okay? Was he going to make it to San Diego? Kade didn't seem worried about him. And why was it bothering me so much that Trace hadn't checked in? Where was Judson? He'd had an attack made on him. What kind was it? And Derrick... what was he doing right then? He'd come for before, and he'd promised me he always would.

How about Kade? Who was he really? The geek or the dominating asshole? Both? What were we going to do together in this secret place below ground he'd had commissioned? How long were we staying here?

A knock sounded, and he stood in the doorway. He carried a protein bar and set it down next to me. "In case you get hungry in the middle of the night." He paused. "Or you need something to bribe the ghosts to leave you alone."

I threw a pillow at him, and he laughed. "The lights will become movement based around midnight. If you get up and move, they'll turn on. Otherwise they don't work until six. That's to save electricity. I don't want to be too obvious on the power grid. Right now, thanks to the electrical equivalent of a VPN, they don't know we're down here. I'm keeping it that way."

I shook my head. "I'd understand Latin better than what you just said."

"*Dulce somnii*, Everly." He winked at me. That might not be the exact phrase for sweet dreams but I'd understood it perfectly, and I was impressed he knew it right off the bat.

"*Securi dormient*, Kade."

Chapter 16

I didn't sleep the whole night. Every time I got over the idea that I was hearing noises of the dead all over me—and up until now I'd never have thought myself so susceptible to this sort of thing—the stupid jet engine air conditioning would turn on, scaring the bejesus out of me. I rolled over, pressing my head into the pillow. There was no natural light underground and I'd have had no idea what time it was except for the digital clock on the dresser telling me it was six in the morning.

I yawned before I pulled myself out of bed. This was going to be a long stay underground. I shoved on the shorts that were too big on me and rolled the waist, hoping they'd stay up. Wishing I had a hair elastic to put my locks up in a ponytail, I made my way out. He hadn't shown me where the kitchen was, but I'd find it. Coffee was too important right now not to be successful.

It wasn't far, but then the whole bunker wasn't huge. I did stumble upon two more bedrooms, making the total, as far as I could tell, four for the location.

Kade sat on the counter drinking coffee. His eyes

widened as I came in, either because I looked like hell or because he was surprised to see me up and about. Maybe he'd forgotten I was there. Until I had caffeine, I didn't really care. I could play denial all I wanted, but I really missed having Trace or Warden with me. Even the way Warden snored. There really was nothing like having a person hold me in the dead of the night.

Internally, I sighed. *Pathetic, call thyself Everly.* And now I was speaking oddly in my own head. Yes, coffee. Soon. Now.

Without a word, Kade prepared the hot brew for me and placed the cup, handle toward me, into my exhausted hand.

I took a sip. Then a second. Finally, he spoke after he'd seen me do that. He was a smart man. "Did you sleep okay?"

"No." I drank down more of what was going to get me through the day. "New place. New noises." I didn't say I'd been fearful. Kade had been sweet since I got here, but he'd been just the opposite back at Judson's. I didn't necessarily want to give him any fodder for being an asshole if that side of him reared its ugly head. "And your AC is loud."

He nodded. "That's true. I've learned to tune it out. The one downside. But it's hard to maintain temperature down here, and it's kind of extreme."

"I guess I'll get used to it." I rubbed my eyes. "How did you sleep?"

"Oh, I almost never sleep more than two hours at a time. Not since I was a kid. I got my two hours. I've been up ever since. Watching the screens. Tweaking the code."

Maybe that was Kade's problem. Maybe he was grumpy because he was so tired. I finished my coffee and the smart man poured more in the glass. I could have kissed him, if that wouldn't have been so weird and awkward. "Will it ding you if it finds one of them?"

"It'll do more than ding. Huge alarm, yes." He rubbed his chin. "I was going to go work out. Want to come?"

That sounded great. "Yes, I'd love that."

"Come on."

I walked with him to a room that was the same size as the kitchen. It almost seemed like he'd built the thing in a series of squares and rectangles. Square here. Rectangle here. Attach. Like he'd fit together a Tetris board.

There was a treadmill, a bike, some weights and several yoga mats. I got down on the one the farthest to the left and stretched. It had been a long time since I'd done this. Not since I'd had my head knocked around. I didn't want to overdo it. But I did need some exercise in the worst possible way. I could practically feel my thighs spreading.

I stretched for ten minutes while Kade got on the treadmill. I shouldn't have been checking out his ass while he ran. I really should have kept my gaze to the floor. But there it was. He had a tight, tight ass, and it was a lot more entertaining than counting the wood planks on the floor while I did my half-cocked version of yoga.

I'd always liked cardio a lot better than stretching and weight training. But in the meantime, I had to be gentle on myself. Of course, I'd had crazy sex and not thought about it. I could probably do a mild jog. When this was over, I was going to run a marathon. I was determined to do so.

I got on the bike. I was going to do a mile, maybe two, at the most. Ten minutes later I panted and wondered if I was going to get through this at all. Amazing how much cardio endurance I could lose in such a short period of time. I gritted my teeth. I always got through these things. I pushed to two miles and got off the bike as fast as was possible for me.

Kade still ran like it was nothing in the world to do so.

"I'm a runner." I shouted at him. "Pay no attention to how pathetic I look right now."

He looked over his shoulder. "What?" He stopped the treadmill. "I can never hear anything when I'm on this thing. It's loud. You okay?"

I nodded, putting my hand on my hips. "Sure."

Kade got off the treadmill and pulled his shirt over his head, wiping his face with the shirt. He had well defined muscles, and when he turned around to use the same shirt to wipe off the machine, I got a good look at the scars on his back. Whoever had hit the Letters had done so with a heavy-duty stick of some kind that had left matching permanent scarring on all of them. Did that just happen or did they have to do it consistently?

But Kade had done something to his back that the others didn't have. At least the two I had seen. He was tattooed on his shoulder blade. I stepped toward him to get a better look. My first impression was correct. It was an elaborate representation of the Joker from the Batman comics. With green hair and yellow-rimmed eyes, he had a blue body and a red background behind him. Truly, he was manic looking. I rubbed the back of my neck. Why would he have chosen that particular image and put it right there on his back?

As though he read my mind, he spoke with his back still facing me. "I like the Joker better than Batman in some ways."

"Why is that?" I walked toward him to get an even closer look. The colors were really amazing. "Because he's the bad guy? You're like Bruce Wayne down here in this cave."

He shook his head, turning around. "The Joker is out

there with his crazy. If they're two sides of the same coin, then the Joker isn't hiding it. He's just… who he is."

I put my hands across my chest. "Is that who you think you are? An evil dude who plots and kills people?"

He placed his hand on my shoulder. "That's who we all are, Everly. Even Trace and Warden. You sleeping with them didn't change that. And if we ever give in to the chemistry between us, your magic won't suddenly make me any better either. I'm going to be this way every day of my life. We're bad men, even if we're the lesser of two evils in your life. This happened to you because of us. Don't forget that."

I didn't know what made me do what I did next. It was just that right then he reminded me of the little boy that I'd lived next door to for years. I'd babysat him three days a week for almost a year. When he'd been scared, he'd struck out at me verbally until I'd figured out that in his ten-year-old way he was asking me to help him.

I put my fingers over his, and I squeezed them tightly. "You don't scare me. Not with your crazy tattoo. Not with your mean words. Not when you dragged me out of the bedroom the first day at Judson's. I'm not sure who you are, exactly. And now I'm not sure you know either. But you're going to be okay."

A muscle ticced in his jaw. "I've got to go check the screen."

I stepped back. "Have at it."

He pointed at me. "Go take a shower and then come see me. I'll show you the emergency exits. I meant to do that yesterday."

That was right. In case someone invaded our graveyard space and we had to run for our lives. It was hard to imagine, except that I'd been shot at on a beach and had to run from a convenience store after Warden paid twenty thousand dollars for a car. I shook my head. I might have to run for my life from here, too. I was getting good at it.

Of course, maybe someday I'd stop running and figure out how to fire back. I turned and walked toward my room. Then maybe I'd get a Joker tattoo on my back and wish I could wear my crazy on the outside, too.

━━━━

"ANYTHING?" I walked into the surveillance room to find Kade tapping on a tablet.

He looked up before he set it down. "No, but Warden says to say hello to you. I messaged him for info on being chased and his work on bankrupting The Alliance. Instead, he wants to know about you."

I cleared my throat, heat hitting my cheeks. "Tell him hello back."

"Maybe I could pass him a note in gym class." He slammed down the tablet. "Tell him yourself." He pointed at the tablet. "It's safe. And if he's communicating, he's either so hard up for you that he's lost his fucking mind or he's using his safe one, too."

He'd never used one the whole time we were together. Could he have? Did he not bring it? Or was he just living in the moment with me? I didn't know. Maybe I'd ask him sometime. But not now with Kade being prickly.

He rose, and I followed him down the hall. Kade pushed aside a bookshelf. "I did this myself. If the people who built this place with me switch sides, they don't know about this." The bookshelf slid over. It was on some kind of slide. I stared at him for a second, but I didn't have time to consider it long, because he was going so fast I had to hurry to catch up. I ran after him. The hallway was dark, low, and long. If I had to bend, he had to stoop, but I supposed it didn't matter. If we had to get away, this would do it.

We came to a fork in the way. He stopped. "Remember left. Right takes you back to where you were. It's meant to throw them off if they were following. Assuming they could get this far to begin with."

"And suddenly I'm not in *Batman*, I'm in *Goonies*."

He snickered. "You're funny. Did you know that?"

"Everyone thinks they're funny. Most of us are not." I really didn't think I was funny. I'd never been. My father was stiff as a board. It wasn't like we cracked a lot of jokes at home. Maybe it was hard to be funny with your daughter after you murdered her mother.

Kade pointed upward. "There's a ladder here. It'll come out on the other side of the highway. You have to climb up through the sewers. It's not pretty, but you'll get out."

I stared at him. "In this scenario, you're not with me?"

"Well, hopefully I am, but maybe I'm dead. Or killing people behind us. Just know how to do it, okay?"

I nodded. "Yes. What are we doing now?"

He took my hand and pulled me along so that I followed him back. His hands were callused. They weren't smooth like he spent all day working on computers, but then again, he'd constructed this place, which meant that he was capable of doing a lot of different kinds of work.

"So your job for The Alliance was to build tech to track people?"

He nodded. "Among other things. It's not really my job, it's more like my role. My job is that I run a tech company I created. I've actually sold it. I'm supposed to be transitioning it but it doesn't need transition so they don't ask anything of me. I have a lot of free time. Do you see the difference? Job versus role?"

"As I am almost about to receive my bachelors of arts from an institution of higher learning, I am fairly certain I can tell the difference intellectually between job and role."

He turned for the sole purpose of winking at me. It was sort of a dick move and what did it say about me that I found it so fucking attractive? Well, that I was sick in the head, but I'd already established that so that wasn't exactly new information.

"Gets your back up if I question your intellect? Storing that away for future information."

I shook my head. "And to think that some guys woo a girl with roses. You do it with insults."

"Sure." He grinned broadly now. "If you were the kind of woman who wanted flowers I'd be so bored with you right now. I like that you get that look when I jab at you that says you both want to hit me across the head and fuck me. But all you do is jab back. So many small intricacies of fucked up right there, I can't even begin to pick them all out."

Okay. This was enough. "I'll tell you what? You are obviously obsessed with this topic. Yes, I slept with Trace and Warden. I'd probably sleep with Derrick, too, since he seems inclined and so do I. I think you're really hot. But you have to get your panties out of their bunch about the fact that I slept with your friends." I shrugged. "They both understood it was temporary. The only one who didn't seem to get that memo was me. Both of them did a number on me. And I'll be honest, even if you were into the idea, I'm not sure my heart could take another run at that."

He stared at me in the terrible fluorescent light. "I don't do this. I mean, ever. I don't mean ever. I mean obviously not never. I'm bumbling through this. Let me put it this way to you. If we had been in college at the same time, you wouldn't have spoken to me. You are only even throwing it out there that you might be interested because I'm Alliance."

I stepped forward, fingering his shirt. It was soft, cotton. "You don't know who I'd talk to. I like smart men. But I don't do relationships. We might have met at a bar. Gone home together. It wouldn't have been this complicated."

Kade flared his nostrils. "I never went to a bar. I was too busy on my computer trying to figure out how I could move my way up in The Alliance. There's never a moment off."

"Then maybe we wouldn't have met. But we did meet now. And I'm not attracted to you because you're Alliance. I'm attracted to you because I'm fucked in the head." I imitated his wink. "I want to get out of this hallway."

He nodded once. "Come on."

We walked back in silence. The closer we got to his lair the more I heard a noise I didn't recognize. Kade dropped my hand and rushed forward. "Fuck. That's the signal. The satellite has one of them."

I ran after him. I'd just landed in this war, but really, fuck them. I wanted to see the face of one of them—one of the guys who had decided that a stranger with nothing to do with any of this had been expendable and could be shot on a beach. Or used as a means to get Trace to talk.

Two men stood talking. One of them had a gun strapped to his back. He shook his head at what the taller, bald man said.

"Who is who?" I stared from the doorway.

Kade sat in his chair, and I came up behind him, leaning forward so I could get a better look. He pointed at the screen. "The tall one. That is Henry Laparra. If you met him, he'd tell you to call him Hank. Ten years ago you would have thought he was hot. He's Australian, although he hasn't lived there in thirty years. You'd like his accent."

I ignored him. "Where is he now?"

"Not far, actually, which is eating at me. Biloxi, Mississippi. I could be there in a couple of hours." He picked up his tablet. "Not me. Can't be me. I have to stay here and keep looking. Nope, I'm going to call in what I'm supposed to do." He slammed his free hand down on the table. "Not my fucking role."

I put my hand on his shoulder, but he didn't seem to notice. He tapped on the tablet rapidly. "Derrick will take some people and go in."

"That's a good thing, right?" I dodged around the other side of the chair. "Isn't that sort of the point here? Get the bad guys?"

He blinked rapidly. "Henry has been a thorn in my side my entire life. Even before I knew about The Alliance he was a problem. My father had children later. My mom was young. I think... I think he found her and had me so that he could continue The Alliance legacy. If I'd been a girl, maybe they'd have kept going."

I sat down so I could listen to him more. "Keep going."

"Hank used to come to my house all the time. I didn't know why. The man is fifteen years older than me. I used to wonder when I was five why this twenty year old was hanging around my kitchen. When I was ten I used to think he was fucking my mother." He shook his head. "Five years later I would of course know what the fuck was happening. Alliance." He spun in his chair again. "I thought for a while they were just... friends. Like now that I was written into The Alliance, my father would turn to me like he'd done Hank."

He rolled his eyes. "But Hank was the son my father

always wished I was. Somehow at five, he already knew I wasn't going to be an Alliance leader."

"And Hank was?"

"Yep." He got to his feet. "Henry liked my dad a lot. I don't think I've mentioned to you that my father was one of the five. He was a leader. A big one. But he died, very suddenly of a stroke, and by the time I came for training at eighteen he was gone. The five you see now were there. Young leadership. The next breath."

"That didn't go well?"

He waved toward the screen. "See him? I was a seven-teen-year-old kid. Trying to live up to my father's legacy. And Hank went after me like it was his job. Oh, they go after everyone. We have a one-to-one hatred, the five of us to the five of them. Hank went after me. Hard."

My stomach clenched. "My father doesn't have marks on his back like the five of you."

He shook his head. "He wouldn't. That was what the five of them did. They initiated that. Before that? No beatings that left permanent scars. Hank gave me mine. And he was so fucking joyful about it. Told me he was the son my dad always wanted."

"Was that what your dad said or what Hank said?"

Kade rolled his eyes. "Hank. But trust me I have every reason to believe it."

"I'm sorry." Sometimes that was all I could say. "And now you have him. Why would he be in Biloxi? Is there something special in Biloxi?"

"Casinos. He loves casinos. Owns two in Vegas. He's a secret partner. But he loves to win. I swear he gets hard from it."

I pointed at his screen. "What kinds of things can you do on there?"

He blinked. I understood. From his perspective it had

to feel like a huge jump in conversation. "A lot of things. Why?"

"Well, if he likes to play, maybe you could fuck with him. Bring him up then rig the game so he loses the next one. You know, just enough that he feels nuts. Presumably he's playing slots and whatnot. I don't suppose there is anything we can do about blackjack from here."

Kade widened his eyes. He put his hands on his hips, and a second later he was tapping his feet. "Can't mess with the outcome of blackjack, but I could mess with the lights. The alarm system. I could…" He grabbed me and pulled me to him. "That is fucking brilliant." His mouth came down on mine, hard but then soft. When he pulled back, I was breathless. "You are a genius, and I decided I'm long out of college. Guard your heart, Everly, I'm going to make a play for you."

I sat back in my seat. I was brilliant and he'd kissed me? Both of those facts threw me. Yes, I was brilliant, but I had never done something to fuck with someone else before. Well, maybe Lexxie Donata. But she had deserved it She'd taken my shoes in gym class and thrown them on the roof. I'd managed to get her in trouble. But it hadn't been this.

Kade furiously typed on his computer. I backed away, letting him do it. I needed space from that kiss, too. I hadn't expected to be dizzy from his kisses or to want more of them so quickly after. I wandered away, eventually finding a room where he had games hooked up to a screen. I sat down. It had been a long time since I'd played a video game, but I eventually found one I knew. I sat down to play, forcing my brain to turn off.

That worked for about an hour. Then I couldn't take it anymore. I shut it off and went back into Kade. Had he managed to do it?

Kade must have heard me come in. He spoke, not looking at me. "The fact that he's the one to make himself visible doesn't surprise me. He thinks he's invincible."

"Did you do it?"

He pointed to the screen. Henry played poker. He drew a card.

"Oh, too bad. That might have been a winning hand." The lights went off in the room with The Alliance leader. "Looks like it's void now."

I grinned. "First step or has he already had a long night?"

"Long night. Just such a string of bad luck. Oh, the lights are coming up, now."

Only the room looked quite different. Derrick stood there, surrounded by five other men. They all wore black. I had no audio, but I knew what I saw. I cried out, covering my mouth just as it happened. Guns raised. And five seconds later Hank and everyone else at the table, including the dealer, were dead.

"Bye, asshole." Kade spoke as Derrick looked up, as though he could see us on the screen. Maybe he could. I shook too hard for rational thought. He nodded. Kade shut it off.

Chapter 17

"I came up with the idea and now he's dead."

Kade rose fast. "He was always going to be dead. You just helped me fuck with him beforehand, which improved my bad mood. What did you think was going to happen? Are you going to freak out on me?"

Red crossed my vision. "I just saw someone get shot by someone else I know. I... I don't know how I'm supposed to react but it's going to take a second. Okay?"

"Fuck." He looked away. "Sorry."

I put my hands on my knees. "This isn't the first person I've seen D kill."

"And we're back to using letters. Do you have a rhyme and a reason for when you shift to calling us letters or do you just suddenly feel like you can't speak full names?"

Why couldn't he just give me a second to deal with this? Why did we have to talk right at this second? "You're overthinking it. Sometimes I say one thing, sometimes I say another. I don't know that I have a rhyme or reason."

"Huh." He put his arm around my shoulders. "Let's have a little food. Brunch. I mean, we ate breakfast but...

heck, I have a better idea. We can…" The tablet dinged, cutting him off. "Hold that thought." He hit the tablet. "Good work."

There was a pause and then Derrick answered. "Yeah. So you were watching. I thought it likely."

"I deleted the feed."

Had he? I hadn't even noticed. I sank down in the chair again.

"Good. We need to figure they saw it anyway. No way were they not watching Hanky boy. I got in without anyone making note of who I was."

I rubbed my eyes. It was good to hear Derrick's voice even though he'd just shot someone right in front of my eyes. "That was because you covered the man bun. And don't you usually kill people with a baseball bat?"

"Is that my sweetheart?" Derrick's voice picked up. "Were you watching, too?"

"Kade and I are glued together right now. Where he goes, I go."

There was a pause. "Gotcha."

"So yeah, you need to go into hiding. For real this time. Your job is done. For now."

Derrick was silent so long I wasn't sure he was still there. "I will. I have some things to grab in the meantime. Few more days. Then I'll go under."

"Coming here?" Kade rubbed his eyes. "You know you can."

"Maybe." Derrick made a noise in the background that sounded like he set something down. "Take care of Everly, Kade. For now, she's still gentle. We haven't had the time to really destroy her soul yet. Everly, Kade's the kindest out of all of us. Even if he pretends that's not true."

Derrick must have disconnected the communication. Kade just shook his head. "He's seriously fucked in the head. Don't believe half of what he says. Alyssa's death took what limited sense he had left and twisted it."

"I think he understands things better than the rest of us do. Or he just sees the world through a different lens."

Kade shook his head. "Be that as it may, I'm holding with the idea that Derrick is just fucked. Come on. My original idea stands."

"Which was what?" He'd never gotten that out there in the first place.

"They're busy right now. They'll have Derrick on alert. And they'll be rushing toward Biloxi to clean up that mess. Then, they'll have to have a quorum. We can't be without the five. Now we're down to four. So in the meantime what we need is for your father to get his shit together and get this done. We need to be there at that meeting."

I tried to breathe. "So this idea you had has to do with my father?"

"No." He tapped the table. Kade was always moving unless he typed, which I supposed meant that he was even moving then since typing require movement of his fingers and wrists. "We can deal with your father tomorrow. I think we're going to go pay him a visit. Much as I hate to leave here. Tonight, we're safe. Tomorrow, too. It'll take them some time to regroup. So let's go get a drink."

A drink? He wanted to go get a drink? "Do you not have alcohol here?"

He shrugged. "A little red wine and some cheap whisky. We can drink that or you can let me take you out on Bourbon Street."

I did like that idea. What I didn't like, however, was the idea of running for my life away from Alliance crazies down Bourbon Street. "Are you sure that we'd be safe?"

"I can never be 100% sure of anything when it comes to The Alliance. But I can tell you that I am going to risk it tonight and go get a drink. Or five. On Bourbon Street. They are going to look for Derrick not me. And I bet they don't know what the fuck to do with you."

Fuck it. "Yes, I need a drink. Or five."

"Can you handle five?" He grinned at me, maybe the broadest I've ever seen him do before.

"I guess we'll see." And to think I'd always been a two drink woman. Never more. I was breaking all kinds of rules lately.

IT WAS a good thing there were so many different kinds of dress on Bourbon, because I was still dressed in Kade's clothes. No one even batted an eye.

"Could we get me something to wear while we're out here?"

"Sure," Kade yelled back at me. There was some sort of parade going on that was making things louder than normal. I didn't even know what it was. Not Mardi Gras, but there were all kinds of celebrations that went on in New Orleans all year. "If you want to wear tourist clothing. We could get you lots of I want to get drunk t-shirts."

I grinned at him. That wasn't exactly what the shirts said but there were a few with that general idea on it. "I could take one that says New Orleans. That actually fits. And some pants."

"I will get you some clothes. Or maybe I just like to see you in mine. It's kind of… hot. There might be some kind of evolutionary, anthropological reason for that."

I side-eyed him. "Are you going to club me over the head and take me home to your cave?"

"Not tonight."

"Ah." I pointed at him. "But you do have a cave."

"Much more of a lair, right?"

We walked into a bar together. It seemed less busy than a lot of the others. The bouncer stopped us at the door. "I'm going to need to see IDs."

I sucked in a silent breath. I was twenty-two, almost twenty-three. I'd waited forever to be twenty-one, drinking in ridiculous frat houses and dorm rooms until I could go to a bar. But I wasn't getting into this bar tonight. I didn't have an ID. I had nothing. I was... completely without proof about who I was.

"Here." Kade handed the bouncer two cards. I blinked. The bouncer handed it back and then we walked inside.

I grabbed Kade's hand. "Where did you get that?"

"I printed one up for you at home. It's not your actual birthday on there or address. But it's your photo and you're over twenty-one so it's not a hard sell."

We sat down next to each other at the bar. I eventually ordered an old fashioned and Kade got a Manhattan. We drank in silence. Eventually, he turned to me. "Do you go to bars a lot?"

I raised an eyebrow at him. "Shouldn't you know that? Didn't you guys stalk me before you took me?"

"Derrick did. I just have your basic background report." He finished his drink. I still had half of mine left. He ordered another one.

I took a long sip of mine. "What does my basic background report say?"

"That you're a hot girl studying social work and your father needs to be controlled. Your address. Oh and that you sleep naked." He winked at me. "Just kidding about that last one."

I pointed at him. "You must be because I do not sleep

naked. Ever. What if there is a fire in the middle of the night?"

"Then you'd be naked standing on the street giving the fire department quite a show. They'd probably give you a blanket."

I took a long drink. I didn't usually consume this much so fast. But since drunk was the goal, I was going to get there. "That would be nice since I'd be cold."

He grinned. "We're just going to keep going with this scenario? Back and forth? With this hypothetical idea of you being stranded naked on the street because you slept that way?"

"I sleep in pajamas. They're not sexy, but they work."

He tilted his head slightly. "Anything you're in would be sexy."

"I can't figure out if you like me or if you just say things like that to egg me on. Like you're going to get me to respond to that and then you're going to be really mean and tell me you don't want me. Besides, you really want to fuck me when you know I've been with Trace and Warden?"

He set down his drink. "I think what I like best about you is how you don't pull punches. You just say things that most people wouldn't even think. It's like boom, you open your mouth and the most unbelievable shit comes right out of it."

"I didn't have to take advanced psych to know avoidance when I hear it, and you, Kade, with your nasty mouth and unrelenting attitude, avoided my question very nicely there."

He waved his hand. "I don't give a fuck that you slept with them. I do want you, but not permanently. I want to get the itch that is you out of my head so I can stop thinking about scratching it."

"Because that is sexy." Still, even as I jabbed at him, I had to admit I liked that he wanted me. Yes, it turned out I was needy. I wanted my pseudo-enemies to want me. And it would be nice to not be left… feeling squishy inside after he was done with me. Kade didn't inspire those feelings. It was more like confusion mixed with wanting to kiss him so hard he bled.

I blinked as realization hit me. That really was how I felt. I wanted to use him the way he wanted to use me. To get rid of the itch.

"Finish your drink. We're going back to your hidey-hole and then you can fuck me. A couple of times. Maybe. It might be a one off. Then we'll deal with my father and get on with it. I don't want to cuddle you."

Kade seemed to sip slower. "Is that how you think it's going to be with me? You tell me what to do and I do it?"

"If you want to pretend you're in control of this you can go ahead and do so. The only thing you're delaying is coming hard. I must warn you that most of the time I'm pretty bored with sex." His friends had broken that record lately, but I thought it best not to mention that right this second. I really didn't know how Kade did with pressure. "I'll probably end up in the shower humming away my boredom."

He jumped to his feet, and faster than I could believe had his hand in mine. He threw money down on the counter. "I can promise you that you won't be bored."

"We'll see." I knew I poked a bear when it came to Kade, but I couldn't seem to stop doing it.

"Let's go buy you some clothes."

Well, I hadn't expected that. "I offered you sex and you said clothes?"

"We'll have sex when I'm good and ready, Everly, and

not because you goad me into it on some sort of power play. You want clothes. You'll get clothes."

Good lord he was frustrating. "Well then maybe I won't be interested later."

He shrugged. "I'm sure I can do with my hand better than anything you could do."

I gasped, and he shrugged. "Not so nice is it? Guess you'll have to prove yourself in bed, too."

This had taken a turn I hadn't expected. Well, if he wanted to have a contest to see which one of us could be better in bed, then we'd go ahead and do that. After we bought me clothes, apparently.

IT TURNED out that I could buy just about anything I wanted in New Orleans late at night. There were vendors selling knock-off clothing all the time. I didn't care about labels, most of the time I purchased things that were on sale that fit well. My father was cheap. I'd always thought it was because he was an accountant and cared about money. Now, I wondered who he was saving money to kill next.

With my arms filled with bundles of clothes in cheap plastic bags, we went back to his mausoleum. I was still feeling a buzz from my drink. I probably should have eaten more before I drank but that wasn't the point.

"Do you want to be buried here?"

He opened the door to let me in, and I was once again struck by how completely off it was to be in a city of the dead, hiding from a secret organization bent on killing my captors. One of whom had just bought me knock-off clothing.

"Are you going to kill me?" He put a hand on my shoulder. "Should I be afraid?"

"My father kills people. Maybe it runs in the family." We made it to the bottom of the stairs, and I turned to regard him as he was right behind me.

"Your father farms it out. He's never done the dirty work himself. And you're not a killer." He searched my face for a second. "Although I think you probably could be." He pointed at my eyes. "There's a spot in there that is hard. I see it. You're vulnerable, sure. But you're also tough as nails. Anyone else would be cowering in the corner. We're passing you around, taking chances with your life, and yet it's you who has us spinning in circles. What is it about you, Everly? You're pretty. You're smart. Funny. Yes, but a million women are." He took a long breath. "So why am I all twisted up about you?"

I kissed him. It surprised him. He didn't respond right away. Kade stayed so stiff I wasn't sure he was going to move at all. But then his mouth pressed into mine. And that wasn't the only thing. He pushed me hard into the wall. I oomphed, but I loved it. I held onto him for dear life.

"You done saying no?" I bit down on his lower lip. "Or playing whatever game you're doing in your own head. You want me. I want you. Let's get it out of our systems."

He tugged on the end of my hair. I loved the bite of pain. Somehow it represented my entire relationship with Kade thus far. I wanted it, but it hurt nonetheless.

"You make me so fucking hard." With that, he ground against me. A surge of heat pushed through me.

"You make me so fucking nuts." I kissed him again, harder. "Dragging me around. Ordering me out of the room the first day like you were king of the fucking manor. Calling yourself K. You like to be in charge. Guess what? You'll never be when it comes to me."

He lifted an eyebrow infuriatingly slowly. "I'm going to

hold you to that. I never, ever get to own you Everly. Promise me that I don't."

That seemed like an odd thing to ask me to swear to. "Why?"

"We own everything. I like the idea of not owning you. If you promise me that we keep going now. If you can't, this stops here. I don't need another ant in my life."

I ran my hand down the side of his face. He needed to shave, but I'd always found that not quite put together look sexy as hell. "That is such an incredibly... disgusting analogy that you keep making. Gross. Stop doing it."

"Doesn't make it any less true." He held my gaze steady. I could get lost in those dark eyes. That was part of what made him so dangerous. "I want that promise from you."

It wasn't going to be a problem assuring him I wasn't going to be one of his ants. "I promise. You'll never own me."

"Good." His mouth was on mine, and this time he kissed me again and again. And again. He tasted like his Manhattan, and I wanted to drown in the sensation. I didn't rush him. I closed my eyes. I'd spent so little time on foreplay in the past. Maybe that was the problem with all my previous experiences. Maybe it came to time. The Letters were older. They didn't rush to the end just to get there.

Kade moaned, the smallest sound. It was almost a sigh. The sound made me shudder, desire rushing through my body. He didn't give of himself easily. Even that little bit of sound was a huge amount from him. I grasped onto it. We could play our games again after this was over.

I tugged at his t-shirt, and he took it off. I ran my hands over the muscles on his chest, loving the visceral feeling of my fingers on that part of his skin. He stared in my eyes as

I did it, and I wished I could read him better than I could. I really didn't know what he was thinking.

But I knew what I was contemplating, and it was just how hard his muscles were. I walked closer to him; leaning my nose down onto his shoulder, I breathed in his male scent. I could scent the night on him, the alcohol, the bar, the jambalaya from the food truck we'd walked past. But beyond that was the clean scent of his soap. I bit down on his skin, just to mark him, just because I wanted to.

He shuddered. "Use your teeth anytime."

We pulled each other's clothes off. I was going to be completely naked with him in the front hall. If anyone came through the front door of his mausoleum, they'd catch us totally nude. I grinned. If anyone was able to come through that door without us noticing, let them look.

He took a step back, staring at me for a second. It was a long glance, and after a second, I wondered if he found something lacking. I lifted my chin. Let him dare to criticize. I'd make him pay.

Kade leaned forward, kissing me on the end of my nose. "You know you're beautiful. Like sometimes it hurts to look at you because you almost don't seem real."

"You know you're built like a Greek god, right?"

He didn't answer me, instead grabbing his pants. He pulled a condom out of the pocket and placed it in my hand. "Hold that for me." Sure, I could do that. He hadn't asked so much as ordered, but right then I didn't mind. The condom indicated completion and that was the goal. "I'm going to fuck you against that wall."

I pointed at the wall behind me. "That wall?"

"Unless you'd prefer another one?"

I shrugged like it didn't matter, like my heart wasn't racing with excitement. "That one seems fine."

"Great." He backed me into it. I wrapped my arms

around his neck and kissed him. He returned the caresses. Eventually, he ran a hand down my body, stopping at my breasts. He squeezed them, his lips never leaving my own. I stroked the length of his back where I could reach, digging my fingers into his skin because I wanted to.

I pulled back just enough to reach his cock. Between us, I stroked him several times. He closed his eyes before he flared his nostrils. "Careful. Too much of that and we'll have to pause a minute before we go any further."

"What's your recovery time like?"

He opened his lids. "Find out later. Lean on that wall."

I pushed back, following his direction. I'd never had sex standing up before. He could lead me through this, and I'd gladly do as he said. My core clenched in anticipation. Every part of me wanted to get off with Kade right now.

"Hand me that condom."

We really weren't doing a lot of foreplay but that was okay. I didn't need it, didn't want it. No, this whole night had been foreplay. I wanted to get to completion. I placed the condom in his hand, and he tore the packaging before he rolled it onto himself.

He grabbed my leg and pulled it up, placing it so my thigh straddled his ass. I held onto him, my back to the wall. This was awkward but not so much that I didn't want to keep going. "Hold on."

Kade pushed inside of me. There wasn't a lot of movement I could make. No, in fact, the best thing I could do was not move. I needed to stay still. It was hard, as my hips wanted to surge toward him, but if I let them, I was going to fall over onto him and this was all going to be over very fast.

Porn sometimes made things look easy that were absolutely not that way. Yes, I'd watched some with boyfriends in the past. This should have been simple. It was not. That didn't make it any less... hot.

I wanted to see if we could pull this off.

Anticipation filled me as I called on all my patience not to tell him just to lay me out on the floor and fuck me hard. He jerked his hips, moving his cock in and then out of me. I closed my eyes. Sometimes just feeling was the most difficult thing in the world.

He'd told me not to let him own me, and I didn't plan on that at all. Another round of his jerking inside of me, and I knew I couldn't let this continue. It felt amazing, and it wouldn't be hard for me to come, but he had all the power here. I didn't want him to see that.

Maybe I'd been wrong earlier. Maybe sex really was a game. Or better yet a power struggle.

"Flip me over." I opened my eyes to look at him. "Take me from behind."

He stared at me for a long second. "If that's what you want."

"It's what I want."

Kade pulled out of me fast. He hissed in a breath as he did. I was wet, hot, ready, and yes I was going to be pressed with my breasts against the wall. But this way he'd never know, never see if this moved me. With Kade it was better that way.

I couldn't give him too much.

Chapter 18

I turned to face the wall. My heart beat fast. Already worked up from the little bit we'd done, I had to find my center before I started weeping like a baby just from having him touch me. Why was I so raw? I didn't know. But Kade never gave me a chance to find my center. No, he was back inside of me faster than I could fathom.

I'd wanted to turn from him, but what I hadn't considered was how deep he'd be inside of me in this direction. From behind, there was always deeper penetration and Kade was large. He filled me up so far it was almost painful.

I moaned and his hand came to my front, slipping in front of me even as he slid all the way in from the back. He found my clit, and he rubbed. I gasped.

"I've got you, Everly. You aren't going to fall."

Distantly, I wondered if that wording worked on many levels and not just the obvious "I wasn't going to fall on my face" reference he was likely making. I stopped thinking. It was hard, but I had to force myself. The things he did to my body should be illegal for how they wrecked me, and I just wanted to enjoy them, not get lost in my head so I missed the moment.

He breathed on the back of my neck. I couldn't see it, but I could feel his nose pressing into my hair. "You fucking smell like strawberries. My new favorite scent."

I held onto the wall. I couldn't talk. There was only Kade, his dirty mouth, and the shit he was saying to me that was as hot as any aphrodisiac ever could be. But his hand was making his thrusts even more effective, and I trembled with the need to come. I wanted to. Oh, it was so close but still it held off. Why couldn't I just come?

"Give it to me, Everly. You make me so hot. So unbelievably hot. I want to feel you explode. I need your noises. I need to feel your cunt squeezing against my cock."

I exploded. His words must have been all I needed. I couldn't breathe, couldn't do anything but come apart in his arms. He hardly made a sound when he came, didn't shout, didn't say my name, just sighed as he climaxed inside of my body.

We stood there together, me holding onto the cold wall, neither of us saying anything as we panted, trying to catch our breaths.

"Was it disappointing?" His voice was low, almost harsh. He was still inside of me. I could feel him. He wasn't as hard anymore, but I wouldn't call him flaccid either.

I shook my head. "Not in the least."

"Good." He pulled out slowly.

"To say the least."

He turned me around in his arms, and stared at me. "Come to my room."

I blinked. "Why?"

"Less noisy in there."

As the air conditioner loudly blasted cold air on my

naked body, that sounded like an excellent idea. "Do you snore?"

"Maybe." He winked at me. "Don't come if you don't want to. I was being nice. I only sleep two hours at a time. Suffer the whole night if you want to. Life's full of stupid decisions."

I ALMOST DIDN'T GO to his room just to make a point. I didn't really know what the point I'd be making was, and my grandmother used to say that I shouldn't cut off my nose to spite my face. I kind of thought that applied here. After a quick shower where I changed my mind ten times, I put on a t-shirt we'd bought that said NOLA on it, and I padded down the hallway to his room.

The problem with Kade—and maybe it wasn't a problem, maybe just the opposite—was that it wasn't so easy to pretend he was nice. Both Trace and Warden could act downright sweet for periods of time. Kade never really gave into that. He might have seemed that way for a little bit, but he never let me forget he was really in this to win and I was just a minor player thrown in his way.

Sex was one thing. I could turn around and slightly detach emotionally. Sleeping was another thing altogether. Curled up in a bed with him, I was vulnerable. Still, it was loud in my room, and I didn't think I could do another night like that.

Chapter 19

I made my way down the hall to his room, entering to find him standing by the left side of the bed in his boxer shorts. I was pretty sure that he'd been wearing briefs earlier. Maybe he slept in one and wore the other kind during the day?

He turned when I came in. "Hey."

I nodded toward him. "Hey."

The air conditioner blasted through the place, the noise slightly dampened in here, but still too loud to be comfortable. How did he live like this without noticing it all the time?

"You really don't hear that?" I pointed upward. "It really doesn't make you cringe in agony?"

He shrugged. "I have actually cringed in agony in my life. Maybe I just have worse hearing than you."

"Maybe." I rubbed the back of my neck. "So you sleep on the left?"

"I'll only be here two hours. Then you can feel free to roll around the bed."

I chewed on my lip. "I'm not really a roller. Not usually.

I often wake up in exactly the same position I went to bed in."

He motioned toward the bed, and I got into the right side of it. We moved around for a while until we adjusted, each of us on our respective sides. Kade flipped off the light, bathing the room in total darkness. I guessed he didn't have any remarks on my comment about my sleeping habits.

I hated questioning the things I had said. But Kade wasn't an easy person to speak to. With him, perhaps I might as well get comfortable with the concept of silence. For whatever reason, it wasn't as easy to be silent with Kade as it was with Warden. He cleared his throat.

At least a minute passed when he spoke again. "Are you stiff in the morning? Staying still like that?"

I smiled, knowing he couldn't see it. Apparently, I wasn't the only one who needed to fill the silence. "No, usually I'm okay. Why do you only sleep two hours?"

"I don't know. But I wake up fully aware that I've got to get back to doing something, anything, that I'm completely wasting time lying in the bed. I try to shut it off, but it doesn't work that way. I get up, get to doing something. Every night."

I couldn't imagine that. I loved sleeping, craved it. The warm, scrunchy feeling after a good night's rest when for those brief seconds, everything seemed like it might be right in the world. Of course, there were other mornings when I was bleary eyed, in need of coffee, and hating the sun for rising. Either way, I wouldn't trade sleep.

There was nothing so important it required me to get up and do it every night.

"Must be very hard for you to turn off your brain. I'm sorry."

He sighed. "Used to it. You should go to sleep. We have to deal with your father tomorrow."

"Deal with him how?"

He didn't answer instantly. When he did, I didn't love his response. "I'm working on that."

I rolled over. "Whatever that means."

"When I know you'll know. Either way, your dad will be made to work faster. By now he knows Henry is dead. He'll know how that happened. Word travels fast in our circles. He's going to hustle."

My father, with his high cholesterol and blood pressure issues, was just as likely to have a stroke as anything else. I rubbed my eyes. I hadn't felt particularly tired, but now lying in the bed and generally not wanting to deal with any of this crap at the moment, sleep seemed like a really good idea. I had my back to Kade and I wasn't going to pretend that wasn't purposeful. It was. Even in the dark he could make me feel… raw, exposed, and not in the naked kind of way. In the he could see all the way to my soul and find it lacking sort of a deal that I couldn't say I'd ever quite experienced before.

"Goodnight, Kade." I whispered my words in case he'd already gone to sleep.

He reached out his hand placing it firmly on my back for just a second. When he pulled it away, it was as though he'd left an empty space where his hand was for just that brief moment. "Goodnight, Everly."

Sleep drifted over me. I dreamed I was on the back of a motorcycle. The loud, screeching of tires on pavement assaulted my ears. That had never been my favorite sound and after my mother left, I'd made it a point to never get on a motorcycle unless I had no other choice. I'd unfairly blamed the vehicles for my mom's departure.

Still, I held onto the driver for dear life, my head

pressed against broad shoulders covered in leather. I breathed in the smell. It was familiar and beloved.

Three cars sped up next to us, one darting in front of us so close on the highway we had to swerve to not crash into the back. I screamed out my alarm even as the driver of the motorcycle stayed silent. A bullet whizzed by my head, and I cried out again. Still, the driver didn't respond or act like he noticed at all.

What was happening? The car next to us, a black SUV, slowed down enough that I could see the person holding the gun clearly as though neither of us tore through a three-lane highway at high speeds. With my heart plummeting into my stomach, I recognized his face. I knew it as well as I would ever know any, it was my father.

He fired.

I sat up in the bed, my heart in my throat. I couldn't breathe. No, I had no air. Couldn't breathe. Couldn't. I held onto my head. My heart pounded in my head. Surely, I must be breathing. I'd be dead. Was I dead? Was I…

"Hey," strong arms came around me, "Everly? Are you okay?"

It was Kade. I knew that voice. But I couldn't think. Couldn't breathe. And then suddenly I could. But it wasn't a normal breath. No, it exploded out of me. A sob wracked my body. Tears flowed out of my eyes, and I shook. I couldn't stop. I wanted to, but I wanted to breathe. I had to cry. It was all I could do.

"Everly?" He tugged me against his bare chest. I couldn't stop my shakes. "Bad dream? Something else going on?"

"S-sorry." I managed to get that out. I would have pulled back from soaking his chest if he'd have let me. When I tried, he didn't let me go.

He stroked my hair. "Must have been a hell of a dream."

"My father shot me." I managed to get that much out before another round of sobs overtook me. Kade didn't say anything, made no moves to stop me. If this freaked him out or annoyed him, he didn't show it. Instead, he stayed silent, seeming okay with waiting until I calmed down.

It wasn't a short process. I didn't know how much time passed, but it was the longest I could ever remember crying before. I was clearly not okay, that much registered in the disaster that was my brain. I'd been muddling through this, making myself be fine, not focusing on just how fucked up it was that my father murdered my mother. I'd hated her my whole life, blamed her, resented her, been absolutely horrified that a woman could leave her only child and never return. Instead, she'd been dead.

If there was an afterlife, and some days I had my doubts, did she hate me for it?

My eyes burned, and I wasn't sure I so much stopped crying as I used all the liquid in my body. I had no more tears left to shed.

He took my head in his hands. In the darkness, I could barely make out his strong features. He hadn't put on any lights, and for that I was grateful. The glare might have killed me right then.

"If it means anything, and I don't know if it will, your father didn't kill her himself. He paid someone to do it. He hasn't held a gun in his hand, ever. We all had to do it in training but that wasn't protocol during his training."

That didn't help. "Hiring someone to do it only makes him cowardly and evil. It doesn't lessen the stench."

"There is no evil." I didn't know if I agreed with that, but he kept talking, and I didn't argue. "There is justice. There is redemption. There is revenge. You can have all of those things. We can make him pay. We can make him hurt if that's what you want. Stay with us long enough to get what we need, and we can bring him down."

I didn't necessarily want that either. "Then I'll be all alone. Maybe that's selfish. What is the matter with me?"

"If you're fucked up then you fit in perfectly with the rest of us in this life. And nothing has to be solved at three in the morning. Come on lie down."

He sort of helped me, sort of moved me until I lay back down. I reached out to touch his chest. "I got you all wet."

"The good news is that I dry." Kade covered us both in the warm covers just as the too loud air conditioning blew through the room again.

"Did I disturb your two hours?"

He covered me up with the blanket. "Don't worry about that either. Sleep. No more dreams. Just sleep."

I didn't think I would, but I must have almost instantly. Sobbing myself dry took a lot out of me. I didn't think I dreamed anything else the rest of the night.

I woke up, knowing it had been a long time since I moved. I wasn't a roller in my sleep but this time I was stiff. I'd slept too long and my body punished me for it. It was hard to open my eyes. They were glued shut. My head pounded. Yes, I officially had a crying hangover.

I couldn't move, which took me a long time to figure out, much longer than it should have, which just showed how tired my brain still was. Kade had a strong arm around my waist, essentially pinning me to the bed. I blinked, which hurt, but I had to clear my vision. I faced him. His eyes were closed in sleep. He looked almost... peaceful. But his grip on me was strong, and I wasn't going to have an easy exit without disturbing him.

He was actually asleep. Had he not gone to bed until

recently? He'd explained that he always got up to do things. How was he still here? The room remained pitch black thanks to the lack of outside light in the mausoleum. What time was it?

The clock on his bedside table said it was almost eleven. My stomach growled, hunger catching up to what my brain had already registered. I had to pee, too, which meant I was going to have to get out of the bed.

I scrunched, sort of shifting my weight, and Kade made a sigh in his throat, a second before his eyes fluttered open. Recognition hit him all at once, and he lifted the hand pinning me from my waist to the top of my head. He briefly cupped it before he stretched, letting go of me altogether.

I took that chance to rush from the bed. His bathroom was clean; everything looked orderly, and straightened. Quickly, I relieved myself, making use of the sink to splash cold water on my puffy face. I couldn't seem to feel anything at all inside. It was as though my meltdown robbed me of any emotions. I was sure they'd come back. Just hopefully not when Kade was there to witness it.

I'd definitely not earned any points in his book.

He'd probably cataloged how to use this against me at some point.

Kade had gotten out of the bed. His defined abs once again on display thanks to his being shirtless. He turned to look at me. "Hey."

"Hey." There didn't seem to be any point in making conversation. "Sorry about last night."

He shrugged. "It happens."

With that, he moved around me, entering the bathroom. I took that chance to escape the room. Getting dressed seemed to be all I could concentrate on. One task at a time, and putting on undies counted as a task. Every little thing had to be thought about, as though I couldn't autopilot anything at all.

By the time I reached the kitchen, Kade was already there. The smell of coffee was the best aroma ever, and I practically moaned when I entered the room.

He held out a water bottle to me. "This first. Then that, for today."

I could have punched him. "I need the caffeine."

"You need the water. You want the coffee. I get that. Drink the water first unless you want to add dehydration symptoms to today's agenda. You might even already have some."

I hated know-it-alls. Still, he wasn't wrong, and I wasn't stupid. Or at least I wasn't totally that way. I took long pulls from the water. He was right. The taste of the life sustaining liquid was the best thing ever. I closed my eyes, and before long, I'd finished the whole bottle. I set it down.

Kade stared at me, one eyebrow raised. "I just got a little hard watching you do that."

I picked up the cup of coffee from the counter. "That so?"

"Yes. But I'm going to ignore it, because despite my fascination with your sucking abilities, you look like death worn over. You need food. I'm going to make some eggs."

I sat down at the table. I could always count on Kade being Kade. That much I knew, and I hadn't been acquainted with him that long. That thought was jarring. It felt like I'd known the Letters a long time. Yet, it had only been a… week? Maybe longer. I'd lost track of time.

"I wouldn't say no to eggs."

"Good. Then I won't have to force you to eat them."

He was so charming in the morning. Almost afternoon. Whatever. All the time. I rolled my eyes. We were back to normal.

▭

I ENDED up following him into the main room. The computer algorithm continued on the display. It seemed that no one had been found since Henry, and I was pretty sure we wouldn't find any of the other leaders. Who would be so stupid as to show themselves now?

Kade picked up his tablet and handed it to me. "Derrick wants to talk to you."

"To me?" I stared down at the screen. Sure enough, D had texted K and wanted to text with me. Kade typed on his keyboard, ignoring my question.

Hello? I sent to Derrick not knowing if I'd get a response. He'd reached out to Kade two hours earlier and might not be right there.

Everly? The response came back.

It's me. I answered him. *How are you?*

I didn't want to think about him taking out Henry in the casino, but the image flooded my mind regardless. I wasn't afraid of Derrick. Or maybe I wasn't because he wasn't actually with me that second. It was just something I had to catalog in my little internal folders that made up my brain. Derrick was capable of raising a gun and ending a life. Of course, this wasn't news to me. He'd killed on the beach with a baseball bat. That had been heated, he'd been saving my life. I guessed maybe this was different because it had felt so cold, so calculated. There was no heat in it. The silence on the camera had made it feel very bam you're dead.

I'm fine. Just wanted to tell you that I won't be coming to Kade's place to see you, but I will catch up with you on your next stop, whenever you go to Judson. You're safe with Kade and I want to take care of some things.

Oh. Okay. Thanks for letting me know. I wasn't sure exactly what I was supposed to say to Derrick. I'll miss you didn't seem exactly right. I missed Trace, I missed Warden and damn my fucked up heart for feeling that way. I didn't know Derrick that well yet. The sad truth was between the sex and his unexpected kindness in the middle of the night I'd probably miss grumpy Kade too when this was over.

I was apparently able to have feelings for three men at the same time, even though none of them were particularly relationship worthy.

Yep. Talk soon.

I set down the tablet. Kade didn't turn. "Come stand next to me. I want you to look just like you do. I'd rather avoid taking you to New York City. Some of my euphoria from yesterday has worn off. Much as I love Manhattan, and I'd love to dress you up and take you around, it isn't the time for it. If your dad can be motivated without me physically holding a gun to his head right now, I'd prefer it."

"You'd like to dress me up?" Why was that the part of that I focused on?

He still hadn't looked at me. "You're sexy, Everly. You know it. After yesterday you clearly know I want you. Once is not going to be enough for me. That's unfortunate, but it is what it is. Yes, I'd like to dress you up, take you to fancy places, and fuck you in expensive hotel rooms. But I wouldn't put it past the Alliance leadership—the remaining four—to be looking just for that right now. We have to outthink them. I woke up with clarity. I'll give that credit to you. Forcing me to stay in that bed with you and sleep longer than usual gave me some... ideas. Maybe I do need more sleep."

Well, if I'd convinced him that the basic human need to sleep applied to him then I supposed this wasn't wasted time. "Ah, okay. My father?"

"Stand here." He pointed next to him, and even though I hated being ordered around, I complied.

He pressed a button and a second later my father appeared on the screen. "Kade, I am going as fast as I can."

My dad looked tired; dark circles marred his face. My heart panged. I couldn't help it. I clearly had a thing for monstrous men and maybe all of that stemmed from some sort of subconscious knowing that my dad had never been a nice man. Maybe my genes predisposed me to be fine with bad people. Oh hell, I was overthinking this shit again.

Anger took over the sadness.

"Jeb." Kade spun around in his chair. There was the constant movement again. "Look how bad Everly looks. That's just a few nights with me. Want to see just how fucked up I can make her?"

237

Chapter 20

What was he doing? I wished he'd cleared this with me so I'd at least know what to say. A surge of annoyance moved through me. How did he know I wouldn't suddenly turn on him and tell my father to run or betray them? Well, probably because I'd wept like a baby on his chest after I dreamed my father shot me.

That had probably clued him in on what I was likely to do right now.

"Honey." My father's voice broke. "Are you okay? What did they do to you?"

I tried not to feel it, the sadness and love that hearing his emotion did to me. But he was still my father. We hadn't gotten to talk, and I wasn't going to get over a lifetime of feelings in a week for the man that raised me. Even with that being the truth, I needed him to get this done so the assholes who had tried to kill me could be brought down.

"Should I start at the beginning? I've been shot at, punched so hard I got concussed, left in a strange mall, and watched people die. But that is all because of The

Alliance and not these guys. Unless you want to count the fact that they kidnapped me to begin with. Of course, that is your fault. And you killed my mother. No, Dad, I'm not okay."

Kade lifted his eyebrows slightly. Maybe I hadn't done what he wanted. I didn't know. If he wanted me to follow directions, he had to fucking give me some.

"Okay." He held up his hands. "Just do what they say and they'll leave you alone. Do you hear me, Kade? Leave her alone."

Kade put his hand on my back before he tugged me, hard, against his side. "Too late. She's mine now. If you want her back, you're going to get this done within the week. Otherwise you don't find the body."

I hoped he was lying, but with Kade I never could be sure. I wouldn't put it past him to make me come and then make me vanish. Or maybe not. He was... sweet, somewhere in there where he didn't let people see.

"I'll do it. I'll get it done by the end of the week." He nodded fast. "Leave her alone, Kade. She has to be able to have a life when this is over. She has to be able to go back to something. You know what happens to the people who can't go back. They end up dead like Derrick's wife."

Kade took a long breath. "You're going to want to never bring up Alyssa again. Just get your shit done."

The screen went off. He turned to me. "Good work."

"I'm not usually in the habit of telling my father who I am fucking." I rubbed my face. "I don't suppose it matters. If he thought I was a virgin, he was deluding himself."

He sighed. "I hadn't planned on adding that to the whole thing. I just thought he'd see how tired you look and he'd know things were really bad for you. But you really went for it. Well done."

A proximity alarm sounded and Kade jumped to his

feet. "Someone is in the graveyard." The screen turned back on and Kade grabbed his mouse, turning it so the camera angles shifted until we could see who walked around.

With his head down, Judson strode toward us. He had on a black coat and dark gray pants. It was completely inappropriate for the weather—he looked more like he'd come straight from Vermont—but there was no mistaking him. Even with his head down, he looked like he belonged. Judson would always seem that way. It came somehow from both entitlement and not giving a shit.

"Son of a bitch. He couldn't call first?" I got the feeling Kade wasn't so much speaking to me as he was just talking aloud. He ran toward the front, presumably to let Judson in.

I sighed. Just when I got some sort of steady feet with these guys, it would shake up. Had something else happened, or was Judson just here to visit? I stared at the screen, the old graves in the background showing other people's lives, how they ended, a brief write up of dates and one sentence of what they'd done on the outside of the mausoleums.

It was almost like looking at a movie.

I heard the bang as Kade opened the door to our hideout and the sound of their voices reached me. I stared down at myself. It was bad enough Kade and my father saw me this way—wrecked—but now I had to live with Judson knowing I was destroyed, too.

I ran a hand through my hair. Apparently, I needed all five of them to think I was pretty. I had to pull it together. Whatever was going on had nothing to do with me.

The movement on the screen caught my attention. Judson wasn't the only one there, someone followed him. A big, tall man with broad shoulders and a visible shotgun he didn't hide carried in his arms.

"Oh fuck." I ran out of the room. Neither Kade nor Judson knew he was there. I tore down the hall. "Gun. Gun. Gun."

Both men, standing by the door, had no idea the gunman was coming. "Man with a gun."

I don't know what I thought to do, but I rushed past them out the door, charging toward the man with the shotgun.

Kade grabbed my arm, yanking me back as he slammed the door in front of me. "Did you fucking not look behind you?"

He wasn't yelling at me but at Judson. The other man's eyes were huge. He shook his head. "He must have been on me since Montana."

"Fuck. We're made. I have to blow this place. Everly, do you remember where to run?"

I did. We hadn't been here long enough for me to forget. I grabbed Judson's arm, dragging him with me. "This way."

He didn't move. "We're not moving."

He pulled a gun that he'd apparently hidden beneath his inappropriate coat. "You're armed."

"We're all armed all the time."

Now, I knew that wasn't true. "No you're all not."

"Well, I am."

A shot rang out, banging into the door. I turned to Kade. "How long will that stay bulletproof?"

"Against that level shotgun? Not forever."

I grabbed on Judson again. "Listen to me. I get it. You have a big dick. You're willing to prove that by shooting the guy on the other side of the door right now. But are you really going to put yourself up against a trained killer just to prove you can? Maybe if you caught him by surprise or came up behind him. This man fearlessly walked here knowing that at least the two of you were here. He's not afraid of you. Let's go. Come on."

"Do it." Kade nodded. "I am, at least. If you want to stay here and die, you can go ahead, brother. We'll miss you. I, for one, am not being a jackass. I have to blow this place. I don't want them getting the intel." He ran past me. "Everly get the fuck out of here. Judson is a big boy. He can decide what he wants to do."

I paused for one more second, silently willing Judson to come along. I didn't know what Kade meant by blowing the place, but given that he'd constructed this in the first place, I was pretty sure he actually meant blowing it up.

"Come on." I held out my hand. "Don't make me do this alone."

Judson tilted his head for a second before nodding once. He put his hand on my back. "I remember how to go. He drills everyone on the escape plan." Judson urged me forward even as he shoved the gun back into his belt, hidden away from view. "Now it doesn't seem so outlandish."

"Kade plans for everything. He's amazing."

Judson shot me a look I couldn't understand as we ran down the tunnel that Kade had taken me down the first day here. I was going to lose even more clothes. It was a stupid thought but all I could focus on as I charged forward. I was glad I'd gotten dressed and not stayed in pajamas.

A boom sounded behind us, and I whirled around. "Kade?"

"He's fine. I can guarantee he didn't blow anything with himself still in there. He's not that altruistic. Trust me.

We all have plans, and self-sacrifice isn't on the list of things to do."

That was interesting. "The Alliance doesn't inspire that kind of action?"

"Not from us," Kade rushed toward us. "I'm not committing suicide in the name of the cause. Move."

I pushed myself back against the wall as he practically ran me over to press on a button that opened a lid. I glanced upward as the sounds of the outside hit me.

"It's like we're going up a sewer drain." I felt stupid as soon as I'd said it, but this whole thing was just so bizarre I wasn't sure I could have been more articulate.

They both ignored me. Or maybe there was just no response to that statement either of them could make. Kade climbed the ladder. "Going first to check that it's safe."

I nodded. "Thank you."

"Yep." He disappeared upward.

I turned toward Judson. "So what brought you to this neck of the woods today?"

He grinned. "I wanted to check on Kade. He'd been remarkably uncommunicative. Of course, now I know why. Trace, Warden, Kade, and Derrick are all in knots over you. How are you doing that?"

It was more like the other way around. I was a mess over all of them. But this was Judson and I couldn't help but play with him a little bit, even given the situation, which didn't call for levity. "I don't know. You're the one who likes to tie things up, Doctor. How am I managing to do it?"

He lifted his brow. "Maybe you'll find out. Going to move through all of us?"

"Are you willing to share?"

Kade poked his head down. "All clear. Come on. Hurry up."

I had meant my jab back at Judson to be easygoing, but now that I'd said it, I wanted to know. Was he willing to share? The others hadn't seemed to care, each of them knowing someone would come before or after. How did that work for Judson and what he told me were his sexual preferences? Once he tied up a woman was she his and his alone?

I climbed the ladder, finding myself on the side of the road next to Kade. Judson was fast after us and Kade quickly shut the lid that did in fact look like a sewer covering. We stood, the three of us together, exposed on the street. Would there ever come a time when I didn't feel like I was being watched? Now that I thought about satellites and surveillance it was as though being outside meant being tracked.

"I have the plane."

Kade nodded. "Good. Take her somewhere."

Hold on. I grabbed his arm as though I could stop him from leaving, even though he'd made no moves to do so. "Where are you going?"

"I have to set up a location for us elsewhere. We can't be without a base."

"Do you just have a bunch of mausoleums sitting around waiting for use?"

He smiled slowly. "Not mausoleums, no. But other places. This was my favorite." He cupped the side of my face. "Don't worry. I land on my feet, and I'm good at blowing things up. It was my special skill in The Alliance. It was what they decided I should be doing for them. I'll find you again. You can count on it. In the meantime, Judson won't let anything happen to you. Despite his being an idiot today, he's actually rather good at staying alive."

"I know better than to let this happen." Judson looked away. "I've had things on my mind, and I made an error in judgment."

Kade shrugged. "No worries. Just lost years of work building that thing. Just means I get to do it again. I like projects. Take our prisoner somewhere safe. We still need her father. But I call dibs on killing him." He stared at me for a second. "That is if she doesn't kill him herself."

Me kill my father? I snorted. "You've got the wrong impression here. I'm more likely to just ignore him for the rest of my life."

He stepped back. "We'll see."

Judson took out his phone. "It's a burner. I'm calling the pilot. I'll tell him to get the plane ready to go again."

"That's good. Get her someplace else." Kade pointed at me. "Do I need to get rude to you? Isn't that how Trace and Warden left you? With mean words."

I shook my head. "Always have to do the opposite of everyone else."

He winked at me. "Be good. I'll see if I can continue to hustle your father along. Then you can be done with all of us."

Judson nodded with his head. "Let's go. A car is going to get us a mile down the road."

Kade took off running in the opposite direction just as a warm rain drizzled down on us. I hurried to catch up with Judson. He was the prettiest of all the guys, but I wouldn't have called him effeminate, not even when I first met him. Now, slightly dirtied from our climb, he looked the most disheveled I'd ever seen him.

"You didn't have to take me," I called out to him. "I could have stayed with Kade."

"I think you might have blown up Kade's life even more than the explosion did." He turned around. "I didn't know we were all so desperate for affection. Maybe I should have invested in weekly meetings with escorts for all of us." He held up his hand. "I don't mean prostitute. Don't get yourself all worked up. Just a female to talk to. We've clearly all been alone too long."

It wasn't lost on me that his mind had gone so quickly to prostitute when mine hadn't done that. I kept my face serene. If there was one thing I'd learned about all of them, and Judson wasn't proving to be any different, they had layers on top of their layers to sludge through to find the men underneath.

The question was did I feel like doing it again? I didn't know. I guessed I'd find out. "So where are we going?"

"I'm still trying to decide that. I have until we board the plane to tell the pilot. Anywhere you want to go?"

He couldn't be serious. "We're on the run, right? I mean there are satellites bearing down on us right now that will find us and then The Alliance will send men to kill us. Where do I want to go? Where do you go to hide?"

"Truth is, I don't hide. Not well, anyway. I can't maintain it for very long. First off, I have a practice to run. Unlike Warden and Kade, I can't just vanish and continue on remotely. I have to actually see my patients."

That made sense. "Trace must have to teach and show up for work, too."

"Right. But he has these so-called research trips he can go on that allow him to disappear. Again, I can't really disappear. That being said, I also hate it. I don't like running."

Yes, he'd stood there like he was going to kill the man after him as though it was no big deal. "What do you propose we do then? Go stand in the middle of somewhere busy and start shouting we're here come and get us?"

"That's stupid. I'm also not that. No, but I think there

has to be something I can do to be useful. I was trying to be that for Kade. I thought he might need help. I didn't realize he was… distracted."

I shook my head. "I didn't ask for this. You understand that, right? Whatever you think you know about what has gone on with me and the others, it wasn't exactly my choice. You all took that from me. If I've made the best out of it, then so be it. I'm not going to apologize or take your judgment. Go ahead and choke on, Doctor."

He laughed, a surprising sound. "Not one person in a million would speak to me like that. Not even my own mother spoke to me with that sarcasm. My sister, when she was alive, everyone spoke to me with deference. Pretty much since I came out of the womb."

"Then you're overdue." A car pulled up ahead and the driver must have spotted us because he came to where we were. Judson opened the door, and I climbed inside. He followed me, telling the driver to take us the airport.

It had been so long since I spoke that I almost forgot what I'd last said when he answered me. "I suppose that you're right. Go ahead. Keep verbally assaulting me. It's kind of hot."

I rolled my eyes. "You don't think I'm hot. That's not how you would think, anyway."

"Think that you know me?"

That was a good question. "I'm finding that I'm an excellent judge of character and the longer this goes on, the better I'm getting at it."

He looked out the window. "I think you're very pretty if that means anything to you. I don't, however, care very much if someone is attractive or they're not. I'm much more interested in what makes a person tick on the inside. That's where… sexual desire comes from for me. That spark on the inside. I know where we're going."

His abrupt change of subject caught me by surprise. Judson jumped from one thing to another. I was still stuck on the 'he found what was inside attractive not on the outside.' In fact, I loved it.

"Where are we going?"

He crossed his arms over his chest and leaned back, his head against the headrest. Judson closed his eyes like I hadn't asked the question. It took me a second to realize he was really not going to answer my question.

I stared out my own window. Every time I changed which one I was with I had to get used to being treated like I didn't have choices again. But maybe I never did. Maybe I'd simply adjusted to the cage that was Kade like I'd done with Warden and Trace. I had to figure out how to ignore the bars that were Judson now.

Or maybe I wouldn't get used to it.

I closed my eyes. We couldn't be terribly far from his private airport, but if he could pretend to be asleep, so could I.

We stayed in silence the rest of the way and all the way through takeoff. He must have communicated where we were going with the pilot or maybe these Alliance lunatics could speak telepathically. I rolled my eyes at my own joke. He'd probably texted him when I'd closed my eyes to feign sleep.

This wasn't the plane I'd been on with Trace. No, this one looked like it belonged solely to Judson. It had the initials JS all over the place, even engraved on the handles of the chairs. I'd never actually seen anything so ostentatious before. It made me smile. If Judson was the kind of person who could be teased—and I didn't know if he was —I'd do so right now.

He tapped on his phone, and I chewed on my lips,

wondering if I should just keep quiet. "What kind of doctor are you?"

That seemed a pretty good topic to broach. He didn't look up from his phone. "I'm a plastic surgeon."

I hadn't expected that. I didn't know what I'd been thinking, but it hadn't been that. Maybe I watched too much television. I kept picturing him in blue scrubs as he ordered people around operating rooms to save their lives in trauma or something.

Of course, a plastic surgeon had improved my life. Without him, I'd be horribly scarred on my face. They did tremendous good. They just weren't that red headed actor running around *Grey's Anatomy*. Yeah, I might have had a thing for him. I sighed. My mind was going in all kinds of directions.

"Did you always want to be a doctor?"

He lifted his gaze before he answered. "Are you making conversation for the sake of filling silence?"

"I'm talking because I'm interested. I'm not going to stay in silence with you for the next however long we're together. I'm a talker. If you don't like it, drop me with one of the others."

He rubbed his chin. "I wanted to be a doctor, yes. It was also what The Alliance thought I'd be best at. My family has a history of working in medical care. We're good at it. That being said, my grandfather was an oil baron so we have a history in that, too. I didn't know which way I was going to get shoved. But the cost benefit analysis placed this as my top usefulness. That's what I'm doing."

I opened and closed my mouth. "You're talking about yourself like you're a commodity."

"That's what I am. In your own way, that's what you are, too. Sure, you're left alone. You're female. You can't be in The Alliance. Fine. But I would bet money that even before you knew about us, you would have ended up married to an Alliance man. You'd never have known it but that's what would have happened."

I shook my head. "I have always managed my own personal life. My father had nothing to do with it."

"For now. Five years from now you'd suddenly have met someone. Alliance loves to marry Alliance."

He'd officially made my temper rise. "I was never going to be a pawn."

"Eighty-twenty you were." He stretched out his legs. "Play denial if you want. It's a dangerous game."

"Like your sister was a pawn?" I shifted in my seat. "Only she knew what she was doing when she married Derrick even though she shouldn't have."

He leaned on the side of his chair, his gaze hardening instantly. "They've been talking to you about Alyssa."

"That's what happened right?" I wasn't going to be intimidated. "That's how she got to continue. Marry Derrick, Alliance. And maybe get to continue on engraved airplanes living the life she was born to. Only it got her killed. So let's not make this out like it's all hunky dory. That's not how this works. Every second of it sucks. Go ahead and live this life. It's not like you had any choice right? You're all victims in your upper level echelon of privilege and leadership?"

He cleared his throat. "Whatever you think that you know from watching the outer tier of this circle you've only recently become aware of, don't fool yourself into thinking you understand. You don't. You never will. Yes, it got my sister killed. She didn't know when to keep her mouth shut. Make sure you don't make the same mistakes. She mattered, and they killed her. You don't."

Ouch. I'd walked right into that one.

Chapter 21

I must have dozed off, because I woke up as we were landing in Boston. I'd never been there, but as per usual lately, I was being taken all kinds of places I'd never seen before. Although I doubted I'd get much touring time wherever we were ultimately heading. Not to mention, I once again didn't have the right clothes. Hot. Cold. Hot. Cold. Blow up clothing, leave them in Vermont, abandon them in Florida…

I once again had nothing to wear. A cold wind blew at me the second the main cabin door opened, and I shivered. Judson must have noticed because he took off his coat and handed it to me.

"You'll be cold."

"Less than you will. I was in Vermont this morning. I'm dressed for this weather. You're not. We'll need to amend that."

I'd just been thinking the same thing myself. "I keep having to get new clothes."

"Some people would love that." He put his hand on

my lower back, escorting me off the plane. The cold air hit me hard, and I ducked my head further into J's too-big-on-me coat. It smelled like whatever cologne he wore. It was a dark but pleasant smell and not one I knew, meaning that it wasn't in any magazines or department stores I'd been in.

After I got to the bottom of the stairs, Judson charged up a little bit until he was slightly in front of me. He took my hand in his gloved ones for a second before he let go and handed me the gloves. I raised my voice to speak to him over the noise on the runway. "I can't take your gloves and your coat."

"You can and you will." He didn't look at me when he spoke, and I took the gloves out of his hand. There was something about the way he'd given me that order that made me want to do what he said. It was different than Kade, who I might have tried to openly defy just for the sake of argument. I didn't mind pushing at Judson if he was wrong, but there was something in his manner that simply made it easier to comply. It was actually… a relief.

A car waited around the corner from the private runway, and we got into it. "You haven't told me where we were going."

He nodded. "We're going to my home. I have one in Boston. It makes it easier to get to the lodge in Vermont."

"The lodge? Is that what you call your island home? The lodge?"

He shrugged. "Like the engraved plane my father gave me on my thirtieth birthday, he named the house in Vermont, The Lodge. All of it is ridiculous. I get that. Pretentious or whatever word you'd want to call it. I get it. But I am who I am, and I'm not going to apologize for it any more than I'd ask you to. You don't have to like it. I don't care."

If that was a reminder that rich people had feelings too then I was sufficiently chastised. What did I care what he called his house? Why was I poking at him like that? I wouldn't want him commenting on the way that I lived, or if the reverse was true, if someone was poor, I'd never mention the details of their lives in a disparaging way either.

"I apologize."

He stared at me for a long moment. "We're going to my house. We'll be safe there overnight. If your father comes through tomorrow with all the paperwork we need, then we can just go back to the house in Vermont. We're close. If he doesn't, then we'll spend tomorrow doing some things they'll never look for. After that we'll go from there. If we get attacked in my home, I'll deal with it. Despite evidence to the contrary, I am capable of defending myself —and you. I've been distracted. That's managed."

"Because you were worried about Kade." I could understand caring about someone to the point of making mistakes.

He rubbed his eyes. "Yes. Among other things. Do you like movies?"

"I… I do like movies."

He nodded once. "Great. So we'll try this differently than we did in Vermont. You're a guest in my house. Kade had wanted all the electronics out of our lives there so that you couldn't call for help. I think if you were going to do that, you've had ample opportunity at this point. I am going to treat you like I would if you just came to stay with me. We're tired tonight. It's been a long day and not the one you were expecting. We'll watch a movie and get some kind of take-out food."

"Thank you." Even as I answered him, my mind

reeled. Judson was right. He didn't seem like the kind of guy to make the mistake he'd made earlier with the assassin. He was meticulous, even down to how he'd tucked in his clothing.

He was right. I hadn't had the kind of day I'd been expecting. He hadn't liked how Kade—their resident tech genius— had stopped communicating. He'd indicated to me that he'd spoken to Trace and Warden and found their behavior off.

"Did you do it on purpose?" I lifted my lids and held his eye contact, which was hard. There was something about the intensity of his gaze that made me want to drop my eyes. Still, I swallowed through the instinct and didn't do it.

He pushed a button and the partition between us and the driver went up. Maybe the man wasn't Alliance. Or maybe he wasn't Alliance enough. As he'd reminded me on the plane, I didn't know much. Not when it came down to it.

"You're very smart."

A shiver moved through me. He didn't make that sound like a compliment. "Is this where you kill me for being too smart?"

He shook his head slowly. "This is where you have my attention. How did I give myself away?"

"It wasn't one thing. It was everything. And you may have mentioned that you screwed up a lot."

He drummed his finger on the side of the car. "Not one person in a million could have read me that way. But then again, you managed to pretend you didn't speak sign language the whole time you were at my lodge, and you can do that, too. You're actually better at this than your father was. Yes, I knew the assassin was there. I didn't bring him. I used the opportunity. I expected to kill him. Then we'd be down one assassin after us, and I'd have convinced Kade to give you to me for your own safety and get back to work. I didn't expect him to blow up the place and go even deeper underground. However, I should know by now that Kade doesn't respond exactly like I anticipate most of the time."

I didn't know if I should feel better that I'd figured him out or be alarmed that he was so manipulative. Then again, this was a game of the world they played. Trace moved people around like chess pieces to get to Mars on his timetable. Warden could empty bank accounts by getting people to invest badly. Kade used satellites like toys. Judson faked scenarios where people could be killed to get me away from Kade and with him.

"Is this a usual thing for you, Doctor? Or am I just so dangerous you can't let your friends play with me anymore?"

His smile was slow. "When I figure that out, I'll let you know."

"Maybe you'll never figure me out." Even as I said that, I knew it wasn't true. He would. This man, who'd once told me he liked to tie up women for sex but now added that he only found what was on the inside sexy, would probably know me in half a second. I wasn't nearly as interesting as I pretended to be.

I was just a girl in over her head who'd finally figured some things out.

He didn't answer, and I didn't know if that was a good thing or a bad thing. I'd have to wait and see. With Judson, I'd bet that was the case more than it wasn't.

HIS HOME TURNED out to be on something called Marl-borough Street. If this was just one of his homes, I wondered what the others outside of The Lodge looked like. I almost asked him if this one had a name, but we'd come to a sort of truce since I'd called him out on his lie earlier. I didn't want to screw that up. The street seemed full of Brownstones, and Judson's was no different.

He gave me a thorough tour. J had different homes, but if he took as much interest in the details of all of them as he did with this one, then he must be constantly preoccupied with real estate and construction. The house was just over six thousand square feet. I'd never have known that on my own except that he told me on the tour. It had an elevator. I'd never been in a house with one before, but Judson said it was a good investment for getting older.

I stared at him until he rolled his eyes at me. "Yes, I plan to get older."

We took the elevator upward to the roof where I quickly wished I had my coat again. I had to admit, the view was gorgeous and the decks—two of them—really beautiful. I smiled at him. "The elevator doesn't go all the way up. There are four steps to get up here. You'll have to give up going up here when you're old. Unless you can install one of those lifts on the railing to go up four steps."

"Oh, I won't be here when I'm old. I'll sell it before then."

He was so all over the place on this subject. "Where will you be?"

"I like the house in Aspen. I think it would be great to wake up every morning there. But that'll have to be after I close the practice and after we get this Alliance stuff worked out. That may put a big hold in my plans. I may have to be more readily available toward the end of my life than I planned on being."

I supposed that made sense. In the meantime, with all of his money, he had incredible houses. Or I guessed he did. The two he had were pretty exceptional. Of course, he'd inherited the one in Vermont when his parents died.

The thought reminded me of something I'd said earlier. "I'm sorry that I brought up Alyssa. I didn't know her. I shouldn't be talking out of turn."

He nodded once. "Come on. I'll show you the rest of the place."

I guessed that was all the acknowledgement of my apology I was going to get. Had he accepted it? I wasn't sure. Judson did get focused and stay on a topic. I liked it. I bet I could learn a lot if he started to talk about something I didn't know about. Like say… getting tied up during sex, which he had indicated once was his preference. What did that mean exactly? How did he tie the person up? I wasn't going to ask that.

We were definitely not there in this part of our relationship.

The house faced south, that seemed to matter to him, and as we walked from room to room he showed me the small details he'd paid attention to when he'd worked with the architects to renovate the house.

"It was a mess when I got it, but that's why I got it. If it hadn't been falling apart it would have been out of my price range."

There were things out of his price range? When it came to money above a certain level I had no idea how expensive was too expensive. He owned multiple homes all around the world but this would have been too much if it hadn't been falling down? Couldn't he have sold two of the others to get it at any price? Or did he not want it that badly?

I didn't know anything about that or what I could ask

Judson and what I couldn't ask him. This probably fell in the do not discuss zone. Although he'd brought it up in the past. I tuned back into listening to his house description. I just hadn't cared about anything in my life as much as he did about this house.

Six bedrooms. Four bathrooms, all of them en-suite. A family floor and room for an au pair. "Are you thinking someday you'd like to have children?"

He nodded before he continued. "I'd like to have kids. If I could figure out the right woman to do that with and how to make sure things were solid and not as fucked up as they are now. Yes, eventually I'd like to have them. I guess I'd better get moving on that. I'm not getting any younger."

"Men can have babies for a long time. It's women who have to watch their fertility, and these days that's less than they used to. But then I don't have to tell that to you. You're the doctor."

He shook his head. "I'd like to be young enough to play with them. I don't want to be a dad who can't keep up with them."

"My dad wasn't a play with you dad. He was more like a watch you from a distance sort of dad."

"That was my father, too." He rocked back on his feet. "I'm really going on about this house, aren't I?"

Manners dictated I tell him he wasn't, but my good breeding had fled out the window a long time ago with the pseudo-kidnapping that I had going on. "You clearly care about it a lot."

He smiled. "I do. Come on. You have to be hungry."

I wasn't, actually. "Speaking of keeping up with people. What I really want to do is run. I need to clear my head, to move my body. I'll probably be hungry after that. Is there any way I can do that?"

"I have a gym here, but maybe what I'm hearing you say is that you want to run outside?"

He had read me correctly. "I'd like to in a way that doesn't equate running for my life. I'd like to go for a jog where no one is chasing me. I don't have the right clothes so I suppose that's not possible."

Feeling deflated, I let out a long sigh. "I took for granted being able to change into appropriate outfits whenever I wanted to in order to do whatever activity I was going to do at that moment. I didn't realize that was going to go away."

The doorbell rang, and he grinned. "Well, I may just be able to make that come true."

Judson rushed past me and then down the stairs. I took off after him. What did he mean? Standing at the door was a man with packages. Judson handed him a tip then took the packages from him. "I got you clothes."

My mouth fell open. "You did?"

"I did. I texted Marco in Vermont and had him tell me your sizes, and then I ordered them and had them delivered."

My mind had to keep up with what was happening here. "When did you do this?"

"In the car. Anything can be delivered here."

I walked toward him, leaning in to give him a side hug. "Thank you. Although it's risky. You don't want people coming here. You need to be safe."

"Everly, I'm fine. You've caught me in my deceit. I knew the dude was there. I let him come. No one is getting near here that I don't want here, end of story. Get changed. We'll go for a run together. I'll see if I can keep up with you."

I took the packages from him, pulling back from the side hug that had gone on longer than I'd planned. I hoped that hadn't gotten weird. He didn't seem to have reacted, but I wasn't sure I'd ever be able to truly read Judson. He was too… guarded. Although, he'd clearly gotten happy that he'd been able to surprise me with clothes.

"Where should I stay?" I needed to know so I could change my clothes.

He pointed upward. "My bedroom is the biggest. Take any of the others that you'd like."

"Thanks."

Since there were five others to choose from, I didn't think that was going to be a problem. I ended up taking the one closest to the stairs. I'd debated it for a minute or two and decided I liked the access to get out as fast as I could should I need to. That was a double-edged sword because it also meant that if someone invaded the house, they'd get to me quickly. Ultimately, I'd sided with escape. How had this become my life?

I changed into running clothes. My brand new sneakers were tight on my feet, but they'd loosen up after one run. I probably wouldn't have picked bright pink ones but that was fine. I was just glad to have them. Judson had thought about just about everything, including toiletries, and I quickly put my stuff away.

When I got downstairs, he waited by the front door. "Thank you for all that stuff."

"Sure. It's a nice jog around here. With the weather cold and the sun down, there won't be too many people on the sidewalks. The houses will be lit up from the inside. Lots of red brick. Want to go?"

I nodded. That sounded like heaven.

Judson was a good person to jog with. He paced with me very well and then after a minute or two, increased it, which made me work harder to keep up with him but not too fast to make it impossible. He wasn't chatty and that was fine, too. I worked on concentrating on my breathing. There was a huge physical difference for me between running outside and doing it on the treadmill. I could already feel it in my joints. I was going to ache harder when I was done with this, and I wasn't sure that was a bad thing. I needed to be stronger, physically, emotionally, and mentally. I didn't know what was coming exactly, but I could tell that much.

Or maybe nothing was going to happen. Maybe getting taken was the extent of my drama. I'd never forget it, and I'd go back to my ordinary life.

I didn't know how long we ran, but it was longer than I usually did before we rounded a corner and I realized that Judson had led us back to his house. At the foot of his Brownstone, I grabbed my knees and tried to catch my breath. All right, maybe I wasn't such an awesome runner after all. I might have overdone it trying to show off, a little.

Judson put a hand on my back. "You're really good. Let's run together every day."

"Sure." It might kill me. But here I was again trying to prove something. What was it about Judson that just made me want him to think highly of me? I shook my head. I had to pull it together. "Now, I'm hungry."

He grinned slowly. "Me too."

We ended up eating sandwiches from his favorite place. They delivered. I ate ham and cheese while he tried to decide what to watch on television. Eventually, he handed me the remote. I stared at it like it was a foreign object.

"Don't guys not do that? Don't you all want to own the television remote?"

He rolled his eyes and took a bite of his turkey. "That never made any sense to me. Why hog the remote? Unless you want to be alone, in which case just watch television by yourself. I can't settle on something. You pick."

I could have been really evil and picked something only I liked to watch. I had a real thing for watching QVC, particularly when they were selling creepy looking dolls. No one else ever wanted to watch with me, but I wasn't going to do that to Judson right when he was being reasonable. We could go back to screaming at each other another time. My endorphins pumped pretty high after the run, and he actually seemed mellower.

I settled on a cooking show. The host was in a small town in China, learning how to cook a local delicacy. I loved to watch other people make meals I knew I'd never attempt. Judson crossed his feet in front of him on the coffee table, which gave me permission to do the same. It had shocked me we weren't eating in the dining room, but this was J being informal tonight. Again, maybe it was the run.

He got up and crossed the room, keeping his eye on the television. A second later he poured what looked like whisky into two glasses and brought one over to me. Okay, I could really like this version of Judson. With a plop down on the couch, he sat back next to me.

The whisky burned down my throat but it was a sensation I loved. It reminded me that whisky wasn't just any drink. It was to be consumed slowly.

"I love that you picked a cooking show. I could watch them all night."

A memory dawned on me. Back in Vermont he'd been the most interested in the taste of dinner. Yes, Judson was a foodie. "We have that in common. I do love to eat. That's why I have to run."

"I think I know what we're going to be doing for our time together."

I raised my eyebrows. "Running and eating?"

"And watching other people cook on television."

I clinked my glass against his. "Sounds like a plan."

His easy smile warmed me as much as the whisky. "A little break before I have to start ordering people killed." He took another sip.

And my good mood plummeted. I choked on the sip of whisky I'd taken and set it down. "Wow. Okay."

I shouldn't have been shocked. Kade had done that right in front of me. Derrick did the deed. It was just that had seemed like a distant, far away moment that had gone away when the mausoleum blew up. Nothing had changed. Judson could kill someone or order them killed, too.

"Little too much honesty?" He lifted his lids in what was clearly a frank assessment of my reaction.

"Sometimes I forget. In these small moments with you guys, you become just people to me. Interesting men that I could... like." Or love in the case of Trace, Warden, and Kade. I wasn't going to say that to Judson. That was too far. "And then I remember when you guys say or do something or someone tries to kill us, that while you are those things you're also these people secretly running things who battle against other people who have little regard for human life. And maybe you guys don't have much of it either. But then my mind turns again. You're a doctor. You must care about people."

He shook his head. "I don't. Not particularly. I said that to shock you, to see what you'd do. Thanks for your honesty. I value that. We can act like ordinary guys because we pretend to be ninety percent of the time. But I think you probably know about pretending. I think you probably fake quite a lot in your life. You're much more than you seem, Everly. Don't let it get you killed." He took another sip. "Not by me. Don't worry about that. You're safe with me."

I hoped that was true, but as I'd already determined, Judson was a liar. The question had to be though, was he telling the truth right now?

Chapter 22

I must not have been too scared, because I conked out right there on the sofa next to him, not waking until the program changed to late night cooking. I used to study with it on. The voice grated on me, and it would keep me awake when I had to study past my bedtime. I rubbed my eyes. I'd been right to use it for that, considering it had just woken me up. I glanced over at Judson.

He was asleep, his head leaning back and to the left on the couch. I wouldn't have thought it was possible, but in sleep he was actually even more beautiful than when he was awake. And J was a very attractive man. I wanted to reach out and run a hand down his face, feeling his skin, the slight growth of whiskers and his breath on my fingertips. Of course, I wasn't going to do that. Out of all of them, Judson made me feel the most kidnapped.

I looked toward the front door. I could walk right out. He probably wouldn't even wake up. But I wasn't going to, and I knew it. My father was in New York; release would come soon. If I ran, I'd never know how this panned out, and I'd always be looking over my shoulder. If these five were going to be the secret overlords of the universe then I wanted them to like me, or at least remember me fondly.

Not to mention I was full on head over heels for four of them. Yes, I included Derrick in that list. I shut off the television, and Judson jerked awake. It was funny how lack of noise could be as effective at waking someone as a loud one could be. When the power went out in the middle of the night in my apartment, turning off the usual buzzing that I was used to, it would wake me like my alarm.

"Sorry." He rubbed his eyes. "Guess I fell asleep."

"That's okay. So did I." I got off the couch. "I'm going to head upstairs."

He nodded. "Me, too."

Judson had come awake immediately, and he didn't look tired. Then again, doctors did that. They napped and they snapped to attention. Or at least they did on those doctor television shows, when they weren't having sex in the break rooms.

My mind was all over the place. Maybe I was the exhausted one. I didn't get alert immediately. He walked me to my room, stopping outside the door. "Sleep well."

"Oh I will, assuming that the sheets aren't scratchy."

He blinked. "Oh that's right. You didn't like the ones at The Lodge. I got them changed. If you ever go back, you'll like them better."

He had? "Judson, you don't have to buy sheets for the girl you kidnap. I'm lucky I'm not in the basement with a bag over my head."

J winced, and I wished I hadn't made the bad joke. "Nevertheless, I fixed it. The sheets will be soft."

"Thank you." Maybe that's what I should have said right off the bat. "Goodnight, Judson."

"Night, Everly." He didn't smile, but his voice was warm. "Let me know if you need anything at all."

I nodded. "I will."

I closed the door, leaving him in the hall. The sheets, as I would discover less than five minutes later, were soft.

———

I DIDN'T DREAM, or at least I didn't remember doing so. I'd gotten used to being held by someone, and I did miss the feel of another person in the bed. Judson, however, didn't strike me as the cuddling type. He wasn't really warm and fuzzy. Or if he started to be, the next second he wasn't.

I got out of bed sometime around mid-morning. I hadn't slept this late in a long time. Well, that wasn't true. My exhausting freak out that I'd done with Kade had made me sleep late. Maybe this was becoming a thing.

I showered and went downstairs quietly, in case Judson was sleeping in, too. Of course, the place was huge. He'd probably not hear me even if I sang at the top of my voice. I remembered my tour and found my way to the kitchen. Judson stood sipping coffee, looking up when I walked in.

"Morning. Sleep okay?"

I nodded. "Thanks. Yes, the room is great. One of the best I've ever been in anywhere."

"Good. I do want my places to be comfortable."

He poured coffee into a cup. "I received three messages before dawn this morning making sure that I made you coffee and that you had some when you first woke up. Trace was the first. He wanted to make sure I knew that coffee was pivotal for you and to make sure I had some in the house. Then Warden texted a similar message that was more like ordering me to go buy coffee since I don't always drink it. And then finally Kade sent a link to the nearest coffee shop should I need to go buy some."

I took the offering of coffee, gladly taking down a long sip. It was maybe the best coffee I'd ever had. Had he ground the beans himself? What was this magical brew I'd never tasted before? "This is amazing. Thank you."

"You're welcome. What is it about you Everly that has turned them this way? Trace doesn't send texts reminding people to have coffee. Neither does Warden or Kade. And I spent a good portion of last night worrying if you were comfortable and then leapt out of bed this morning to make sure I had coffee. What is it about you?"

I shook my head. "I don't know." It was time for some truth. "Let's be honest, shall we? Trace was nice to me and then he was a total ass right before we left each other. Warden was the same. Then Kade spent most of his time being a jerk, but lightened up at the end. If this constant emotional spinning is me somehow doing something to them, then you should see it from my end. None of this has made any sense."

He nodded once. "I'm not going to try to take you to my bed."

Well, that was quite a statement. "Okay."

Was there really anything to say in that instance? Judson was gorgeous, he was hot, he was clearly a multilay-ered person with secrets. Yes, like his friends, I could fall for him, but I was clearly a glutton for punishment. They all knew about each other and no one seemed to mind in the least that I was sleeping with multiple members of their little club.

Except apparently for Judson who was not going to sleep with me.

"Aren't you going to ask me why?"

Was he kidding? I set down the coffee. "No. I'm not, because I'm sure the answer would be insulting. You've said you find the soul attractive. If you don't find me that way, then you're essentially saying you don't like who I am as a person. There isn't enough coffee in the world to manage that. I'll say something nasty back to you. Then we'll be fighting. I'd rather figure out how to have a pleasant day with you. Even if it's all surface and I know that you don't like me."

He crossed his arms over his chest. "That's not what the answer would be. Actually, that couldn't be any further from the truth."

Clearly, he was determined to have this conversation. "Okay then. Is it worse? I mean should I ask you for a sedative before you tell me?"

His grin shocked me. "I'm not going to sleep with you, Everly, because the power differential between the two of us is so completely skewed. I'm not sure you could truly consent to the way I would have to have sex with you."

I gulped. Now, that I hadn't seen coming. He handed me back my coffee. "Because of the tying up thing."

"Because of that. We need to have a serious conversation before we have sex, I need to educate you about what I want. And you need to say yes. We need a safe word. And I'm not at all convinced that people in the situation you and I are in can have true consent for what I want. What I need." He cleared his throat. "So we won't. Okay?"

I nodded because I wasn't really sure what to say to that. I didn't know the first thing about BDSM. Not anything real or concrete, in any case. I liked the sound of coming to an understanding first, and if it was going to be that way, and not just sex the way I was used to having it, then we did need to be on equal footing.

He'd opened this door. I walked through it. "Do you always have sex that way?"

"Not always, no. But what I find is that I really prefer to have sex with the rope for at least a good portion of the beginning of the relationship. My need for it does seem to wane as trust is built. Or at least that's how it's been in the past. My kink is uniquely mine. And I get that it won't be for everyone. If it's not for you, I can respect that, too."

I swallowed. "Does the rope hurt?"

"Depends on the rope. But with you, I'd want silk binding." He slid his finger up my wrist. "I want to take care of you, to see that you're safe in those moments. Not hurt. Not necessarily. Sometimes maybe I like to inflict a little pain. I've got a touch of sadist in me. Depends on my mood. I'd let you know ahead of time. That would never be a surprise. And if you didn't want it, it doesn't happen. See, the power is all yours. You meet my need in your way or you don't meet it. But we can't even really seriously discuss this as things are." His hand was still on my wrist. "Your pulse is racing. Just started. Does this frighten you?"

I rubbed the back of my neck. "Entices me. I've never thought about this stuff and suddenly I can picture myself, naked and tied up, with you coming over me. I don't hate the idea."

He nudged me, the slightest brush of our shoulders together. "Good. I'm going to be hard all day picturing that now. Thanks for that. Come on. Let's get you some food to go with your caffeine."

Since I wasn't sure what else to say on this subject, I followed him out. He stopped when we got to the front hall. "Run up and get dressed. Don't forget your coat. I don't want you cold."

I nodded. Judson had effectively rendered me speechless. I was going to be able to follow directions. For a person who said he didn't care about people, he certainly seemed to look after my needs. And then there was that whole thing he had just said about wanting to take care of me while I was tied up.

He was a real contradiction. Or maybe he didn't really know himself.

I hurried up the stairs. Whoever had bought all my clothes had done a really great job. They were more fashionable than I was, that was for sure. Had Judson done it? Like selected them all himself or had the app just let him order women's clothing and have them delivered fast? I needed to ask him about this.

I put on a pair of white pants and matched them with a gray sleeveless turtleneck. It seemed a contradiction in point but maybe it was a fashion statement I missed because I didn't live in a place that got particularly cold. Next, I matched a pair of pointy-toed white boots and a pink pea coat to finish the outfit. I'd really not paid attention to just how much stuff he had bought me.

This was so different than Kade who would have been content to leave me looking basically homeless if I hadn't pushed the issue. My clothing issue in this kidnapping was just ridiculous at this point.

Still, as I looked at myself in the mirror I'd never looked better. Judson had been dressed impeccably, his blue dress shirt rolled at the sleeves, appearing perfectly with his khakis. I'd match him pretty well. Wherever we were going to eat, they wouldn't stare like I didn't belong at the same table with him.

Maybe that was why he'd picked the clothes, he wanted to make me presentable.

I left the room heading downstairs and stopped as I approached the stairs. I hadn't paid attention the last few times I'd done this, but there was a framed picture that should have caught my focus. It was Judson and a woman. I stared at them for a second, focusing on the fact that I was absolutely certain that I saw Alyssa in front of me. She looked like him, sort of. Enough of a resemblance that I was sure that this was his sister. They were twins.

In the photo, Judson had to be at least ten years younger. He hardly looked ancient now at thirty-six, but he was noticeably younger in the photo. Or maybe he just seemed that way because he was grinning ear-to-ear as was his sister.

I turned my head from looking at him to examining his sister. Here was the woman who had shared a womb with Judson, loved and married Derrick, known about The Alliance, and been killed. I didn't know how she died, how they'd ended her life, but I doubted it had been pleasant.

She wasn't gorgeous in the sense that I would see her on the cover of magazines, but then again neither was I. Most women weren't. She had a pleasant face, bright brown eyes that were glowing in the way she grinned.

Her face was round and her hair was brown with blonde streaks in it that I would bet came out of a very expensive bottle. Her hair fell in waves around her shoulders. They might have been in The Lodge in this photo. I thought I recognized the lake behind it, but it could have been any lake since I wasn't sure I could tell one from the other.

What struck me about her, other than her white dress that clung to her like a second skin, was how petite she was. Alyssa was tiny. Next to Judson, she looked like she was maybe five feet tall.

So much had happened in the world of these men because of her. If she hadn't been killed, I doubted I'd be standing here now. Derrick and Judson would probably be engaged in other things other than revenge plots to take down The Alliance. They'd probably never have triggered enough interest in them that my father would have discredited them to The Alliance to begin with.

"We took that the day after she got engaged."

I jumped. I hadn't heard Judson approach.

He took a step closer. "She was already wearing white all the time. I think she did for six months. If you find yourself at Derrick's house, you'll probably see this picture, only with him and not me."

"She's lovely." I took a step back. "I supposed I should really look at the woman whose name I was slinging around."

He lifted his lids. "Oh, she would have loved you. Trust me. Alyssa liked people who spoke their minds. She would have loved how you stared us down, how you ran out the front door of The Lodge barefooted like you were going to get out of there with the sheer strength of your will alone. She would love that you had all of us twisting in the wind. Other than Derrick, of course."

I winced. "Other than him, obviously."

Judson tugged on the edge of my hair. "Food."

"Good idea."

He took my hand in his and squeezed it. "I know the best place for lunch that also serves breakfast. It's not really a brunch place, but you can get eggs all day."

"Sounds good to me." A thought dawned on me. "What's going on with your medical practice?"

"If this isn't solved in two weeks I will have to open it back up. For now, I'm on a sabbatical I gave to myself. I don't want to neglect the staff, so two weeks. Right now, they're being paid with no trouble. After that it'll get a little tighter. I don't like when things get tighter."

The restaurant he took us to was small on the inside and noisy. No one looked up at us, and we were over-dressed for the crowd. Most people were in jeans. Maybe Judson noticed me noticing because he shook his head. "You look incredible. I meant to tell you. Should have told you. The picture you were looking at distracted me. But you are gorgeous. I mean, you always are. But you are particularly lovely today. Maybe I just have a thing for you in those clothes because I picked them out."

That answered that question. "You just chose them on an app?"

"Yes. It's a service app. Kind of a concierge thing. You can get just about anything you want that way." He pointed at the menu. "I can't decide if I'm doing breakfast or lunch."

This was the strangest date I'd ever been on, and I had no doubts that was what we were doing. We weren't two people just eating together, and for the first time with Judson, I really didn't feel like we were kidnap victim and person with all the power. I felt as though I were on a date with a very attractive man who wanted to talk about the menu.

I decided to pretend that was what it was. "How do you feel about Bloody Marys before noon?"

He set down his menu. "I'm in favor of them."

"Good. Then we'll start with that. Maybe you get lunch, I'll get breakfast and we'll share."

Judson was beautiful in the sunlight. Objectively, he was the most strikingly attractive man in this restaurant, so when the women around us looked, I wasn't at all surprised. He was the kind of man women looked at. No wonder he was successful at what he did. If someone came in for a plastic surgery consultation, all he'd have to do was smile and they'd sign right up.

"Thank you for my clothes, Jud." It wasn't until the nickname was out of my mouth that I realized I'd used it.

"You're welcome." He pressed his hand down on top of mine. "Call me Jud anytime you want, Everly. But I'm always going to use your full name. I love it."

Yes, it was the best date ever. I was just going to enjoy it.

———

WE STEPPED OUTSIDE TOGETHER. I didn't know about him, but I had a Bloody Mary buzz going full force in my head. I felt no pain at all.

We'd taken a rideshare to get here so neither of us had to drive. "Tell me the truth. You're not at all scared right now? We're out in public."

"Let them come. They won't live through it. They killed my fucking sister. They're not getting within feet of me and living to tell the tale. I wanted to kill that asshat in Kade's vault. I itched for it."

"Oh." Realization dawned on me but didn't deflate my buzz. "We're baiting them."

He shrugged. "If they come they come."

All right, so maybe he was a little bit crazy. I'd gotten used to a little bit crazy. I was so used to the psycho element of these last weeks that I wasn't even fazed. Okay. If they came they came. Or maybe it was just my Bloody Mary buzz making me this relaxed.

Movement caught my gaze. A homeless man sat by the edge of another building. He held out a cup and had a sign in front of him. I couldn't see the words from where we stood but I'd seen enough of them in my life that I could guess what it said. As Judson tapped on his phone, I noticed how the elderly gentlemen had holes in his gloves. I wasn't wearing any, but I bet I was going to want some later if I was outside. He had only one shoe on and his coat was torn.

Tears pooled in my eyes.

"You okay?" Judson grabbed my arm. "What's wrong?

The Alliance won't touch you either. If ever there was someone who could handle themselves, it would be you."

"That man." I spoke in a low voice so the person of whom I spoke couldn't hear me. He didn't need to know he was being discussed. He'd suffered enough indignities in his life to have to put up with that.

He nodded. "It's very sad. I can give him a few dollars."

I sighed. "In this big plan of yours. The one the five of you plan to implement with The Alliance. When you take over. When you out the current group. Who takes care of him?"

He turned to full on face me. "Who takes care of him now?"

"You made my point for me. No one is. In this game of world domination where you all move chess pieces, and Warden destroys bank accounts, Trace plans the exit from the planet, Kade watches anyone on satellites, Derrick executes with guns and baseball bats. And you… what will you do, Judson?" I didn't even know.

"I run everyone. I've always been de facto leader. I am the tie breaker, the one they listen to when someone has to listen." Well, then someone should inform Trace, but I wasn't going to say that right now.

"Fine. You run things. You make yourselves richer. You gain power. You take control. Which one of you is thinking of him? Of that man and the countless millions worldwide like him? Which one of you does that?"

He didn't answer for a second. "They're not the point. The poor have always been poor, Everly. Since the dawn of time. I didn't make them that way and neither did The Alliance. They are basically not players, not relevant in what we do."

"Well, that breaks my heart." I wasn't even surprised by what he said. "And that's why I'm crying."

I didn't know what Judson would have said to me right then because his phone dinged and he looked down at it. He stared at it so long that I wondered if he'd gotten lost in the words he read. Finally, he lifted his head. "Your dad's done. We should head to New York."

They'd told me it would take months and then every time we brought it up, less and less time. I guessed my dad was motivated, and given that I knew he killed my mother, he was more than capable of getting things done.

The fate of the world hadn't changed in this one conversation. It might have been better if I'd never had it.

Chapter 23

We boarded Judson's plane to head to New York City. When we got on the plane, Derrick surprised us by waiting for us on board. Judson must not have known either, because he startled next to me.

"Derrick?"

The baseball player spun in his chair. "Hey, brother."

"What are you doing here?" Judson strode past me and set his stuff down under a chair. I followed him on. I really had no idea if Derrick and Jud were close. I knew they'd both loved Alyssa and they were in this mess together with The Alliance. But other than that? Did they like each other?

"I landed in Boston. I was on my way to get my girl from you when I got the message. Figured you'd be coming here. Beat you to it." He held out his hand, and I took it. "Hello Everly. You look beautiful. Fancy. Like you could go to a gala with him. I love it, but I like you in your jeans, too. The ripped ones that you wear to bars."

I sighed. "Lest I ever forget you stalked me before you kidnapped me."

His smile was huge. "I am totally nuts. You know that. But I'm forever there for you."

Judson groaned. "What makes you think I'd let you just take her?"

"You took her from Kade. I take her from you. That's how it was going to go. Everly, you're going to miss out. I was going to take you to Montana. Big Sky. That's where I was born. You'd have loved it."

I'd never been there. "I heard that place is beautiful."

Derrick tugged me until I sat next to him. Judson walked over and took the seat on the other side. Twenty seats on this plane and we were lined up like we were sitting in coach where I'd officially gotten the short end of the trip by sitting in the middle seat.

Of course, it was Judson and Derrick. They were both gorgeous.

Judson stared out the window. "I wouldn't have given her to you."

"I'm not a doll you can just pass around." Of course that was ridiculous. I'd pretty much been just that for some time.

They ignored me. "You have to share. That's how this works."

"Share, yes. Give in to your every whim when you feel like acting up? No." Judson turned to me. "My sister made the mistake of thinking she could control Derrick. I warned her that was ridiculous. No one controls Derrick. He's actually smarter than the rest of us combined. But he is really good at living in this constant manic state. It isn't fixable. This is how he is. Don't make that mistake."

Derrick laughed, which startled me. "And Judson is really good at pretending that he controls the world. It bothers him when he can't. He's not king of the universe. We don't have to bow."

I closed my eyes. This was going to be a long fucking flight and it was supposed to be short. Their phones both dinged and they dragged them out to look before Judson jumped to his feet.

A wave of anxiety hit me. "Something wrong?"

"They've accepted our re-entrance into The Alliance. Haha, that of course means they're acting like they ever had any valid reason to kick us out. But, whatever. They want to have a meeting to replace Henry's seat today. So we're not going to New York City, but all of us are heading to the meeting spot."

I swallowed. "Derrick, you must be in such danger for killing Henry."

"Nope." He shrugged. "Alliance can't kill Alliance. That's rule number one. I wasn't Alliance when I took him out. As long as they're going to pretend that they could remove us, I'm going to use that ridiculousness to my advantage. They could turn me in to the police. They won't. But they can't come after me for it."

I side-eyed him. "Derrick, they could always come after you. Even if it's twenty years from now. Don't you watch mafia movies?"

He grinned at me. "Not a bad comparison, but I think you're overestimating their love of Hank. The four left had no great love for him other than he furthered their agenda. They weren't friends or family. Now, we may have to manipulate some things to get Judson on there tonight. We don't have the time we thought we had to basically sell everyone on accepting him. Shouldn't be a problem, we have enough supporters, but it would have been nice to have run a campaign of sorts."

Judson strode away, calling over his shoulder. "I've got to let the pilot know he needs more gas."

I didn't suppose these treks we made on these planes

with the guys were really filed in flight records anywhere. Gas up and go? Was that how this worked?

"Are you guys going to leave me here?" I took off my seatbelt but Derrick placed his hand on my arm to stop me from moving.

He shook his head. "Why would you stay here?"

"We're done. My dad did what he said he was going to do. You're supposed to be letting me go."

Derrick furrowed his brow. "That's right. We are."

Judson came back and sat down in his seat. "You can go when we get to Seattle. Your dad will be there for the vote. We'll turn you over there. Unless you have some strong desire to find your way home all on your own from Boston?"

Derrick shook his head. "I say we keep her."

Keep me? "I'm not a dog you found on the street."

"She's right. She's not, and she's not even our hostage anymore. We'll figure things out, Everly. What you want matters in the sense that people have a small amount of self-determination. Smaller than they think they do, but whatever."

I waved my hand. "If you start quoting Kade and his ant metaphor I'm getting off the plane and walking from Boston."

His smile was fast. "Point taken. Presuming you are not getting off, you're coming with us."

"That makes you officially a member of this mess, Everly." Derrick ran a hand up my arm. "Not being dragged, consenting to come along."

The truth was I'd been pretty much doing that since the Caribbean. The captain turned on the engines. It looked like we were on our way to Seattle. I'd never been there but that was par for the course lately.

Both Derrick and Judson tapped on their phones,

essentially ignoring me. If I wasn't their captive anymore, then there were things I was going to demand they get back for me, starting with my cell phone. A person not being held hostage could call her friends and re-enroll in classes. But I would wait until Seattle, since I doubted even Judson's magic app could procure me a cell phone mid-air.

I closed my eyes and pretended I could fall asleep when the reality was I didn't feel the least bit tired. They had said I should stay with them. Or at least Derrick had. That couldn't be reality. I wasn't going to just follow these Alliance guys around here there and everywhere while they did whatever they did. I opened my eyes.

When they weren't battling for their rights and positions, what did they do? I had to figure that out.

We were no sooner in the air than Derrick fell asleep. He leaned in his chair, his legs out in front of him like he didn't have a care in the world. Jud continued to mess with his phone. Apparently there weren't rules about putting away his electronics during takeoff or not using the data plan to communicate. I closed my eyes again. I didn't even have anything to read to try to get through this.

Derrick started to snore, loudly. I gave up pretending I could sleep and opened my eyes. Judson sighed before he smirked at me. "I've told him to get the deviated septum fixed. I even have a guy I recommended that could do it. An ENT I like. But he's stubborn. Been like this since he was a teenager. Snores like he's using heavy machinery."

The night he'd spent sleeping by my bed when I'd been concussed I'd either been too out of it to notice or he hadn't really slept.

"Here." Judson patted his shoulder. "Lean on me and try to ignore it. We can always move, but I have a feeling he'll follow you. He tends to obsess until he gets bored with it."

I almost pointed out that he'd not gotten bored with Alyssa but that was highly inappropriate. When it came down to it, we'd just met. She'd been his wife, and I'd told Judson I wouldn't bring her up again. I'd apologized.

"Everly." He caught my attention. "Whatever you're thinking about, stop. That look in your eyes. The world isn't ending today. I can promise you that. We can survive just about anything. When Alyssa died, both Derrick and I fell apart. But we're still here. I'm wearing pants. I didn't for a couple of weeks back then, I hardly got out of bed. I didn't think I'd ever survive it. How do you live when the person you literally shared the womb with is suddenly ripped from the world? Yet, here I am. You'll be okay. Whatever this is, if you survive it, you'll eventually be fine."

My heart broke for him. He'd lost the person who was probably the most important person in the world to him. I put my head down on his shoulder, and he actually let out an audible breath. I wasn't sure if that meant anything at all, but it was almost like he'd been holding it to see if I would.

"So is this your way of saying that this too shall pass?"

He leaned his head on top of mine. "My mother used to say that."

"One of my nannies. I didn't have a mother. You know the whole father killed her thing."

"Right." He was quiet for a second. "It was strange with my mother. As an adolescent they told me about The Alliance. She didn't know about it. I was asked to keep this secret, this tremendous thing, from her and Alyssa. In some ways, it negated her authority of me. Here was this person who knew things, who was in charge, who I discovered had absolutely no idea how her own world worked. She became pathetic to me. I know that sounds awful. Keep in mind I was a nasty teenager at the time. Raging hormones, shitty attitude."

I remembered the boys when they were like that in school. "It makes sense, actually. That's when we challenge authority. Yours was ripped out from under you and in that sense it empowered your father, right? He knew. She didn't. What a sudden and remarkably distorted view it must have given you about male, female relationships." I rubbed my eyes. We were in smooth skies. Judson had a soothing voice, and Derrick's snores had gotten rhythmic enough they were almost a constant part of the overall plane experience. "But you did tell Alyssa."

"I could never keep anything from her. She had the stronger personality than me. I had a secret. She had it out of me in two days. Then that changed her with Mom, too. It was all kinds of problematic. She knew about it, but wasn't in it. Hated my father for that but couldn't say a word to him. Of course, it all got better when snorey over there showed up. Then she could obsess over him. And he didn't mind her talking about The Alliance."

I started to get the general picture of how things were. "Is your mother still alive?"

He yawned. "No. She didn't make it very long after Alyssa died. My father right after her. Whatever their… dynamic was… my father worshiped my mother. He was done without her. All that Alliance power, all that prestige, and he was a shell for the weeks he lived without her."

It was a bit romantic in a sick, twisted way. Secrets that fueled the family destroyed them. And now here was Judson on an airplane to go take the seat on the Alliance council of the man he'd helped plot to kill. The same council had somehow taken Alyssa from him and the man next to me.

"What was your dad like, Everly? I know you have

some strong feelings right now, and I don't blame you for them, but what was he like in your mind before you felt that way?"

I had to think about that. "He was everything."

There really wasn't another way to describe it. As distant as he'd been, removed in some ways, I'd centered my whole life around him, even staying near home to go to school to be close to him. I'd wanted his approval, and I'd mostly gotten it.

"It was just the two of you."

I yawned. "Just us. Sorry. Maybe I'm tired."

"You've been up and down the East Coast of the United States, the Caribbean, wherever Warden stashed you, and underground in New Orleans. Then I dragged you to Boston. I think you're entitled to be tired. Sleep. We can do the whole who were you before The Alliance changed you game another time."

I smiled. Was that a thing that Alliance people regularly did to get to know each other? "No. You'll clam up and hate me again."

"I never hated you. I saw you as a tool. I see everyone that way. Make no mistake, I'm very pragmatic and narcissistic when it comes down to it. But I won't clam up."

I hated airplanes, but I liked being curled up on Jud's shoulder. I liked Derrick being on the other side of me even if he snored like a chainsaw. Maybe I was just done, because I did fall asleep.

When I woke up, the cabin was quiet. Derrick still had his eyes closed, but he wasn't snoring. His head was at a different angle, which might have helped. Judson had adjusted slightly and that was what had woken me. He was out cold, as well.

I had to pee and that was a distraction from everything else happening. The plane bounced a little bit but not so much that I had to stay in my seat. Did we have fasten seatbelt signs on this thing? I didn't know. I'd not even seen a flight attendant, so maybe it was just us and the pilot.

I rose quietly and made my way to the lavatory. Like everything else on the plane, it had Judson's initials branded on the door. The actual inside of the bathroom didn't. I peed and then washed up, staring at myself in the mirror. The girl who looked back at me wasn't the same one who'd been studying and having boring sex with random men from bars. I'd seen things I'd never imagined —like killers on a beach—and been more places in a week than I could have fathomed doing. I'd met people who I'd never have encountered otherwise. None of this had been my choice but they hadn't abused me.

The plane jerked strongly in the air, and I gripped the sink. Okay, maybe I needed to go back to my seat fast and strap myself in.

I opened the door and walked as fast as I could back to my seat. Derrick's eyes were open and he extended his hand to me, which I took.

"You okay?" His eyes were clear, he was alert. Judson slept on in the seat by the window.

I nodded. "I'm not a great flyer, and it's bouncing."

"Just a little weather. We're almost there." He shifted in his seat slightly, and I buckled myself in. Not that it helped with the bumping, but I did prefer to be strapped in, knowing I wouldn't bang into the ceiling if we hit even harder turbulence. "Why Judson's shoulder and not mine?"

His question distracted me from the bouncing. "He offered it to me. And you were snoring."

"Yeah, I do that. You can kick me, and I'll stop." He patted his arm. "Here, this is me offering it to you."

I shook my head. "I'm not tired anymore."

He stared at me without saying a word, and like I was a

sheep being herded by a Border Collie, I did as his stare instructed me to do. I leaned my head down on his arm. He smelled good, like sandalwood. I decided I really liked the scent. Okay, this wasn't so bad. I wasn't going to sleep, but I could cuddle like this through the bumps at least.

"I'm probably going to have to kill a few of these asses."

And just like that my ease in the moment fled. Maybe it was because I had my head on his arm that I could just ask the question. Maybe I'd lost all sense of self-preservation. What kind of an idiot asked a killer if he was okay killing? Then again, I had my head pressed on his arm and he'd rescued me when I'd been stranded. He claimed to have feelings for me. With Judson right there, he'd probably not get too angry. Or would he? I gave up wondering and asked the question. "Does it bother you to do so?"

"Not anymore. There was a time I said no. These assholes killed my wife because I did. No, I don't mind killing them. I still don't want to kill for them. For us? Yes, I've long since stopped caring." He shrugged, which moved my whole body.

"She didn't die because you said no," Judson must have opened his eyes at some point. I hadn't noticed. I was too busy snuggling with a killer because that was just what I did these days apparently.

Derrick shook his head. "I'm not doing this with you again."

"Well if you are going to insist on bringing that up, then we are going to do it whenever I'm in earshot of hearing it, bro." Judson put a hand on my knee and squeezed. It was strangely reassuring, considering there was nothing about this moment that was okay. The conversation. The turbulence. It all pretty much sucked.

He continued. "I loved my sister the most of anybody

or anything in the world. When you two got married, I was happy for both of you. She seemed to even you out and you gave her what she always wanted—absolute adoration and a constant project to work, namely your life. She got herself killed because she could never leave well enough alone. She had to open her mouth when repeatedly warned to not do so, from not just you but me. And Warden, Trace, and Kade, too. Alyssa would be alive today if she'd behaved."

Derrick didn't answer right away. "In no world is it okay to victim shame her. She's dead. It wasn't like she risked our exposure. She spoke to other Alliance members. Not anyone on the outside. It wasn't a death warrant. They did it to punish me."

"No, they did it to punish me." Judson spoke through gritted teeth. "And you've never been willing to see that. Stop blaming yourself. Obsess over Everly if that makes you feel better until you lose attention. Whatever it takes, Derrick. Your refusing to kill a mid-level banker who stumbled on the wrong accounts and didn't understand what he'd looked at is not why Alyssa isn't here today. It was always about my family. The leadership role. The fact that I told her in the first place. Her death was a fuck you to me. You just got to suffer in it."

I hated to make this all about me, but as I listened to them go back and forth about which one of them was more to blame, it dawned on me, that through no fault of my own, I was in the same position Alyssa had been. I knew about The Alliance. More dread settled in my stomach. At this rate I was going to throw up before we landed.

My head pounded. Derrick placed his nose on top of my head before he planted a kiss there. It was the first time he'd done that. "Are you okay?" His voice was low.

I shook my head. "No. Is it safe to go back into the bathroom? I think I might... I'm not feeling well."

He was on his feet fast before he held out his hand. "I'll walk you there."

"Everly," Judson spoke my name in a calm, slow manner. "You're very strong. This won't break you. We're landing soon. Take some deep breaths. You're fine."

Derrick put his hands on his hips. "If she says she doesn't feel well, you telling her that she's fine won't fix it."

"Actually, it might, since I'm pretty sure she's just stressed out from us talking about my sister's death and you killing people."

They could fight about this all they wanted. I undid my seatbelt and did make it to the bathroom before I lost the contents of my Bloody Mary filled stomach. How long ago had that been? It had been a long time since I puked because of stress, but I'd been that way for most of my childhood. If things got really bad—if I made my father truly mad, if I failed a test I studied for, if some mean girl made fun of what I wore when I was twelve which seemed like the end of the world—I threw up. Now, it only took talk about murderers and murdering to do it to me.

A knock sounded behind me. Derrick's voice was soothing through the door. "Need anything?"

"A stronger stomach."

Since I wasn't likely to get that, I supposed for the moment I was fine.

━━━

THANKS TO THE TIME CHANGES, it was dinnertime when we landed in Seattle. I'd spent the rest of the flight with my eyes closed, pretending I was on the ground. That had worked pretty well, particularly when it stopped bumping.

Derrick and Judson hustled me into a black car, and we'd taken off to who knew where. I still didn't feel well, and it was better that I was just a little bit out of it. We weren't at a hotel but a large house that seemed to be surrounded by cars that looked very similar to our own. Was this the black car brigade?

I followed them inside the house, men I didn't recognize grabbing my bags and circling round the outside of the house when we went in.

A burst of heat hit me when I walked through the door, the vent clearly right above the entranceway.

"Damn, did you break her? How long was she with you, Judson? Two days? Everly, you don't look so hot." Kade strode toward me as two other people rose from where they sat by the window. Trace and Warden.

I gulped. No, I wasn't okay, but I was back with the five of them for the first time since we'd left Vermont. I hadn't given that a thought in the midst of this mess. With me were five guys who had come to mean a huge bit more than they should have.

And I had no idea what any of it meant.

Chapter 24

I looked around the room, cognizant that I had all of their attention on me at the same time. Derrick put his hand on the small of my back. "She's not feeling really well. It got bumpy up there in the air."

"And we were having kind of an upsetting conversation that probably made that worse." Judson walked past me into the living room. "Everything fine here?"

Two more faces I recognized scurried out of the kitchen to greet Judson, one of them signing as he did. Constance and Marco, Judson's staff from the house in Vermont. Apparently, they worked for him here, too.

Trace pointed toward them. "They had this all opened up when I got here. Amazingly efficient considering they traveled to get here in the same amount of time we did."

"They only had to come from Los Angeles, not across the country. Although I guess Warden was in San Diego."

Warden shrugged. "I didn't hustle. I knew how long it would take all of you to get here."

Marco signed hello to Judson who answered him. They talked about the bedrooms and his concern that one of the water heaters might be getting ready to break. Judson asked him to hold off calling a plumber for two days unless it was an emergency. I glanced away.

"Hi." I was basically speaking to the room. So far I'd been doing a pretty good impression of a statue. A just puked on the plane statue.

Trace walked over to me, standing right in front of me and next to Kade. "Hello. You really do look like you've seen better days." He placed a hand on my forehead. "You're not hot. Just a little airsick, huh?"

I nodded. "Guess so."

He really was so handsome. I hadn't forgotten it in the time away from him, but here he was looking just as delicious as he had on the beach while I, apparently, looked like death warmed over. Warden rose from the couch. He approached me as well. With the exception of Jud, they were all around me. It should have been hard to breathe. I should have been begging for space. But the twisted part of me loved it. There was... power in all of them liking me.

"Are you up for a conversation or do you need to go take a nap?" Kade asked me, drawing my attention back to him.

I ran a hand through my hair. "What kind of conversation?"

"Of the serious variety." He motioned toward the couch. "Sit. One of us will get you some coffee."

Judson left the room just as I moved toward the aforementioned couch, which was black leather and reminded me of the one we'd had until I was fifteen years old. Then my father had replaced it without warning. It had surprised me at the time since he didn't like to spend undue money, but he'd said it had never been his style.

He'd killed my mother. Maybe looking at the sofa had reminded him of her. I sat down just as Jud came back in carrying a yogurt and a coffee. He placed it down on the coffee table in front of me. "No coffee 'till you eat this. Way too much caffeine and alcohol today and not enough food. It couldn't have helped."

I actually was pretty sure I'd eaten quite a lot. "If I consumed any more food I'd explode."

He shook his head. "You lost everything you ate. So that counts as no food. Don't argue. Just eat."

I took the spoon he'd put on the tray and took a bite of the yogurt. Constance and Marco weren't anywhere I could see, which meant they'd gone off somewhere. It was just me, and the Alliance men. Just like the beginning of my kidnapping.

They all sat. It was Kade who spoke. That wasn't surprising. It was always Kade who spoke first in the group meetings. Kade who had come to my room to get me after I'd thrown up the last time. That was twice now I'd ended up puking around these guys. It was maybe more than I'd thrown up around anyone, ever, other than my nannies and my father.

"I've spoken to your father. He's here in Seattle. We can turn you back over to him."

I swallowed. So that was that. Judson and Derrick had indicated they might like me to stay somehow, but it looked like I was leaving. Lots of amazing memories that I could never share with anyone. "Okay."

I really wasn't being particularly articulate about this. Was I supposed to be thanking them for the time or something? I'd had maybe the nicest kidnapping ever but that didn't change that our relationship had been screwed up from the beginning.

What was the protocol here?

"Or." Kade leaned forward. "We all texted on the plane. You stay with us. We all like you. I think it's clear you like all of us, or at least we're all starting to feel that way. Maybe more than like each other. Not one of us was ever going to have a normal relationship and now that you know about The Alliance, I'm not sure you can. I mean, how would you ever date someone and not wonder if it was a set up?"

Well... shit. I hadn't really focused on that but now that he said it, of course he was right.

"You're not going to throw up right, Everly?" Warden ran a hand through his hair. "I don't really do puke all that well."

I shook my head. "I'm not going to puke. How would I stay with you exactly?"

Kade nodded. "You'd stay with us. You'd sort of transfer around. Like you've been doing but larger stretches of time. Then when we all came together for things like this you'd be with all of us at this time, too."

Were they kidding? I looked around at each of their faces and they absolutely were not. If I had something to throw I would have done so. "You guys think that I am just going to follow you around for the next however long doing nothing with myself but spending time with you?"

Kade and Trace looked at each other before Trace answered. "You wouldn't have to do nothing with yourself. I'd be happy to give you projects like I did in Vermont."

I could have strangled him. "I had a life before you all interfered in it. I was getting a degree. I had plans. I was going to help people, specifically children."

"Yes, we knew that from your file." Trace shook his head. "Obviously, that can't happen in this scenario."

"Well it could," Derrick jumped on the talking train. "She could live with me permanently and visit you all she wants."

Trace groaned. "I don't think there are all that many

kids she could help in that ranch of yours in Montana in the middle of nowhere without anyone around for fifty miles. Besides, I hate to think of her standing in the snow when you get bored of her and want her gone in the middle of the night."

Derrick held up two fingers. "That happened twice. Just twice."

Okay, I was done. I got up from the couch. "Look, I like all of you, for some reason I can't fathom. I've had sex with three of you." I threw that out there just in case anyone didn't know. "And I would with the other two of you should the situation present itself." I was not going to be left in the snow at Derrick's house in Montana. We'd find some other place now that I had some self-determination back. That was not the point. I had to keep my brain on track.

"Everly." Trace said my name in that low voice of his and it was everything I could do not to just melt into the ground. I was not going to be distracted. "Don't you want to stay around? Don't you want to be with us? We kind of think that you do. Sure, this has not been the most typical introduction and whatever this would be between us would be off the charts different, but do you really want to go back to the way you were living before? Can you?"

Judson held up his hand. "Gentlemen, I think we've given our Everly a lot to think about. We clearly have strong feelings for you. But we have the most important issue in our lives to deal with right now so you need to go to your room."

He was sending me to my room? "I thought I wasn't your prisoner anymore."

"You're not. But you're not welcome to this conversation either. So you don't have to go to your room. You can take a walk. Go get some food. Have a run. Go the movies.

A bar. Anything you want. But you can't stay here in this living room."

Well, that had sufficiently dismissed me. Truth was, I had no money or cell phone. I didn't know anyone in Seattle, and much as I would adore having a tour I probably couldn't do that tonight. After the long flight, I could probably use a shower and a good night's sleep. My stomach would be better in the morning.

I hoped.

I didn't know where my room was. "Which room is mine?"

"Third room down on the left, next to mine," Trace answered.

"And mine," Warden responded right after.

Well, that answered that. I took the long hallway I'd seen when I first entered the house and walked into what had to be my bedroom. Clearly, Constance had done what she'd managed back in Vermont and in the time I'd been having that uncomfortable conversation. I looked around. The room was neat and clean, as all of Judson's houses had been so far. Some people collected toy cars. Jud collected real estate. I didn't even know where I was in Seattle.

I'd ask him in the morning.

I closed the door behind me. We'd gone back to his home in Boston and packed so I had what I needed and for the first time in a long time had no clothing emergency laid out in front of me. I rubbed the back of my neck.

They wanted me to just bounce around visiting each of them in their day jobs while they lived life and I just... did what? Fucked them? No, I wasn't a roaming spread my legs service. This wasn't going to go like that. I didn't know exactly how it was going to go but not like that.

A knock sounded, and I opened the door. Constance

stood there, holding towels. She pretty much pushed her way through the door and shut it behind her.

"What are you doing?" She spoke in hushed tones.

"I'm standing here." That couldn't be what she was asking me, but it was the only thing I could think to say right at that second. It was what I was doing.

Constance shoved the towels down on the bed. "I never in a million years thought I'd have to tell you not to consider staying with these men. They're bad men."

My mouth fell open. She seemed to really like them. Certainly, she had a fondness for Judson. Or at least that was the impression I'd gotten in Vermont. "I think... I think they're complicated."

"Oh don't do that thing women do. Trust me, they're bad men. I've worked for Judson's family since I was a young woman. It never works out for the girls who come and go. His mother was a shell of a person and you know what happened to his sister. Oh sure, individually they seem fine, but they are part of an organization that does those things. I loved Alyssa. I held her the day she came home from the hospital. She was bright with light. That's what this is. I'll stay as long as I can help Judson. I promised myself I would. But you need to turn on your heels and run like hell."

I couldn't breathe. Having delivered that speech, she walked right out, leaving the towels. I sunk down onto the bed. My mind divided into two. Part of me wanted to do just what she said, get up and run. Constance had watched things I'd never seen. She knew Alyssa and mourned her. The woman knew firsthand just how dangerous a situation this was. The other part of me insisted on doing something that made the first part of me feel nuts.

I doubted her.

This was a woman giving another woman a piece of

advice, and I knew even as I sat there that my foolish brain was going to insist that I knew better than she did. I'd spent alone time with all of them. Maybe she didn't understand the small things that made them the way they were, the layers that had to be peeled to discover the men underneath.

I groaned. Yeah… I pretty much hated this side of myself.

I couldn't go anywhere. My dad was coming tomorrow, and I needed to settle things with him at the very least. I had nowhere to particularly go. I had to figure out my life. For now, I had a bed to sleep in and time to talk myself out of being a dipshit.

The sound of cars outside screeched as they took off. It had to be more than just my guys leaving. I crawled over to the window to look. The whole crowd of people circling the house seemed to be leaving. Doors slammed in the house and a knock sounded on my door.

I jumped up from where I crouched by the window to answer it. Derrick stood out there. He'd changed into a suit, which looked funny on him. His hair was slicked back so that in the bun he still looked more dignified than I'd ever imagined him.

"We're going. The meeting is happening. Right now." He touched the side of my face. "You're really beautiful. I just wanted to tell you that."

Trace whistled down the hall. "Romeo, don't make it harder, come on."

Derrick stepped back. "Get some sleep, Everly. You're going to need it."

"What does that mean?"

He didn't answer me.

I stood there watching them all leave. The others didn't turn to look at me, not even Kade, which seemed really off.

But then again this was the meeting of their lives and they had more to think about than me. Apparently, the whole fate of the world fell to this. I was probably not a blip in their minds, and if I was to stay with them I'd have to get used to that. Whoever was with these guys was always going to be second in their minds.

Not to mention they were all eventually going to want wives and to carry on this Alliance nonsense with their children. What would happen to me then?

I closed the door, changed into the pajamas I'd worn in Boston, and crawled into bed. There had been a time in my life when I'd not been able to sleep in strange beds. No more. Boy had I gotten good at falling asleep wherever I was.

A noise woke me a second before my eyes flew open. I reached for the lamp to turn it on when a hand shoved me down on the bed. I cried out. "What the fuck?" I yelled out, terror surging through my veins.

"Right where they said you were going to be."

I didn't know that voice and struggled to sit up, to roll over, but he had me pinned by the center of my chest and there wasn't a thing I could do. I kicked up my legs but someone at the end of the bed grabbed them, holding me down.

"Who are you? What do you want?" I could barely speak. This was a nightmare I hadn't known I'd had, even after being kidnapped.

With his free hand, the man turned on the light. That didn't help anything. I had no idea who this person was. He had dark hair and dark eyes, a chin that jutted out and had a cleft in it. His hair was short, styled so that it was slightly longer on top than anywhere else, but neatly kept. He wore an expensive looking suit. That was all the information my brain could take in about him in the seconds that I stared.

He spoke again, his voice low, his tone amused. "Do you know who I am?"

"My name is Benjamin Gray. Does my name ring a bell?"

Should it? "No, I'm afraid not."

"I sit on the council of The Alliance, an existence you should know nothing about but do. That's okay because you won't know about it very long. You have been given to me in trade for Judson Smythe's seat on the council."

What? "That doesn't make any sense."

"Well, of course not. They'd not have explained it to you. Why would they?" He patted my arm like we were friends and shivers of dread tore into me. Whatever this was, whatever this lunacy turned out to be, it was going to be very, very bad.

I forced myself to look at the man holding me. He had his head bowed. I couldn't see his face but blond hair fell forward, it was long. He wore all black with a red sash—the kind that a beauty queen might have—across his chest. He bobbed his neck slightly, adjusting, and that was when I got a better look at him. He wasn't a man at all. In fact, I was pretty sure he was a teenager. What in the ever-loving fuck was going on?

I had to stay calm, had to think. Surely, whatever was happening could be resolved.

"You see, there is always a gift that the new council members make to the senior member of the council. The five men you've been spending time with were all my trainees at one point. As idiot over there is." He nodded toward the asshole holding my legs. "They know me. They know I have a certain proclivity toward young brunettes. The gift is almost always a young woman who is somehow connected to The Alliance. It's simpler that way. Your father screwed them over. Taking you made sense. Or at least that's how Kade explained it to me. He does like to talk, that one. Anyway, here we are. You're mine until I kill you. They needed someone to blame. Your father was unfortunately that man and you, as they say, are the sacrificial lamb. It's nice to meet you, Everly. I don't know how long I'll keep you. You're going to wish it wasn't very long."

He slammed a cloth down on my face and as I fought against it, I breathed in chemicals that knocked me out. Colors passed before my eyes.

And then... nothing.

━━

I WOKE UP ALONE, nauseated, in a basement that smelled like mold. I coughed, trying to breathe. I wasn't tied down, wasn't restrained at all. I was just alone in the pitch black basement.

I didn't know how long I would stay there, how long I'd even get to live. Tears flooded my eyes, and I let them fall. Somewhere I could hear the sounds of what I thought were rodents running in the walls above my head, voices traveled down to me. I couldn't make them out, but they were all men, and they seemed to be chanting, repeating words over and over together. It was almost sing-songy.

I tried to remember through the haze in my head what Ben had said to me. I was his prisoner because the five Letters had given me to him. I couldn't believe it. He was lying. He had to be. I'd gotten to know them, and despite Constance's warning, I was sure that they'd cared about me, really had. They wanted me to stay with them.

Or maybe it had all been a show. An elaborate ruse like

the one Trace did with the man he wanted to fund the trips to Mars. A long con they'd all engaged in. They'd kept me calm and gotten their jollies off in the meantime.

That phrase. My grandmother had used it. I sniffed. What was going to happen now? I had to hold faith. This was a huge mistake. In fact, when the guys found out what happened they were going to come and get me.

Weren't they?

Afterword

Dearest Reader

Don't kill me. I did warn you in the beginning this was going to be a long, dark trip for Everly before we got to her Happily Ever After. Stay tuned for news about Kiss Her Goodbye #2 coming soon. And if you could leave this book a review I'd be so grateful. Also, please join me in my reader group on Facebook Rebecca's Randomness where we talk about all things books all the time! https://www.facebook.com/groups/RebeccasRandomness /

In the meantime, maybe you'd like to check out some of my other titles, like Kidnapped By Her Husbands (Wings of Artemis #1) https://amzn.to/2QmjAJ4

Please turn the page for a complete listing of my novels and visit my website at www.rebeccaroyce.com to sign up for my newsletter.

I promise, there is a lot more to come in Everly's story.

RR

Afterword

About the Author

As a teenager, I would hide in my room to read my favorite romance novels when I was supposed to be doing my homework.

I am the mother of three adorable boys and I am fortunate to be married to my best friend. I live in Austin Texas where I am determined to eat all the barbecue in town.

I am in love with science fiction, fantasy, and the paranormal and try to use all of these elements in my writing. I've been told I'm a little bloodthirsty so I hope that when you read my work you'll enjoy the action packed ride that always ends in romance. I love to write series because I love to see characters develop over time and it always makes me happy to see my favorite characters make guest appearances in other books.

In my world anything is possible, anything can happen, and you should suspect that it will.

I'd love to hear from you! Please visit my website at www.rebeccaroyce.com to sign up for my newsletter and learn about my books!

Here's where you can find me online:

www.rebeccaroyce.com

Rebecca's Randomness Reading Group https://www.facebook.com/groups/RebeccasRandomness/

https://www.facebook.com/authorrebeccaroyce/
www.twitter.com/rebeccaroyce
Instagram: rebeccaroyce79
Cheers!!
Rebecca

Other books by Rebecca Royce...

Always

Evermore

Endless

Wards and Wands

Hexed and Vexed

Curse Reversed

Meow, Baby (novella, Coming Soon in Petting Them antho written with Ripley Proserpina)

Tragic Magic (Coming Soon)

Safe Haven

Everywhere and Nowhere

Dimension X (coming soon)

More coming soon....

Soul Bound

Prisoner of the Dragons

More coming soon....

Shadow Promised

Strange Days

Weird Nights

Bizarre Years

More coming soon...

The Warrior (completed series)

Initiation

Driven

Subversive

Redemption

Justice

Warrior World (spin off of The Warrior, completed series)

Deacon

Micah

Jason

The Westervelt Wolves (completed series)

Her Wolf

Summer's Wolf

Wolf Reborn

Wolf's Valentine

Wolf's Magic

Alpha Wolf

Angel's Wolf

Darkest Wolf

Lone Wolf

Fallen Alpha

Alpha Rising

Alpha's Strength

Alpha's Sacrifice

Alpha's Truth

Alpha Enticing

Hidden Alpha (coming soon)

The Capes (completed series)

Seductive Powers

Adrenaline Rush

Last Ascension

The Conditioned

Eye Contact

Embraced

Unlawful (coming soon…)

The Outsiders

Love Beyond Time

Love Beyond Sanity

Love Beyond Loyalty

Love Beyond Sight

Love Beyond Expectations

Love Beyond Oceans

Love Beyond Flames

Love Beyond Lies (coming soon)

Cascade (completed series)

Haunted Redemption

Phoenix Everlasting

Fragility Unearthed

Persuasion Enraptured

Reverse Harem Story (completed series)

Unconventional

Unexpected

Undeniable

Kiss Her Goodbye

Hard Truths

Book 2 coming soon

Stand Alone Titles

Planet Bear

Under The Lights

No Quitting Allowed

Mr. Wrong

Bite Marks

Bitten Surrender

The Vampire and The Virgin

Demon Within

Crimson Lust

Call Me Crazy (coming soon)

Writing with Ripley Proserpina

The Storm

Lightning Strikes (coming soon)

Thunder Rolling